HEALERS OR BUTCHERS?

They are powerful. They are greedy. And, they can be deadly.

They are the DOCTORS FROM HELL — eighteen of the most chilling examples of medical doctors who have strayed from their sacred oath as healers to sexually abuse, mistreat, mutilate, defraud, and actually kill the patients who trusted them.

They are men like Dr. James Burt. who butchered his female patients with his so-called "love surgery." Or Dr. Dennis Kleinman who sexually molested his patients while they were unconscious. Or Dr. Pravin D. Thakkar, who impregnated his women patients, then performed abortions on them without their permission.

After reading the true stories of the DOCTORS FROM HELL, you'll think twice before you make your next appointment.

DOCTORS FROM HELL

FRED ROSEN

PINNACLE BOOKS
WINDSOR PUBLISHING CORP.

PINNACLE BOOKS are published by

Windsor Publishing Corp.
475 Park Avenue South
New York, NY 10016

Pinnacle and the P logo are trademarks of Windsor Publishing Corp.

First Printing: November, 1993

Printed in the United States of America

For Leah, the Saloon, and Mr. Jordan.

ACKNOWLEDGMENTS

This book represents the efforts of a group of individuals, besides the author, who gave freely from the sweat of their collective brow.

My editor at Zebra Books, Paul Dinas, was incredibly supportive, and offered sage advice at crucial points. I am also indebted to his colleague Beth Lieberman, who introduced me to Paul, and has always been very encouraging. And, without my agents, Frank Weimann and Jessica Wainwright, the whole package never would have come together.

My colleague, Stacey Greenspan, deserves much of the credit for doing the bulk of the research. Her energy kept me going during the rough days.

Thanks, too, to R.W. Gennari, Paul Silverman, Ruth Rosen, and Edward Friedman who researched some of the later chapters, and Carolyn Colwell who offered support and insight.

This book would not have been possible without the cooperation of the many State Medical Boards around the country, who do a fine job in keeping records of doctors who abuse the right to practice medicine.

In addition, I would like to express my appreciation to the staff at the Huntington Public Library, in Huntington, New York, who run one of the finest libraries in the country and were always cooperative in providing research, particularly on-line support.

My students at Hofstra University also deserve credit for the insights they provide me on a daily basis.

Most of all, I want to express my sincerest gratitude to the victims, attorneys, and others who bared their souls and trusted that I would do right by them. In particular, I would like to thank Jan Phillips, Carol Seymour, Leona Cohen, Billy Condon, Bill Quinn, John Collins, and John Lukens.

And as always, Ted Schwarz, who got me into this in the first place.

Table of Contents

Introduction

This is a book about abuse. But it's not about abuse by a parent, sibling, teacher, or boss. It's about doctors who terribly abuse their patients.

Who among us, except doctors, take an oath that they will heal the sick? They take an oath, the Hippocratic oath, that they will heal the sick and comfort the afflicted. They are looked at by our society as healers. We go to them when we're in pain and we expect them to make us better.

But there are too many doctors who spit on that oath. For their own warped reasons, their oath is tainted with a dark side. They provide pain instead of pleasure, anxiety instead of relief. They do not relieve suffering; they create it.

They are truly doctors from hell.

Some of the cases you are about to read are more well-known than others. James Burt, "The Love Doctor" who rearranged women's genitalia with painful, humiliating results, was the subject of a CBS "West 57th Street" report. Cecil B. Jacobson, who was convicted of mail and wire fraud which involved his surreptitiously impregnating seventy of his patients with his own semen, was the subject of much national publicity.

Most of the cases, though, are little known outside the state or area where the abuse took place. Some abused patients secretly, like the convicted abortionist Dr. Abu Hayat. Others were actually open about it, daring the state medical boards and the courts to reprimand them, like Doctors Valentine Birds and Stephen Herman of Los Angeles, who sold AIDS-stricken patients a phony concoction that they claimed would help alleviate the symptoms of their disease.

What all the doctors in this book have in common is the betrayal of trust. The betrayal of that trust is a national tragedy, so much so that a National Physicians Data Bank has been formed to keep track of complaints against doctors throughout the country.

Not surprisingly, the largest amount of doctor/patient abuse is sexual. Doctors are quick to exploit patients, who are at their most vulnerable when they come to see them. From the smallest children to the most mature adult, you will find the stories of their abuse at the hands of their beloved physicians in this book.

What was surprising and disturbing was that within the category of sexual abuse, there were an astonishing amount of cases across the United States involving women. There are more cases of women being abused by their doctors than any single group.

As you will see, ironically much of the sexual abuse chronicled here went on because it was tolerated by the patients themselves. Usually, the abuse takes the form of unwarranted sexual contact, anything from simple touching to attempted rape. More often than not, this type of abuse goes unreported, because doctors who engage in sexual abuse, be it heterosexual or homosexual, always pick patients who are the likeliest of victims and the least likely to report them.

Over and over again, as I conducted interviews for this book, I was told that I had a tremendous responsibility to report the truth about these doctors, and to, in a sense, raise people's consciousness, to make them realize that they didn't have to be victims and that if they were, to do something about it.

I humbly hope I have lived up to that responsibility.

As you read the names of the victims, you will notice that in some cases their names first appear in italics. In those cases, I have used a pseudonym to protect their identities.

There but for the grace of God go we.

Fred Rosen
November, 1993

Pain and Damage

Chapter One

Dr. Ming Kow Hah
Queens, New York

Where was the skull? Dr. Ming Kow Hah knew that he hadn't taken it out. It had separated from the rest of the fetus during the abortion. So where was it?

Dorothy Alou must have known something was wrong. She was bleeding profusely, more than she should have been had the abortion been going well. In fact, she had bled so much, she was going into shock. But with her legs in stirrups, she was powerless, totally vulnerable as Dr. Hah went about his fishing expedition.

Second trimester abortions can involve extreme pain. Because the fetus has been carried by the mother for an appreciable length of time, to the point that she may have felt it moving inside her, this makes the abortion process very debilitating emotionally. As for the physical aspect, second trimester abortions frequently involve, in the degree of pain and the time it takes to complete the procedure, great similarities to labor.

Still, whatever the difficulties, Dorothy Alou was determined to go for an abortion and the doctor she chose to perform the procedure was Dr. Ming Kow Hah.

Hah had been practicing medicine in New York State, since being licensed on May 15, 1972, when he was thirty-five years old. He'd settled in Elmhurst, one of the many ethnically diverse, suburban neighborhoods in Queens, a borough of New York City. The awning fronting the building, which doubled as his home and office, displayed the words "Medical Clinic."

Here was a place where people went to be healed; to have their problems taken care of by concerned, sympathetic, and, most of all, qualified personnel.

It was to that office that Dorothy went on April 23, 1990, where she requested an abortion. Hah examined Dorothy and wrote in his records that she was eighteen to nineteen weeks pregnant, and that there was no fetal heart tone. He diagnosed, ". . . second trimester pregnancy . . . missed abortion . . ."

The State Medical Board later noted that "in order to proceed safely with the performance of an abortion on this patient, a reasonable and prudent physician must obtain a sonogram, necessary to corroborate fetal demise and gestational age. The Respondent's [Hah's] physical examination was adequate to measure uterine size but he failed to obtain a sonogram which is an objective measure of gestational age."

Instead Dr. Hah reportedly told Dorothy, "Come back tomorrow and we'll do the procedure."

The next day, Dorothy returned, but upon examin-

16

ing her again, Hah told her that "she was too big" for him to perform the procedure in his office. Instead, Hah inserted eight laminaria into her cervix and directed her to meet him the next day at the Econi Surgi-Center for the an abortion.

Laminaria are dried, rounded stems of seaweed. When inserted into the cervix twelve hours before abortion, the seaweed stems will gradually expand as they absorb moisture, passively dilating the cervix in a gentle and painless way. This makes it easier for the physician to insert the instruments necessary to complete the abortion.

The use of laminaria is common medical practice. What happened the following day was not.

At about 4:30 P.M. on April 25, Dorothy met Dr. Hah at the Econi Surgi-Center, an outpatient facility, also in Queens.

Assisted by an anesthesiologist and a nurse, Dr. Hah gave Dorothy intravenous Brevitol to relax her, and injected her with one percent Lidocaine to dull the pain. He then began the abortion by removing the laminaria. In the process, he ruptured the amniotic sac; at this point, cloudy, green amniotic fluid came out of her cervix.

That fluid was indicative of fetal distress and possible demise.

The method of abortion Hah had chosen was a common one: dilation and evacuation. He inserted a tube into Dorothy's uterus that was attached on the other end to a pump. When Hah turned on the pump, the suction from the tube freed the fetal tissue from the uterine wall and pulled it through the tube and out of the body into a small container.

Essentially, Hah was removing the fetus in pieces

17

with the exception of the head, which separated from the rest of the body and remained, according to a report prepared by the State Medical Board, "somewhere inside the patient."

During the course of his attempt to remove the head of the fetus, Hah lacerated Dorothy's uterus so badly that it moved into her vagina. In delivering the uterus into the vagina, he tore it from the right pelvic sidewall attachments.

Dorothy was bleeding excessively now from the uterine laceration. Had she been in a hospital, they would have started giving her blood. But, Hah had failed to have blood available prior to the abortion just in case it was needed.

According to a report later prepared by the New York State Board of Professional Medical Conduct, "A reasonable and prudent physician faced with a uterine laceration in an out-patient facility would have terminated the procedure immediately upon detecting the lacerated uterus and transferred the patient to the nearest hospital setting where the repair of the laceration would have been performed through an abdominal incision. The retrieval of the fetal skull necessitated a laparotomy, which could not be performed in an out-patient facility."

Clearly, Dr. Hah should have stopped. Instead, he continued probing Dorothy with his medical instruments, feebly attempting to suture the slice in her uterus that he had inflicted, even though he knew the fetal head was still someplace inside Dorothy.

As her life's blood seeped out of her, Dr. Hah continued.

"The failure to immediately terminate the procedure and the persistent attempt to repair the lacera-

18

tion in an out-patient facility led to the significant injuries sustained by [Dorothy Alou] as a result of [Dr. Hah's] gross incompetence in his handling of the initial complications that developed during the abortion procedure," the New York State Regents Review Committee would subsequently state.

It was later estimated that at 6:15 P.M., when Dr. Hah or his anesthesiologist finally called an ambulance, Dorothy Alou had already lost approximately two liters of blood.

Upon the arrival of the Emergency Medical Service personnel. Dr. Hah lied and told them that he had performed a tubal ligation — a sterilization procedure where a woman's fallopian tubes are tied off — when in fact he had performed an abortion.

What had started out as a simple abortion had turned into a nightmare.

Dorothy was rushed to Elmhurst General Hospital, where the results of Hah's handiwork became apparent to the surgical team working on Dorothy: 2500 cc of blood was found in her peritoneal cavity; her uterus was lacerated; the left infundibular ligament in her uterus had been severed; her bladder had been lacerated as well.

The damage was so extensive that the surgical team had to perform a hysterectomy, a right oophorectomy, a salpinectomy, and bladder repair. As for the missing fetal skull, it was finally discovered inside Dorothy's abdomen and removed.

For Dorothy, it was like she had never been to a doctor but rather one of those backdoor abortionists — men and women who, because of little or no medical training, inflicted harm on thousands of expectant women.

But Dorothy Alou had gone to a trained professional, a medical doctor, where she expected the best in medical care. Instead, because her uterus had been removed during the emergency hysterectomy, Dorothy was, in effect, sterilized. She could never again bear children.

Dr. Hah continued to practice on other patients.

The next month, on May 15, 1990, *Sylvia Kahn* went to Dr. Hah with complaints of abnormal uterine bleeding for approximately three weeks and abdominal cramps. A pregnancy test was performed with negative results.

Hah then obtained consent from Sylvia to perform an endometrium biopsy, that is, a biopsy of the uterine lining. Instead, he performed a dilation and curettage without obtaining Sylvia's consent.

Botching one operation and performing another without patient consent. What else was Dr. Hah capable of doing before he was stopped?

On June 1, 1990, *Jane Smith* went to Dr. Hah's office with complaints of postmenopausal bleeding, abnormal itching, and bumps in the vagina. Hah's pelvic exam showed the presence of herpes warts (condyloma) and an infection of the endocervical glands (chronic cervicitis). Neither was life-threatening. However, his physical exam showed that Jane was "post left mastectomy," meaning that her left breast had been cancerous and removed.

Anyone who has ever had cancer is in danger of getting it again. It's important to be closely monitored and tested by your physician for any reoccurrence of the disease. Dr. Hah did not follow this procedure.

20

That same day, Dr. Hah cauterized Jane's cervix prior to receiving the report of a pap smear, which is meant to detect cervical cancer. He also failed to perform a dilation and curettage, which is a procedure to open the cervix and scrape off the lining of the uterus with a sharp instrument called a curette, to rule out cervical cancer as a cause of Jane's postmenopausal bleeding.

On November 16, 1990, the State Board for Professional Medical Conduct, a division of the Department of Health, served Dr. Hah with a statement of charges including professional misconduct and a summary suspension order, temporarily suspending his license to practice medicine.

After the Department of Health and Dr. Hah presented their entire case, the Board decided to revoke his license on January 17, 1991, on grounds of gross incompetence, gross negligence, negligence and practicing the profession fraudulently.

On July 26, 1992, Dr. Ming Kow Hah's license to practice medicine in the State of New York was irrevocably revoked by the State Board of Regents.

That was the end of Dr. Ming Kow Hah's medical career in the State of New York. Or was it?

Even after his license was revoked, the State's Health Department received an anonymous tip that Hah was still practicing medicine at his home office in Elmhurst, Queens.

"I see women come in and out of the clinic very often," a woman who lived across the street from Hah's home and office was quoted as saying in *The New York Times* on January 1, 1992.

Was Ming Kow Hah practicing medicine without a

license? If he was, he would be liable, finally, for criminal prosecution. The job of discerning the truth fell to the state bureaucracy.

"When someone's license is revoked and [that person] is therefore unlicensed to practice [yet continues to do so], it becomes a matter of unlicensed practice. That complaint ends up with the State Education Department which has an Office of Professional Discipline, which investigates complaints against unlicensed professionals," says Richard Barr, a spokesman for the Office of the State Attorney General.

To get the goods on him, *Lauren Winter*, an undercover investigator from the State Education Department, made an appointment with Hah.

"She said she was pregnant [when she was not] and it was arranged for her to go in with a urine specimen from one of her colleagues who indeed was pregnant. When it seems to confirm pregnancy, if he offers to perform a medical procedure at that point, he's gone too far enough in the view of the law to have committed a crime of unauthorized practice," Barr continues.

Hah fell for the bait. He tested the urine and when it tested positive for pregnancy, Hah offered to abort Lauren's "baby." At that point, before any procedure was begun, Lauren gave a signal and the state investigators that were shadowing her closed in.

"We arrested him on January 13, 1992, for the unauthorized practice of medicine, and he was indicted on January 17," said Barr.

Charged with the unauthorized practice of medicine, what is known as an E Felony offense in the

State of New York, if convicted Hah faced up to four years in prison.

While his case wound through the court system pending trial, there was a question that hung over his story like a pall.

Why had he been allowed to still continue to practice despite the fact that his license had been revoked? The answer appeared to be in the state's weighty bureaucracy.

While the State Education Department's Office of Professional Discipline is charged with the duty of investigating people suspected of practicing without a license in various professions, including medicine, there were only three investigators to keep track of literally thousands of cases.

Dr. Hah was caught. How many more unlicensed practitioners remain free to maim unsuspecting patients?

If Dorothy Alou, Sylvia Klein, and Jane Smith were looking forward to a conviction and a long prison sentence, they were disappointed.

On April 30, 1992, Ming Kow Hah pled guilty to one count of the unauthorized practice of medicine, but was given a conditional discharge and one year probation.

His probation ran out in 1993.

Chapter Two

Dr. George Burkhardt

How many chances should a doctor have if he practices on patients while he's a drug addict? One? Two? Maybe, none.

Now, the doctor might claim that he's not under the influence while practicing. But what if, during this addiction phase, said doctor performs surgery and removes a perfectly healthy organ. What then?

For Sarina Povio of Fort Lauderdale, Florida, the answers to these questions are not the stuff of philosophical rumination. She lives with them everyday, as she looks in the mirror and sees a deep, dark empty socket where her right eye used to be.

Dr. George Burkhardt of Plantation, Florida, operated on Sarina while addicted to cocaine.

Plantation, Florida, is an upscale suburb of Fort Lauderdale. As you ride along Broward Boulevard through the heart of town, row upon row of bright green lawn shines in the ever present Florida sunshine, broken occasionally by the blight of strip malls and antiseptic-looking office buildings.

The building where Dr. George Burkhardt practiced was cold, modern, and antiseptic-looking like all the rest. But inside the building where Burkhardt practiced, his office was anything but cold.

Sarina Povio came to see Dr. Burkhardt in the summer of 1986. Burkhardt had decorated his office in nineteenth century style, with brightly colored chintz, drapes, soft cushions, and shiny hardwood floors. There was a bentwood settee upholstered in bright blue and red fabric and paisley borders. An old-fashioned daguerreotype of an ice skating party hung in one of the office's niches.

The only medical touches were the old wooden wheelchair that serviced some invalid from one hundred years ago. It was set in a far corner of the room. Leaning against a mantel was a pair of ancient wooden crutches that Dickens's Tiny Tim might have used. The illusion of the past was broken by the archetypal frosted glass window with a sign that requested patients to sign in and the receptionist behind it who greeted incoming patients.

On the walls staring down were Currier and Ives prints and family snapshots from a later time, the 1940s: a couple posed in front of a Cadillac, a studio portrait of a stately older woman and perhaps the one most effecting, two little boys opening presents on Christmas day in Tipton, Indiana.

On the way to the examining room, the nurse's area contained records which were stored in vertical files draped in more red and blue chintz.

Entering the examining room finally, Sarina was seated in an old-fashioned dentist's chair, which included a drill console, from which a few drills hung down menacingly. Upon further inspection, the porcelain rinsing bowl was filled with a plant; a corner porcelain sink was fitted with spigots and a floor-length ruffled skirt.

Sarina had noticed a little sore on her gums that wouldn't heal and had gone to her dentist for a diagnosis. He sent her to a pathologist who did a biopsy and diagnosed the sore as a mild form of cancer. That was how she was referred to Dr. Burkhardt, an ear, nose, and throat specialist, for an examination.

After a preliminary examination, Burkhardt got scans done of Sarina's sinus and eye area to make sure the cancer hadn't spread. The tests indicated that it had not. The idea then was to surgically remove the cancerous lesion on her gum.

Sarina had no reason to believe Burkhardt was anything but a competent physician. Hailing from Indiana, Burkhardt attended three universities as an undergraduate: the University of Chicago, Butler University, and Stanford University. After crisscrossing the country in pursuit of his bachelor's degree, he finally decided to go south and attended medical school at the University of Miami. Upon his graduation in 1966, he'd done his surgical internship/residency at Jackson Memorial Hospital in Miami from 1966 to 1968. He followed that up with a residency in otolaryngology at Tulane University Hospitals in New Orleans from 1969 to 1971.

Eventually, he settled in south Florida, where he was licensed to practice medicine in 1967. He became affiliated with a number of hospitals in the south Florida area, including becoming an active member of the staff at Plantation General Hospital in

26

Fort Lauderdale.

Plantation General Hospital is a small, private hospital. It was to Plantation General Hospital that Sarina was admitted on July 8, 1986. The next day was her operation.

That evening, Burkhardt came to her room. In his possession was a consent form that he wanted her to sign. It said that in the event he found cancer in her eye, he had her permission to remove it.

According to Povio, Burkhardt claimed that since the cancer was local, there was nothing to worry about. The consent form was a formality that the hospital insisted upon. Reluctantly, Sarina Povio signed it.

"What could I do? He scared me so much I felt I had to give permission. But the last thing I said was, 'No matter what, don't take my eye,' " she later told a national woman's magazine, *For Women First*.

When Sarina awakened after the operation, it was to the shock of her life: Despite what she said, Burkhardt had removed her right eye. She naturally figured that the cancer was a malignancy and that was the reason.

Within two years, her life was in shambles.

Because Burkhardt had removed an excess amount of her facial bones, she couldn't wear a glass eye. Sarina was left with an ugly, gaping hole where her eye used to be. The hole descends to her mouth. If by chance she coughs or sneezes when she's eating, the food comes out the eye socket.

Once employed as a salesclerk in a bakery in a Plantation supermarket, Sarina claimed that she was forced to quit her job after the operation because of her appearance. And the best that doctors could do to help her cosmetically was a pair of rose-colored glasses with a special side panel to hide the hole in her face. Still, curiosity seekers gazed at her empty socket.

Her marriage didn't fare any better. She was constantly on edge and fighting with her husband, actions which she blamed on the emotional state the operation left her in.

Could anything be done to alleviate her pain and suffering? The answer came two years after the operation, when her attorney, Richard Goodman, read the pathology report that had been done on the eye after it was removed. He discovered that the eye had been *free of cancer*, and that Sarina had never been given this information. All along she thought her eye was cancerous and that was why Burkhardt had removed it.

In a deposition later taken by Goodman, Burkhardt said that during the operation he got alarmed when he felt a soft spot in the bones surrounding Sarina's right eye. Concerned that the cancer had spread, he became convinced that the whole eye had to go, in order to save Sarina's life.

In addition, *Burkhardt had not done a biopsy during the operation.* The biopsy would have determined whether or not Sarina had a malignancy. As for the reason he removed a perfectly healthy eye without biopsying it, Burkhardt explained it in his deposition to Sarina's lawyer in this way.

"I didn't do it," Burkhardt said, "because it runs the risk of sending malignant cells through the operative wound and therefore defeating the purpose of the surgery."

* * *

Meanwhile, Sarina, as well as the south Florida medical community Burkhardt was a part of, was in for another surprise.

On June 1, 1987, investigators with the Miami Field Division of the United States Drug Enforcement Administration paid a little visit to the Medical III pharmacy in Plantation, which was located near Burkhardt's office. They were curious regarding the large amount of cocaine the pharmacy had been dispensing. The pharmacy's records revealed that Dr. George Burkhardt had purchased a large quantity of the drug from the pharmacy.

Four days later, on June 5, a DEA investigator visited Burkhardt, who admitted he was addicted to cocaine and surrendered his DEA registration certificate, order forms, and several controlled substances.

According to the DEA records, the pharmacy sold Burkhardt 610 grams of uncut cocaine in twenty-nine months between 1985 and 1987.

In other words, during the time of his operation on Sarina, Burkhardt was heavily addicted to the drug, though he claimed not to be under the influence when he operated on her. But because he never sold any of the cocaine, he was never criminally charged.

Four days after the DEA visit, Burkhardt entered the Cottonwood de Tucson Treatment Center in Tucson, Arizona, for treatment of his addiction to cocaine.

A later report by the Florida Board of Medicine, dated April 27, 1988, made it crystal clear how Burkhardt's addiction affected his patients. "Respondent (Burkhardt) is unable to practice medicine with reasonable skills and safety to patients due to his addiction to cocaine," the report states.

The Board could have revoked Burkhardt's license. Instead, they chose to suspend it for two months and put him on five years of professional probation (that ended in 1992), during which time, his urine would be tested for the presence of cocaine.

Records indicate that Burkhardt's colleagues in the south Florida medical community rushed to his defense and helped him with his treatment program. Sarina, though, was not appeased.

If anything, the discovery that Burkhardt had been a drug addict during the time of her surgery made Sarina angrier. Despite his denials, she became convinced that Burkhardt was under the influence of coke during her operation.

She proceeded with law suits against Burkhardt, Dr. Lanny Gavar, the surgeon who assisted Burkhardt during the operation, Plantation General Hospital, where the operation took place, and the Medical III pharmacy, which, according to the DEA, sold Burkhardt the inordinately high amount of cocaine.

Eventually, Povio received $450,000 in settlements from Plantation General, Gavar, and Medical III. Even though he lacked malpractice insurance, Burkhardt refused to settle. He insisted that he was not under the influence of drugs and had acted properly when he removed Sarina's eye.

"This case is fraught with irresponsibility," Sarina's attorney, Richard Goodman, told the *Fort Lauderdale Sun Sentinel*. "Burkhardt's operating with a heavy cocaine habit and then says, 'Go ahead and sue me. I don't have any money.' "

Burkhardt's attorney, James Sawran, riposted by

asserting that there was no evidence that the cocaine impaired Burkhardt's professional judgment.

In a published report, Burkhardt said of his cocaine abuse, "It screwed up my personal life, but not my professional ability."

Burkhardt finally agreed to an out-of-court settlement in the middle of April 1992. All the parties to the settlement, including Burkhardt, Povio, and their lawyers, agreed to keep the financial terms a secret, and not to talk about the facts of the case to the press or anyone else. Most importantly to Burkhardt, he did not have to admit that he'd done anything wrong.

"We are glad the case is behind us," was all Povio's attorney, Richard Goodman, would say to the *Sun Sentinel*.

Sarina Povio now had her financial settlement, without an admission of guilt. Still, it was something and she could move on with her life

When last contacted, Sarina was apparently having experimental dental implant surgery to improve her appearance. Regardless of its success or not, every day she has to look in the mirror and see what the results of her surgery by George Burkhardt were.

Chapter Three

Dr. Shakir M. Fattah

Dr. Shakir Fattah began his postgraduate training and practice in Iraq under one military dictatorship and finished it under another.

The first was a swift *coup d'état*. On July 14, 1958, the army, led by General Abdul Karim Kassem, seized control of the Iraqi capital of Baghdad and proclaimed Iraq a republic. Shakir M. Fattah was just one of the many Iraqi citizens who watched helplessly as Kassem and his men killed King Feisal and Crown Prince Abdul Illah.

In early 1963, Fattah and his countrymen watched helplessly again as Colonel Abdul Salam Aref, a former colleague of Kassem's, led a coup which overthrew the Kassem regime. Kassem was executed, and bloody internal strife followed.

Practicing medicine in such a political climate was precarious. In 1964, Fattah chose to leave Iraq and headed for the more democratic climes of the United State of America.

In the States from 1964 to 1968, Fattah focused his

practice on internal medicine, and his postgraduate training in Canada from 1968 to 1972 in cardiology. Clearly, regardless of what others would say of him later, what could not be denied was his extensive training.

Eventually, Dr. Fattah moved to Ohio, which licensed him to practice medicine. He currently practices internal medicine at his own clinic in the suburban community of Massillon, Ohio.

Fattah had come a long way, but what began as a journey of hope would turn into a rendezvous with death.

It all began in 1978.

Seventy-six-year-old *Sarah Jones* had been a patient of Dr. Fattah's for three years when she showed up at his office persistently, between March and June of 1978, complaining of pain in the right side of her abdomen.

While such a complaint would warrant most doctors to take a related history, and perform a physical examination prior to a diagnosis, Fattah did none of this. Instead, he prescribed medications meant to relieve Sarah's symptoms and sent her home.

Sarah's problems were only beginning.

After two office visits in September, Fattah hospitalized her on September 24, with Sarah still complaining of abdominal pain. He prescribed Librax, a medicine used in the treatment of irritable bowel syndrome.

During her hospital stay, various tests were performed, and all were negative. Yet, despite her persistent, severe abdominal pain, at no time before or during this hospital admission did Fattah perform a pelvic examination. The State Medical Board of Ohio would later state, "Dr. Fattah had not performed a pelvic examination . . . as would be required early in evaluating a patient with abdominal pain where the cause is unclear."

On September 27, Fattah discharged Sarah with a diagnosis of "spastic colon." Yet, while in the hospital, Fattah prescribed Demerol, a pain killer, for her abdominal pain. "The prescribing of Demerol would be excessive for a diagnosis of spastic colon," the State Board would later say.

Fattah disputed the State Board's contention, claiming he gave Sarah the powerful painkiller because she suffered from arthritis in her spine and all her joints. Yet his own records indicated that Sarah complained of abdominal pain and nothing else when he prescribed Demerol.

The next time Fattah saw Sarah it was in November. Now she complained that she had pain in the right side of her abdomen constantly. Without further workup, Fattah prescribed various medications, including Demerol.

Dr. Fattah continued to prescribe Demerol to Sarah through August 18, 1979. After that date, according to the State Board's "Findings of Fact," Fattah prescribed additional medications without physically examining her. The "Findings of Fact" continues by stating, "Fattah did not see her in a professional capacity for over a year after September 4, 1980."

Fattah saw Sarah again on January 18, 1982. Now she was complaining of pain in her colon (colitis). Her blood and urine analyses were negative, but Fattah failed to document any physical exam or diagnosis. Instead, he prescribed more drugs for her symptoms.

Again on March 8, Sarah complained of colitis and abdominal pain. Dr. Fattah's diagnosis: "irritable bowel syndrome" like before, and he prescribed medication to treat it.

Finally, when Sarah came to Fattah's office on March 10 complaining of nausea and abdominal pain, he hospitalized her.

During this, her second stay, abdominal ultrasound tests revealed an extensive accumulation of fluid in Sarah's abdomen. Two days later, on March 17, Fattah requested a consultation with another physician. That physician took fluid samples from Sarah's abdomen and also performed a pelvic examination. While the results of the pelvic exam was normal, the examination of the abdominal fluid revealed cancer cells.

Several additional tests were inconclusive, until a CT scan revealed a mass, but it was unclear where it was located and to what extent it had affected Sarah's organs. The radiologist recommended another ultrasound.

Despite the fact that the CT scan was inconclusive, Fattah held a conference with Sarah's family regarding the "extent of the malignancy" and her poor prognosis. Fattah's progress note also indicated that Sarah's course was "progressively and rapidly downhill, and that she would be treated symptomatically," which wasn't any different than the way she had been treated by him anyway.

It was not until April 20 that Fattah obtained another pelvic ultrasound, which finally identified a cancerous growth that had spread throughout the uterus.

Sarah died on May 18, 1982, as a result of "adenocarcinoma [cancer] of the pelvis."

Could Dr. Fattah have found the cancer before it

was too late? The State Medical Board would later state simply, ". . . proper investigation of the cause of [Sarah Jones's] abdominal pain would have included a pelvic examination and, if that were negative, a CT scan of the abdomen. Sarah Jones had persistently complained of abdominal pain for four years before Dr. Fattah pursued those measures."

Still, physicians are human beings. They do occasionally make mistakes and to condemn a man for life because of one error might seem harsh.

But how about two, or three, or four, five, six, seven, eight, nine, ten, eleven, and twelve errors of similar nature?

On December 21, 1978, *David Tyler,* forty-three years old, who Fattah had been treating for high blood pressure, came to his office and complained of pain that began in the back of his neck and went down to his arms. These painful episodes, which lasted from five to ten minutes, started in the evening and were accompanied by heavy sweating.

David said that he'd stopped taking his blood pressure medication two days before. Could that be the cause of his problem?

His blood pressure was high, 160/110. Fattah stated the symptoms were due to his "risen blood pressure," and told David to resume his blood pressure medication.

What Fattah did not do was order an EKG or document a physical examination.

Two weeks later, on January 2, 1979, David complained of the same episodes, which were now lasting fifteen minutes. Fattah had David hospitalized for a week. According to his discharge summary, Fattah

36

had treated him with bed rest and medication, discharging him when his blood pressure came down to normal and his pain disappeared. But something else was going on.

An EKG showed heart problems, which Fattah did not follow up with any other tests or a referral to a cardiologist.

One year later in April, Fattah prescribed Ionamin, an appetite suppressant that increases blood pressure, along with Lopressor, a hypertensive medication.

By the time David showed up for a visit on May 29, 1979, he'd lost thirteen and a half pounds. While his blood pressure wasn't unusually high, he complained of afternoon dizziness and stated that he'd fallen off a ladder two days before. Fattah told him to reduce his dosage of Lopressor by half.

In July, 1980, when David was hospitalized for an unrelated condition, his EKG showed a "complete left bundle branch block." Again, Dr. Fattah failed to perform further tests.

On August 25, 1980, David Tyler was rushed to the hospital in severe pain. His chest felt like it was caving in on him and pain radiated out to both shoulders and arms. His breath was short, and he was sweating profusely.

David Tyler died six days later of a heart attack.

The State Medical Board would later note that despite the fact that as early as December 1978, Tyler's clear symptoms suggested heart disease, Dr. Fattah did nothing to follow it up. Even after his January 1979 hospitalization, when it had become clear that Fattah was dealing with coronary disease in a relatively young man, he failed to follow up with tests to ascertain exactly what the problem with his heart was.

"Dr. Fattah had neither taken the appropriate steps

himself nor obtained a cardiology consultation to evaluate [David Tyler's] condition and to determine whether surgery was appropriate to prevent potential catastrophe."

One thing was certain: Potential catastrophe had become a real tragedy. A man was dead.

Practices in small towns like Massillon see a variety of cases, and Dr. Fattah's clinic was no exception. One of his patients was eighty-five-year-old *Mary Mc-Graw,* who had emigrated to Frankton from Texas.

Like many senior citizens, she suffered from degenerative arthritis with low backache from time to time, and her vision was impaired due to cataracts and vascular changes in her eyes. But other than that, she was a spry woman who enjoyed life.

When she came to see Fattah on December 17, 1980, she was suffering from headaches. Without examining her, Fattah prescribed a powerful medication, Darvocet-N 100.

But one month later on January 17, the headaches had become severe, and she was also complaining of nausea. But what was she *really* suffering from?

One possibility was the pressure was building up inside her head due to a brian tumor, aneurysm, or some other mass inside her skull. The second possibility was a disease syndrome almost unique to older patients, polymyalgia rheumatica with temporal arteritis. The polymyalgia rheumatica syndrome can lead to rapid deterioration of vision and other neurological changes. If recognized early, however, it responds dramatically to the administration of a steroid called Prednisone.

The State Medical Board later noted that instead of

entertaining these "very real and serious possibilities," Dr. Fattah "had merely treated [Mary McGraw] with pain medications and various other medications he had apparently continued from her prior treating physician [in Texas]."

In July 1981, Mary stated that she felt the same. Fattah prescribed more medication.

On October 3, 1981, Mary complained that her left shoulder hurt, that she had fallen on her left hip, and that her "vision is not as good."

Again she complained of vision problems on January 5, 1982. She said that she was confused at times, that she had day and night confused.

Did Dr. Fattah order any diagnostic tests? Did he perform a neurological examination to address Mary's complaints of severe headaches, nausea, vision problems, falling, and confusion?

"At no time during the period from December 17, 1980, through January 5, 1982, did Dr. Fattah order diagnostic tests or perform a neurological examination," the State Medical Board's report would later say.

On February 4, 1982, Fattah admitted Mary to the hospital. She was barely conscious. Mary became comatose on February 7 and died on March 20, 1982, due to "cerebrovascular accident."

Strangely, in Fattah's admitting history and his discharge summary, which he dictated two months after Mary died, he failed to mention Mary's history of severe headaches or vision problems. Instead, those reports inexplicably indicated that Mary was admitted to the hospital "because of persistent vomiting, loss of appetite and a change in mental status."

The State Medical Board said that Fattah should have tested Mary for polymyalgia rheumatica syndrome, which if left untreated would cause blindness and other neurological changes, and which is treated with the steroid Prednisone. Dr. Fattah would counter that he could certainly not treat a patient for a condition such as Mary's that was not life threatening with what he characterized as "huge amounts of dangerous steroids."

On direct examination by his own counsel, Dr. Fattah said, "The problem is you had an eighty-five-year-old lady who presented with vomiting and nausea . . . she went into coma, and the coma was complicated by so many things. She was ninety pounds. . . . The point is that in medicine, you reach a point where you say: This is an eighty-five-year-old lady. She has an occasional headache which is responding to Darvoset which is a mild medicine. If you refer her to a neurologist, what is he going to do? If they find something, I mean, what is the practical part of it? To do tests for the headache."

Frank Ryan ran track. Eighteen years old in 1982, it had been while he was running that he began coughing and having chest pain. Even when he walked, he tired quickly and his breath became short.

On May 18, 1982, Frank's doctor, Shakir M. Fattah, admitted him to the hospital. Fattah ordered some preliminary tests, including a chest X ray and an EKG. The results of the EKG showed some abnormalities. A progress note by another physician indicated that, due to marked changes between the present EKG and an old one that had been done in 1978, "complete investigation regarding [Frank Ryan's] cardiopulmonary system was needed."

Despite this warning, Dr. Fattah ordered no other

tests that day. And Frank's condition continued to worsen.

On May 20, Frank took a shower. After he got out, he complained of chest discomfort. His pulse was rapid at 120 and bounding. ·

Fattah's progress notes for that date stated:

"Patient experienced shortness of breath on taking a shower this A.M. Pulse rate increased to 128. Acute myocarditis [heart attack] cannot be ruled out."

Two days later, Frank tried to take a shower again, with the same result. The chest pain was so intense, he had to return to bed. His pulse rose to 130, his blood pressure dropped to 80/64, and he was told to stay in bed.

When Frank's pulse rose to 144, Dr. Fattah was called. Fattah failed to note either this incident or the results of the EKG that had been done upon his order at 11:10 A.M. That test showed cardiac irregularities "which suggested that something was happening to the right side of the heart, the side that is related to pulmonary [lung] circulation."

Instead of further investigating the possibility of some sort of lung or chest disorder, Fattah ordered cardiac medications, digitalis and Inderal, to treat Frank's symptoms.

Despite all this activity, Fattah's progress note for May 22 was succinct. "Patient remains symptomatic. Shortness of breath and chest pain. . . ."

A few days later, on May 24, a stress test was done, but was discontinued because Frank experienced chest pain and fatigue. An echocardiogram was also done that day. Finally, on May 25, Fattah noted: "Echo shows tricuspid valve prolapse because of his obstructive pulmonary disease, patient will be sent home on Lopressor 25 mg."

The State Medical Board later noted "that a physician should have sought to discover why such a thing was happening."

Instead of investigating further, Fattah discharged Frank. He gave him a prescription for Lopressor, a medication oriented toward treatment of congestive heart failure.

Congestive heart failure in an eighteen-year-old athlete who ran track?

It would eventually be the State Medical Board's view that there had been no evidence of congestive heart failure in Frank Ryan. And why was he being discharged when he still showed symptoms for which, in the State Medical Board's view, "there is no adequate explanation"?

Considering his severe symptoms, it was therefore not surprising that approximately six hours after Frank left, he was readmitted to the hospital at 11:55 P.M. A progress note initialed by Fattah, though it is unclear whether he was in attendance at the time of readmission, indicated that the readmission was "because of a sudden episode of chest pain . . . and short fainting episodes."

On the morning of May 26, at approximately 4:45 A.M., the nursing staff called Dr. Fattah. They told him that Frank's pulse was up to 152; his blood pressure was up to 130/86.

By telephone, he ordered the nursing staff to give Frank fifty milligrams of Lopressor, five milligrams of Valium (a tranquilizer), and to administer oxygen to help with his breathing. He also ordered an EKG to be done later that morning.

Apparently, it did not occur to Fattah to look and see if there could be any other cause of Frank's problems other than his heart. Then, things turned worse.

At approximately 7:00 A.M., Frank's pulse was back up to 152. He was nauseous and vomiting. By phone, Fattah instructed the nursing staff to administer Maalox, an over-the-counter antacid.

Twenty-five minutes later, the nursing staff placed an anxious call to Fattah. Frank had a dry cough and appeared "acutely ill." His blood pressure was 130/82, and his pulse was bounding like a wild stallion between 128 and 136. His breathing was rapid and shallow, and he had shortness of breath and chest pain.

By telephone, Dr. Fattah told the nursing staff to obtain arterial blood gases.

Around 8:00 A.M., the dutiful nursing staff called Fattah with the results of the blood gas studies. They showed that the oxygen level in Frank's blood was markedly below normal. Fattah ordered Frank transferred to the cardiac care unit and that the oxygen being given to him be enriched.

Apparently, Frank's condition was not critical enough for Dr. Fattah to rush to the side of his patient. Dr. Fattah was still at home thirty minutes later when he was notified of abnormal results of [further] blood gas studies. He told the nursing staff to enrich the oxygen to a full one hundred percent, obtain additional blood gases, "and to obtain a portable chest X ray stat [fast]."

At 9:45 A.M., Frank was sent for a lung scan. The State Medical Board notes that "It was not until 10:45 a.m., when [Frank Ryan] returned from the lung scan, that Dr. Fattah was in attendance. The lung scan results were consistent with a 'high probability of pulmonary embolism.' "

A pulmonary embolism? That's blood clots going to the lungs. But Fattah was treating him for a heart problem.

At 10:55 A.M., Frank could no longer breathe on his own, and he was placed on a ventilator. It was ineffective.

At approximately 11:20 A.M., Frank's heart stopped. Cardiopulmonary resuscitation was begun. For *two hours,* the doctors and nurses tried to revive him, to no avail.

At 1:30 P.M., on May 26, 1982, Frank Ryan was pronounced dead. The official death certificate that Dr. Fattah filed stated the cause of death as "bilateral (both lungs) pulmonary embolism."

The official questions about Frank Ryan's death would not come until nine years later. By that time, a doctor testifying for the state, Robert L. Polk, would say that "had Dr. Fattah obtained the appropriate tests and diagnosed [Frank Ryan's] pulmonary embolism in a timely manner, the death of this otherwise healthy young man could probably have been prevented. . . ."

It would also be later proved in a court that Dr. Shakir Fattah altered Frank Ryan's death certificate to back up his assertions that Frank Ryan had heart problems.

The State Medical Board would conclude that Frank ". . . needlessly died at age 18 because Dr. Fattah lacked the competence to recognize or pursue significant symptoms and test results. [This] is extremely disturbing."

Debbie Wallace was eleven years old when she came to Dr. Fattah's office on February 8, 1984, with an eye injury. She had been snapped in the eye with a rubber band.

Examining her, Fattah saw a slight tear at the right edge of the cornea and a partially torn pupil that reacted sluggishly to light. She had only eighty percent of her vision.

Dr. Fattah prescribed no treatment.

Debbie returned the next day. Her vision was still twenty percent down in the right eye. In his records, Dr. Fattah noted that "Dr. Stewart [an ophthalmologist] is consulted," but failed to document the substance of that conversation.

Fattah applied a pad to the eye and instructed Debbie to return the next day. On February 10, he noted that her eye was improving and her vision was good.

Fattah didn't see Debbie again until four days later, February 14, 1984. Things seemed to have gotten worse.

Debbie's eye was very congested and red, her vision was less clear than before, and she just couldn't keep the eye open.

Fattah prescribed an antibiotic and told her to continue eyedrops that he had apparently prescribed before without documenting it in his records. He also noted that he would consult again with Dr. Stewart, the ophthalmologist, but his patient record would later fail to indicate that he did so.

Debbie was back in two days. Not only was the eye very congested, there was bleeding in the front part of the eye. Her vision was limited; she only had light perception in the damaged eye.

The State Medical Board would later say in their official record that "At some later time, a note was added to Dr. Fattah's patient record, indicating that Dr. Stewart had performed surgery on February 16, 1984, and that [Debbie Wallace] subsequently had 20/

20 vision in her right eye.

Sounds like a happy ending. Problem was, it was incorrect.

"That statement is inaccurate," the Board continued. ". . . Furthermore, it is apparent from the testimony of Dr. Stewart, and the medical records of [Debbie Wallace's] subsequent treating physicians that Dr. Fattah's patient record failed to accurately reflect his treatment of [Debbie Wallace]."

On February 16, 1984, Debbie, accompanied by her mother, went to see Dr. James V. Stewart, the ophthalmologist. At that time, Debbie's mom stated that Dr. Fattah had "cut a black spot from [Debbie's] right eye yesterday."

Dr. Stewart found a penetrating wound of the right eyeball, with about one mm of the iris sticking out through the wound. The front of the eye was so filled with blood, he could not see how much, if any, of the iris was still intact. Debbie could only perceive light; no vision.

Dr. Stewart hospitalized Debbie and performed surgery. He repaired the puncture wound in the cornea and removed the protruding portion of the iris. He submitted the iris fragment to the pathology lab. The pathology report "indicated that the fragment he had removed was less than 1 mm in size."

Dr. Fammartino, the next physician Debbie saw, examined her on March 6. The history he took at that time "indicated that, during the time [Debbie Wallace] had been under treatment by Dr. Fattah, Dr. Fattah had removed her avulsed iris with a topical anesthesia and sterile scissors in his office."

Dr. Fammartino noted that Debbie Wallace's iris was completely gone.

46

Testifying at a deposition taken on February 25, 1987, Dr. Stewart said that "he had removed only the one mm portion of iris that had been protruding. . . . Since it was later discovered that the entire iris was missing, he could only assume that the rest of the iris had been removed earlier by Dr. Fattah."

As for the note in Fattah's record that he had consulted with Dr. Stewart, Stewart testified that Fattah had called him around February 8, 1984, "stating that he had a patient with an eye injury. He [Dr. Stewart] received the impression that the injury was not a serious one, and that no referral would be made."

Fattah called him over two and a half years later, on December 1, 1986, at which time Fattah admitted that he had removed "the bubble" from Debbie's eye two days before Dr. Stewart saw her. Stewart noted that conversation in his patient record.

Stewart also testified that as of February 24, 1987, Debbie's uncorrected vision in her right eye had improved to 20/30. But there were signs that she was developing glaucoma, her eye pressure was elevated and her visual field was reduced.

The State Medical Board would later note, "The case of [Debbie Wallace] is frightening. It is frightening to find a physician who, without specialized training in ophthalmology, would undertake treatment of eye injuries such as (Debbie Wallace's), rather than making the appropriate referral, and go so far as to remove a 'bubble' from the eye, without knowing it was the patient's avulsed iris."

April 30, 1984. On that date, sixty-three-year-old *Beth Lampley* came to Dr. Fattah. She was spitting up blood.

47

If Fattah examined her, he didn't note it in his records. He prescribed an antibiotic and a decongestant. Back again on October 15 complaining of spitting up blood phlegm, sweating and dry mouth, he scheduled her for a chest X ray the next day.

The X ray indicated that Beth was suffering from bilateral bronchial pneumonia, but that didn't explain why she was coughing up blood. That meant she was bleeding somewhere inside her body. The physician, the State Medical Board would later state, "is obligated to find the source of the bleeding, as it could be the first symptom of a very serious disease."

When blood is found in the mouth, bleeding could have occurred anyplace from the bottom of the lungs up to the lips, which is why investigation of the entire respiratory tract may be necessary.

By October 22, Beth indicated that her symptoms had improved but that it hurt to swallow. Continuing her medication, Fattah instructed his patient to return in one week for another chest X ray.

After that, Beth complained frequently of sore throats, sinus problems, nausea, headaches and earaches, all of which Fattah treated with medications but without documenting physical exams.

On March 4, 1986, Beth complained of spitting up blood again. And again, Fattah didn't examine her but, instead, diagnosed an upper respiratory infection (a cold) and ordered some blood tests and an X ray.

Beth returned three days later, complaining that her throat and ear still hurt but she'd stopped spitting up blood. Fattah prescribed an antibiotic and decongestant, the same type of treatment many doctors give for the common cold.

On May 15, Fattah noted that Beth had again reported blood in her saliva, but that a chest X ray showed no significant change. He told her to continue taking the medications he'd prescribed and to report on her progress.

For the next six months, Fattah continued to treat Beth for symptoms of sore throat, headaches, and sinus problems. Not until November 24, 1986, did Fattah examine Beth's mouth and throat.

He found a swelling under her tongue and performed a biopsy on December 8 that revealed a malignant form of cancer. Beth's daughter elected to take her mother to the Cleveland Clinic for further treatment.

On December 19, 1986, a physician from the Cleveland Clinic performed an examination of her mouth and throat. That exam revealed a cancerous growth that went from the left base of the tongue back to the far side of the right base of the tongue, and extended to the level of the hyoid bone. Cancer was also found on the left floor of the mouth.

The biopsies performed confirmed Fattah's findings of malignant cancer. Four years later on October 11, 1990, Beth died as a result of this disease.

It was a slow death.

In its investigation, the State Medical Board would note, "that carcinoma of the tongue can be a rather slow-growing tumor, with a very prolonged course," and "While it was impossible to tell when [Beth Lampley] had first contracted cancer, her symptoms had required appropriate examination and tests much earlier than November, 1986."

The pain in her right shoulder had lasted for a month by the time fifty-seven-year-old *Julia Swindell* came to Dr. Fattah's office on May 9, 1985.

She described her pain as a "knotted" feeling on the shoulder blade, with intermittent pain and discomfort that had nothing to do with movement.

The board later found that Fattah should have recorded Swindell's complete medical history and performed a physical examination. He did not. In addition, he should have obtained chest or shoulder X rays of the area in pain. He didn't do that either.

Instead, he diagnosed Julia's problems as heart-related and obtained an EKG. Without a further workup, Fattah diagnosed Julia as suffering from "generalized arthritis," and a heart condition including, angina pectoria, and ventricular arrhythmia." He prescribed cardiac medications.

Fattah saw Julia for seven more visits between May and November of 1985. On October 9, she complained of chest pain and weakness. On November 11, she complained again of weakness.

Regardless of her specific complaints, Fattah continued to treat her with cardiac medications, and obtained several more EKGs during this period of time, which revealed very little.

In late November, seeing that she wasn't getting better, Julia saw another physician. He hospitalized her on December 10. On December 13, a breast exam revealed a large mass in Julia's right breast.

Subsequently, Julia was found to have cancer of the breast that had spread to her bones and spleen. The prognosis was not good.

Julia Swindell survived a year and a half longer, and then died as a result of metastatic breast cancer on August 28, 1987.

The State Medical Board would later say that not only had the EKGs Fattah had done shown signs of heart problems, had he X rayed her chest and shoul-

der, the X rays "would have shown metastatic lesions in the bone."

In other words, if the X rays had been done in May when he initially saw her, and not in December, the cancer would have been caught earlier.

This would not be the last time Fattah failed to diagnosis a deadly disease in time.

Elise Foster, twenty-eight years old, had been going to Dr. Fattah for two years when she arrived at his clinic on January 19, 1986, complaining of stomach cramps, vomiting, and diarrhea every few days for the previous three or four months.

Dr. Fattah documented no further history and ordered no tests. He diagnosed Elise as suffering from a "viral infection" and prescribed an antibiotic and other medications.

The State Medical Board would later state that "Dr. Fattah's diagnosis of 'viral infection' was not compatible with [Elise Foster's] statement that her symptoms had lasted three to four months, as viral infections do not generally last that long even without treatment."

In addition, symptoms of several months of abdominal dis comfort, including diarrhea, required a further workup. And, "The specific complaint of diarrhea suggested a lower bowel problem," the State Medical Board continued.

There was no further workup.

On April 16, 1986, Elise came back, with complaints of sharp stomach pains so severe she couldn't eat or sleep, dizziness, and a felling of being "full all the time."

Fattah diagnosed her as having "acute gastritis" (stomachache) and prescribed an antacid and a tranquilizer and sent her home.

She was back on April 24 with the same complaints. Fattah ordered gastrointestinal and gallbladder X rays, which came up negative. Fattah wrote a note indicating that he'd advised Elise to go to the hospital for admission. He didn't even refer her to a specific physician.

At about 11:30 A.M. on April 26, Foster went to the emergency room with complaints of abdominal pain and vomiting. She was admitted to the hospital under the care of another physician. A CT scan on April 29 revealed a large tumor involving the transverse colon and loops of the small bowel. Evidence that the tumor had also spread to the liver was found.

After surgery, chemotherapy and radiation treatments, Elise Foster died on November 16, 1986. She was only twenty-eight years old.

January 25, 1986. Sixty-one-year-old *Ursula Meadows* showed up at Dr. Fattah's office complaining of flu and no appetite for about a month. Fattah noted that she was suffering from upper respiratory infection and a weight loss of thirty pounds in two months.

Thirty pounds in two months is a tremendous weight loss requiring some sort of explanation, perhaps a meticulous history and physical. Fattah did neither, ordering a blood test instead and prescribing an antibiotic and Librax.

Returning a week later, Ursula said she felt better, had more of an appetite but felt dizzy. Her blood tests showed elevated levels of two enzymes, LDH and alkaline phosphate, but he ordered no further diagnostic studies.

The State Medical Board would later write that "Dr.

Fattah failed to take appropriate follow-up steps when the . . . blood tests had shown abnormalities. . . . Elevations of those enzymes would suggest a problem, such as infection or tumor, in the liver. In fact, the combination of the elevated enzyme levels and [Ursula Meadows's] rapid weight loss should have prompted Dr. Fattah to suspect cancer and to conduct further diagnostic testing."

If Dr. Fattah suspected cancer at this point, the record indicates that he didn't follow-up. Ursula continued to get worse.

During her visit on February 8, Ursula said that she had "passed out Tuesday." Fattah noted that her urine was loaded with white blood cells (indicating infection of some sort) and that her lower abdomen was tender. He prescribed a drug that treats urinary tract infections and, on February 15, an antibiotic, noting a diagnosis of upper respiratory infection, though Ursula hadn't made any such complaint nor did Fattah document such physical findings to support his diagnosis.

"Progressive weight loss," Fattah's progress notes of April 5 reported. "Suggest IVP and barium enema. Abdomen lower abdominal fullness. Rule out uterine cancer. Back Monday for pelvic."

Suddenly, on April 7, 1986, Dr. Fattah grimly noted in Ursula's records, "Probably cancer uterus. Enlarged and bleeding. Will refer to gynecologist."

The report of the gynecologist who saw Ursula on April 10 said that Ursula "had stated a history of uterine bleeding two months ago" to her physician, yet no such note appeared in Fattah's records. Upon examination, the gynecologist discovered a suprapubic tumor, uterine bleeding, and an enlarged uterus, the size of a woman who was sixteen weeks pregnant!

The gynecologist admitted Ursula to the hospital for further examination where it was found that she was suffering from endometrial adenocarcinoma, a deadly form of cancer of the uterine mucous membrane.

On May 18, 1986, Ursula Meadows died as a result of that disease. An autopsy revealed that the cancer had spread to the lymph nodes.

And the liver.

And the left lung.

The State Medical Board later said, "A liver scan and gastrointestinal X Rays should have been done. Dr. Fattah had neither performed a complete history and physical nor obtained the appropriate tests."

On February 24, 1990, Doris Purcell, forty-nine years old, came to Fattah's office complaining of a slight cough and "pain in the left side of her rib cage for five days."

Anyone who's ever been to a doctor knows that the first thing a competent doctor does is a physical examination, especially when symptoms are present. Prior to that, the physician, his assistant, or receptionist has you fill out a form with a complete medical history, so he's aware of any prior problems.

The only thing Fattah documented was Doris's weight, blood pressure, and temperature (it was normal). He then treated her for a cold and prescribed an antibiotic and decongestant. And Doris went home like a dutiful patient, as most patients do who trust their doctor.

But Doris returned to Fattah's office on March 9, complaining of swelling in her legs for the previous three days. Fattah noted that she had pain and tender-

54

ness in the left part of her lower chest as well as swelling in the knees and ankles. And she was running a temperature of 100.4°F.

Fattah ordered an X ray. Fattah's radiology report described a "well circumscribed density involving the right upper medial lung field, which appeared to be a right apical pulmonary lesion."

In layman's terms, Doris had cancer of the lung. Yet according to Doris, he told her that her X rays were negative. The diagnosis was made even more chilling by the fact that it was Fattah, and not some assistant, who interpreted the X rays.

The radiology report recommended further diagnostic steps, specifically suggesting a CT scan of the lung. After all, there was a strong possibility now that Doris had lung cancer.

But Fattah did not order that test. Instead, he ordered blood tests and prescribed more antibiotics.

You don't need to be a physician to know that antibiotics are not effective against cancer or that lung cancer is extremely aggressive. The tumors grow very quickly. If not caught and treated in time, it's fatal.

The hourglass had started to run out on Doris Purcell. Unless she got proper treatment before the sands ran out, she would die.

Complaining of chills and pain in the left side of her ribs, Doris returned to Fattah's office on March 15. Fattah ordered and again personally interpreted another X ray, which indicated the pulmonary lesion had not changed size or shape significantly. Still, Doris was running a fever, which would necessitate hospitalization.

Fattah did not record her temperature in her patient record, nor did he note any reference to the X ray findings or order a CT scan. Instead, he noted only that he instructed Doris Purcell to return in one week.

Some patients will stay with a doctor till their death. Others will let their doctors kill them with poor treatment because they refuse to question their authority. A few aggressively take responsibility for their own life. Doris Purcell did the latter.

Doris saw another physician, Dr. *Paul Hyman*. The history taken by that physician indicated that Fattah had placed Doris on "numerous antibiotics, (. . . in addition to the Ampicillin documented by Dr. Fattah)." Doris also reported that after numerous blood tests, Fattah had told her that she was anemic and had "high white corpuscles." And of course, Fattah had told her that her chest X rays were negative.

Dr. Hyman got a chest X ray done immediately, which revealed the lung cancer. Doris was promptly admitted to the hospital and a biopsy revealed adenocarcinoma (cancer) of the right upper lobe of the lung.

Doris eventually received proper care. In fact, Fattah himself would later testify before the State Medical Board that his course of treatment for Doris was "ideal for her," in that she had received timely and appropriate treatment and was now healthy and doing well."

Dr. Shakir Fattah testified that as soon as sixty-seven-year-old *Matt Monroe* walked into his office on July 5, 1989, he knew the man was terminal. That is, he surmised Monroe's condition from his past experience evaluating cardiac patients for surgery, and his care for many cardiopulmonary patients at a cardiopulmonary clinic.

Matt complained of facial distortion, numbness in

the right upper lip, and right eye, a right-sided headache of a week's duration, and a sore right ear. Fattah, who failed to take a medical history or do a physical examination, noted the possibility of a facial disorder commonly known as "Bell's Palsy" and "R/o Brain Metastases," indicating the presence of a metastatic tumor in the brain, a cancer that had spread from somewhere else in the body.

He did not, however, order any diagnostic studies to rule out brain cancer.

Another notation indicated that a chest X ray had been done, followed by a notation, "possible right bronchogenic cancer," indicating cancer in the right lung. The radiology report with regard to the chest X ray noted that the tumor ". . . appears benign, but previous studies for comparison would be needed to assure this conclusion. Otherwise, a CT scan would be helpful, diagnostically."

Matt had a time bomb ticking in his chest. Unless properly treated, what was benign could turn malignant. Dr. Fattah, however, did not order a chest CT scan as had been suggested.

Fattah prescribed a medication to increase coronary blood flow, without noting why and told Matt to come back in a week. Mrs. Monroe would testify later that Fattah told her to call him the next day, which she did.

During their phone conversation, Fattah told her that her husband might have cancer that had spread to his brain and caused the paralysis of his face. He told her that he would have to run more X rays.

Matt came back a week later on July 12, at which time Fattah noted that Matt had lung cancer that had spread. He ordered another chest X ray, and instructed Matt to return in one week. There is no indication that he ever told his patient what he was suffering from.

Dr. Fattah's chart for Matt's visit on July 19, 1989, contains a report of a chest X ray done on that date. Although the radiologist reported that there was no change in Matt's chest tumor, Fattah's progress note for that date stated that the chest X ray had shown "diminution on the right lung infiltrate," meaning that the tumor's size had decreased.

Contrary to what the X ray actually said, when he talked to Mrs. Monroe, Fattah told her that the spot on Matt's lung seemed to be getting smaller, which indicated that it wasn't cancer because cancer got bigger, not smaller. Dr. Fattah said that the lung spot could just be scarring because her husband had broken a rib at one time.

Matt had a third chest X ray at Dr. Fattah's clinic on August 3. Again the radiologist found the tumor unchanged and recommended a tomography, another diagnostic test. Fattah's progress note for that date made no mention of the X ray findings, and he did not order the tomograms as recommended.

On September 19, Matt took a chest X ray for the fourth time. The new one showed the same findings as the last three.

Dr. Fattah gave Matt no further treatments or tests.

On October 17, a fifth chest X ray was done. The findings were essentially the same. The radiologist again recommended tomograms. Finally, this time, Fattah acquiesced, and, on November 17, Matt had tomograms of his right lung done at Fattah's clinic.

The radiologist reported that the tumor, while still benign, ". . . malignant change could not be ruled out." Fattah finally scheduled Matt for a chest CT scan.

58

On November 20, approximately four and one half months after such a test had been recommended by the radiologist at Fattah's clinic, the chest CT scan was done on Matt.

It revealed two masses in Matt's lung, not the one that had previously shown up on the X ray. While the cancer still appeared to be benign, Fattah failed to follow up with any other treatment.

According to Mrs. Monroe, Dr. Fattah had again asked her to call him after the CT scan, and she did so. During their conversation, Fattah told her that it didn't look like cancer, but that he would watch it.

Then, while the time bomb ticked in Matt Monroe's chest, Dr. Fattah did not see him again for nine months.

On August 21, September 4, and September 18, Fattah saw Matt who was complaining of hoarseness and feeling "tired all the time." Fattah diagnosed laryngitis, but did not recommend any treatment.

On September 19, Fattah performed a laryngoscopy, noting findings of "thickening of the [vocal] chords, no paralysis."

On October 11, Matt went to the emergency room of his local hospital with complaints of hoarseness, progressive tiredness, and weight loss. According to the history taken by the emergency room physician, Matt had decided not to see Dr. Fattah anymore but had been unable to get an appointment with another physician in the interim. Matt also told the doctor that he had a history of a chest mass in his lung that was probably not malignant.

Matt was admitted to the hospital under the care of another doctor for evaluation of his chest mass. Chest X rays taken at the hospital on October 11, showed the chest mass, but it had enlarged since the November, 1989 CT, and was highly suspicious for malignancy."

Specimens of tissue were taken from the infected lungs. A biopsy was performed. It confirmed that Matt had a malignant tumor in his left lung.

Because of his generally poor condition, weight loss, and the fact that the malignant tumor was also found to have spread to the other lung, Matt Monroe was not felt to be a candidate for surgery. Matt declined the options of radiotherapy and chemotherapy, preferring just to die in peace.

Two months later, he was readmitted to the hospital. He died on December 11, 1990, from coughing up a massive amount of blood due to his lung cancer.

Dr. Robert Polk, the State Medical Board's expert witness, would later testify that had Fattah not delayed a definitive diagnosis of Matt Monroe's lung tumor for approximately one and a half years, it might have been operable.

Matt might still be alive.

Dr. Shakir M. Fattah was finally called to account before the State Medical Board of Ohio. At stake was his license to practice medicine and surgery in the state, and some said the safety of the patients who came to him with trust at his Massillon clinic.

In a hearing held on November 7 and 8, 1991, the state presented its case against Dr. Fattah, reviewing all of these cases and more, which, it said, proved he was a liability as a doctor.

In announcing its verdict, the Ohio State Medical Board said that "Dr. Fattah's frequent claims of omniscience, in the absence of objective clinical data and in the face of tragic outcomes, shatter the reviewer's credulity. These cases collectively, engender concern for the safety of Dr. Fattah's present patients. It is apparent that Dr. Fattah is a danger to the health-consuming public. His incompetent, unscrupulous practices have already caused disaster for some, potential disaster for others. This matter does not call for remedial sanction, aimed at rehabilitating the physician. It calls for immediate, stringent measures to protect unsuspecting patients."

And then on May 13, 1992, the Board ordered Dr. Shakir M. Fattah's certificate to practice medicine and surgery in the State of Ohio be permanently revoked.

According to Lauren Lubow, Case Control Office for the State Medical Board of Ohio, "Doctor Fattah appealed the Board's Order to the Franklin County Common Pleas Court."

Presiding Judge Evelyn. J. Stratton wrote in her ruling, "Dr. Fattah, in his hearing before the Board, and in his appeal, has done very little to try to discredit or refute any of the testimony presented against him. He presented almost no contrary evidence, no opposing experts, and in fact his own testimony convicts him as much as the testimony of Dr. Polk. His own testimony is contradictory, inconclusive, and often in direct conflict with his own medical records."

And then she cited the case of Mary McGraw.

"After a year of complaining of headaches and other major symptoms, with little or no treatment, [Mary McGraw] expired with a stroke on March 20, 1982. Not only did Dr. Fattah do nothing to try to extend her life by warding off the signs of strokes which were clearly identified by the expert witness, but he

61

did nothing to improve the quality of her life during the final year that she suffered.

"Unfortunately, most of the evidence in this case is extremely tragic. The majority of the patients identified by the State Medical Board involved the death of various patients both young and old. The deaths were largely and collectively the result of Dr. Fattah ignoring major identifying symptoms or grossly mistreating those symptoms. In several cases, Dr. Fattah went even further by treating conditions that he was not clearly qualified to treat, instead of referring those cases to a specialist. The record is replete with example and example of misdiagnosed and mistreated patients that were identified and clearly documented by Dr. Fattah's own records. The numerous examples constitute overwhelming and (not just merely substantial and prohibitive) evidence of Dr. Fattah's failure to conform to the barest minimal standards of care of similar practitioners in the same or similar circumstances. In this case, actual injury to the patient, usually death, was well established."

"The Court affirmed the Board's Order of Revocation; however, the court decision also specifies that the stay shall remain in effect until the matter is finally adjudicated," says Lauren Lubow.

Until that time, Dr. Fattah can still practice medicine and surgery.

Chapter Four

Dr. Abu Hayat

Certain New Yorkers like to trumpet how their city is defined by its culture. It's a city filled with theater and fine restaurants, gorgeous residences and public parks, they say. If they get sick, there's always the specialist they can go to, or the university hospital that gives excellent care.

But that's the New York for the money, the privileged.

For the working poor, the underbelly of the city is a different story. They live in tenements and eat at greasy spoons, their only entertainment: conversations on the corner or what they see on television. As for medical care, it's far worse than the rich can imagine.

With little money, many are forced to go to what are euphemistically described as "clinics," dreary, depressing offices where doctors that are best described as butchers perform their handiwork on unsuspecting patients.

For those poor and undereducated women who become pregnant and decide to have an abortion, they don't go to clinics, they go to abortion mills, where conditions are unsanitary and patients are shuttled in to a doctor like so many cattle to the slaughter. Leading the pack of these doctors from hell was Dr. Abu Hayat.

The island of Hispaniola lies in the Caribbean, sun-drenched and inviting.

On one side is Haiti, a country with the worst standard of living in the Northern Hemisphere. On the other side is the Dominican Republic, which is just barely up the economic scale. Both Haitians and Dominicans know that the United States would afford them a vastly superior life-style.

Rosa Rodriguez and Marie and David Moise were among the lucky ones. Marie and David were from Haiti, Rosa from the Dominican Republic. They managed to emigrate to the United States, where they hoped to lead a freer and healthier life.

They wound up settling in "Alphabet City," a series of tenement-lined, crime-ridden streets on the lower east side of Manhattan. It was there that many recently emigrated Hispanic immigrants went to live.

In place of the rich's fancy restaurants were the neighborhood *bodegas*. The theater was the theater of the streets, anything from drug-related shootings to lice-infested homeless urinating on the streets. Museums were funeral homes with their fancy facades, which the immigrants patronized in inordinate numbers because of the crime and dirt they were forced to live in, and eventually many of them were forced to succumb to.

As for medical help, private doctors and clean

hospitals were a fiction, something they saw on television, on a soap opera or a dramatic movie-of-the-week. Clinics were where they went for inexpensive and frequently inadequate treatment.

The *New York Post* later reported that Rosa was abandoned at the age of sixteen by a man who had gotten her pregnant. When her child was two, she found herself in a family way again. She was working as a waitress, making $150 a week, and still living with her mother.

Another child would be a terrible economic, not to mention emotional, burden to anyone under similar circumstances. Rosa decided to have an abortion.

On October 25, 1991, Rosa Rodriguez, twenty-two years old responded to a newspaper advertisement that promised inexpensive, "pain-free" abortions. Rosa Rodriguez went to a Brooklyn clinic, where she was examined by Margie Miranda, who then took her to Dr. Abu Hayat's office at 9 Avenue A in Manhattan's "Alphabet City."

Waiting in an examining room to be examined by Hayat, Rosa became frightened when she heard screams coming from an adjoining examining room.

"I heard screaming from the room where the doctor went," she would later be reported as saying. "I heard somebody saying not to kill the baby."

Soon, it was her turn to meet with Dr. Abu Hayat.

When she asked why the woman was screaming, she said Dr. Hayat told her, "Not everyone wants anesthesia, and not everyone can pay for the anesthesia."

Then it was down to business.

"The fee for the abortion is $1,500. In cash," Hayat told her.

"I only have $1,000 cash with me," Rosa replied.

Hayat was nothing if not a businessman. He accepted the $1,000, and also took her passport, green card, and a gold and diamond ring as collateral for the remaining $500. By handing over the green card, Rosa was mortgaging her freedom.

The green card legally proved she could live and work in the United States. Without it, an immigration inspector might assume she was an illegal alien who could be deported.

After receiving his booty, Hayat examined Rosa. Hayat examined her manually but did not take a sonogram, a standard procedure during pregnancy to create a black and white picture of the fetus inside the womb and thus determine its age.

Apparently, Hayat didn't care about the fetus's age. Even though she was eight months pregnant — if her fetus were delivered now, it could be viable outside the womb — and in direct violation of New York State law that does not permit abortions after six months, Hayat decided to go ahead with the procedure.

He injected Rosa with an unknown solution to cause the termination of the pregnancy. Next was the insertion of laminaria, the medicated wooden sticks that are put into a woman's cervix to dilate it twelve hours before an abortion. Rosa objected.

"They looked dirty," Rosa would later say. "I asked if he could clean them."

Rosa says that an aide to Hayat "put water on them and rinsed them," rather than sterilizing them. Afterwards, he inserted them and sent Rosa home. She was to return the next day for the abortion.

"And if you have any problems," Dr. Hayat said, "you should call Margie and not go to any hospital."

At about 9:40 A.M. the next day, October 26, Rosa

went with Margie to Hayat's clinic. In the interim, she'd felt the baby moving and had a change of heart.

"I want to stop the abortion."

Hayat told her that at this point, she had to proceed. Hayat tied Rosa's feet to the stirrups that protruded from the examining table. While two assistants held down each arm, Hayat plunged a needle into her arm and injected some sort of drug which knocked her out. She went into the dream world of semiconsciousness.

Like a character in a movie who awakens from a sound sleep to abject horror, when Rosa awoke she discovered her legs and clothes saturated with blood. Hayat simply told her that he had removed the "old medication" and inserted some more. He told Rosa to go home and return to his office the next day.

And then he added these caveats:

- She shouldn't tell anyone what had happened.
- She shouldn't go to any hospital.
- If she felt badly, she should call Margie.

Records at the State Medical Board show on that night, October 26, Rosa Rodriguez experienced "severe abdominal pain and contractions."

Just as the doctor had ordered, Rosa called Margie and told her about her plight.

"I'll call Dr. Hayat," Margie said.

Margie did, and Hayat said that Rosa was not yet ready [for the abortion] and should wait until the next day.

As the night progressed, Rosa grew worse. She called Margie a second time to complain about the pain.

Margie reassured her. She said this was normal, not to get desperate. Why didn't she come to her, Margie's house, and she would take care of her?

Rosa never got a chance to take her up on her offer.

The pain finally became too severe for Rosa, and she told her mother that she was pregnant and in a lot of pain. A wise family friend called an ambulance. She was taken to nearby Jamaica Hospital.

Hours later, at approximately 8:10 A.M. on October 27, 1991, Rosa Rodriguez delivered her second child, named Ana Rosa Rodriguez.

"The baby was bleeding a lot from her arm," Rosa would later testify. "I saw that her right arm was *missing*. They asked me if I wanted to keep her, and I told them, 'Yes!' "

Where was the baby's right arm?

The physicians at Jamaica Hospital, not knowing that Dr. Abu Hayat had botched the abortion, performed a D&C, an abdominal X ray, and a pelvic sonogram, to no avail. They failed to locate the baby's missing arm. That made sense since the botched abortion took place across the river in a different borough.

The arm had probably wound up in the trash outside Hayat's office.

After Hayat's office learned that Rosa had given birth, Rosa claims that an associate of the doctor phoned her at Jamaica Hospital. That associate offered to return her papers and jewelry if she promised not to report the botched abortion to authorities.

Rosa would not tolerate that kind of blackmail. She reported her story to the authorities. Hayat was arrested and charged with assault on both the baby and the mother, and for violating New York State's abortion law.

Had this been the only crime Hayat was guilty of, it could have been considered to be an aberration of a greedy, incompetent man masquerading in the guise of a physician. But after the story of Rosa Rodriguez hit the newspapers and the local TV news shows, which reported all the gruesome details, the publicity it generated caused more than thirty women to come forward to say that Dr. Hayat had botched their abortions.

It soon became clear that Rosa's case was just one of many Hayat horror stories.

Like many Haitian immigrants, David and Marie Moise had very little money. When Marie became pregnant, they decided to seek an abortion.

On March 17, 1991, they went to Dr. Hayat's abortion clinic. They told Hayat that Marie was two and a half months pregnant.

First things first. The price for the abortion, Dr. Hayat told them, was $500 in cash. Apparently, they agreed, and Marie was taken to the second floor of his clinic to begin the abortion. Meanwhile, David stayed downstairs and took a seat in the waiting room.

About a half hour into the procedure David would later recall, Hayat left his patient on the table. He needed to go downstairs to the waiting room, to speak to David.

"Your wife is more than three months pregnant," Hayat allegedly told David. That would make the procedure more difficult than he'd anticipated. Hayat wanted $500 more to continue. If Hayat didn't get his money immediately, he would not complete the abortion and David would have to take his wife home.

David was distraught. He pleaded with Hayat to

finish the abortion.

"What can I do? I don't have any money," David replied.

While his wife waited in stirrups upstairs, in the middle of the operation, David had to think fast. He said that he would bring the additional $500 the following afternoon.

Allegedly, Hayat told him, "Go back home, ask your neighbor to borrow $500."

And with that, Hayat refused to complete the procedure. Hayat and one of his assistants personally assisted Marie downstairs. She was hemorrhaging from her vagina, had severe abdominal pains, and she was still under sedation. David would later say that she was so groggy, she couldn't stand, let alone dress herself without help.

Hayat would not allow him to call for a taxi from the office telephone. David and Marie had no choice but to go home.

That night and into the following day, Marie kept experiencing the pain and bleeding. Finally, at 11:45 P.M. on March 18, David took his wife to St. Luke's Hospital on Amsterdam Avenue and 114th Street in Manhattan.

It was Dr. *Ellen Roberts* who examined Marie Moise upon her admission to the hospital. Dr. Roberts found that Marie had a distended abdomen, a temperature of 103°F, and an irregular heartbeat. And in a scene right out of *Rosemary's Baby,* Marie had a foul-smelling, dark, bloody discharge with little pieces of fetal tissue and laminaria protruding from her cervix.

Husband David told Dr. Roberts how they had gone to Dr. Hayat for an abortion and that Hayat

70

would not complete the abortion because David could not immediately come up with the additional money Hayat had demanded.

The doctors at St. Luke's Hospital performed a dilation and curettage to complete Marie's abortion. Unfortunately, Hayat's barbaric treatment led to infection requiring hospitalization.

Hayat would later deny that he had rendered any treatment to Marie Moise whatsoever. What's more, he was unfamiliar with her name and had no record of ever treating her.

The latter was true. The State Medical Board would later find that Hayat failed to maintain a medical record which accurately reflected his evaluation and treatment of Marie Moise.

In any case, his statements would eventually be contradicted by his employee at the time, Margie Miranda, who specifically remembered Marie and David Moise in the clinic on several occasions.

Hayat could not go on forever abusing patients. Eventually, he would have to pay for his actions.

On November 22, 1991, the New York State Board for Professional Medical Conduct charged Dr. Abu Hayat with the following: "professional misconduct by reason of practicing the profession of medicine with gross negligence; with negligence on more than one occasion; with violation of State Law governing the practice of medicine; with moral unfitness in the practice of medicine, with abandonment of a patient; with fraudulent practice, with failing to maintain accurate records and with excessive tests not indicated clinically."

Most times, a physician is allowed to practice while

the charges are being heard, but Hayat's case was considered to be one of the most egregious and it demanded immediate action.

On the same date that Hayat was charged, the Commissioner of Health ordered "that the continued practice of medicine in the State of New York by [Dr. Abu Hayat] constitutes an imminent danger to the health of the people of the State and ordered that effective immediately [Dr. Abu Hayat] shall not practice medicine in the State of New York and that the Order shall remain in effect unless modified or vacated by the Commissioner of Health. . . ."

On December 3, 4, and 17, 1991, the State Board for Professional Medical Conduct met to consider the charges against Dr. Abu Hayat.

The cases of Rosa Rodriguez and Marie Moise were the first two cited. But it wasn't until the third, the case of *Celia McMurray,* that the full impact of Hayat's actions truly were brought home.

Willoughby Avenue is in the Crown Heights section of Brooklyn. Like "Alphabet City," it is an area that is predominantly African-American and Hispanic.

It was to a clinic at 165 Willoughby Avenue that Celia McMurray, seventeen years old, went for treatment. She was referred to Dr. Abu Hayat.

In September 1990, Celia went to see Dr. Hayat. She was accompanied by her husband and the operator of the Willoughby Avenue Clinic.

Celia was examined by Hayat, given a prescription for antibiotics, and told to return.

As he'd requested, Celia and her mother returned to Dr. Hayat's office on September 18, 1990. Celia was given an intravenous infusion, which caused her to lose consciousness.

What happened during the period of time when Celia was knocked out? What exactly did Hayat do to her?

Celia McMurray remained in Dr. Abu Hayat's office for four hours, and was then given another prescription for antibiotics. She went home.

Later in the evening of September 18, Celia complained of vaginal bleeding and abdominal pain. She was also having great difficulty breathing.

The following day, September 19, she was admitted to the sprawling Kings County Medical Center on Clarkson Avenue in Crown Heights.

Kings County is a city-run hospital, and has an excellent emergency room trauma team. If anyone could help her, they could.

Celia was diagnosed with sepsis. Also known as septic poisoning, the condition is actually an infection caused by the absorption into the bloodstream of disease-producing microorganisms, such as the type one might find on unsterilized medical instruments.

The surgeons at Kings County anesthetized Celia and performed an exploratory laparotomy, a surgical procedure that doesn't require an extensive amount of cutting, and is therefore less invasive. They discovered that Celia's uterus was perforated in the lower segment. Apparently, the damage was extensive because her uterus had to be removed.

Celia's condition continued to worsen. Six days later, on September 26, 1990, Celia McMurray died of septic shock.

As was the case with Marie Moise, Hayat would later deny that he had treated Celia.

At the Medical Board hearing, Jeffrey Rubin, Hayat's attorney at the time, submitted two letters, dated April 30, 1991 and July 23, 1991, "wherein he states that [Dr. Abu Hayat] claims that he never treated [Celia McMurray] at his clinic at 9 Avenue A . . . and that he never performed an abortion on her. Mr. Rubin also reported that [Dr. Abu Hayat] claims that he does not have nor did he ever have possession of a patient chart concerning the treatment of [Celia McMurray]."

The state moved immediately to counter that claim with the testimony of *Dr. Rebecca Parkins.*

Dr. Parkins, who was the chief resident responsible for Celia McMurray's medical care at Kings County Hospital, identified Celia from a photograph. Once it was established that she'd treated Celia, Dr. Parkins was free to offer further relevant testimony.

Dr. Parkins testified that she asked Celia's mother for the name of the physician who treated her daughter.

"It was Dr. Hayat," Celia's mother told Dr. Parkins.

Dr. Harding then asked Celia's mother to have Dr. Hayat call her at the hospital.

Hayat called Dr. Parkins at Kings County Medical Center and told her that Celia McMurray had delivered a fetus at home and came to him with complaints of abdominal pain and bleeding and that he sent her straight to the hospital.

To counter that claim Margie Miranda, who was employed by Hayat at that time, was brought in to give evidence. Margie identified Celia from a photograph. She testified that Celia, accompanied by her mother, was seen *twice* at Hayat's 9 Avenue A clinic in September 1990, and that subsequent to the second visit, Celia's mother phoned Hayat and was "hysterical and crying at the time."

Margie Miranda also testified that there had been a record on Celia McMurray at Dr. Hayat's office and that at the time of Celia's initial visit, Dr. Hayat argued with the operator of the Brooklyn clinic about "payments relative to [Celia McMurray]."

The State Board for Professional Medical Conduct hears the charges against recalcitrant doctors and then makes its conclusions. The conclusions, in Celia's case, went a long way toward solving the mystery of what happened to her after Hayat had given her a drug that put her to sleep.

"On September 18, 1990, [Dr. Abu Hayat] performed an abortion on [Celia McMurray]. During the course of the abortion, [Dr. Abu Hayat] perforated the uterus."

Hayat failed to transfer or make arrangements for Celia's transfer to the hospital after her uterus had been perforated, the Board found. And then, the most damning statement of all.

"On the following day, September 19, 1990, [Celia McMurray] was admitted to Kings County Hospital where the diagnosis was sepsis secondary to a perforated uterus from an abortion. She developed disseminated intravascular coagulation [severe bleeding] as a result of the sepsis and died on September 26, 1990, as a result of the coagulopathy."

Almost as an afterthought, the Board noted that Hayat "failed to maintain a medical record which accurately reflected his evaluation and treatment of [Celia McMurray]."

No matter how damning all of this was, the Board still wasn't through. The trail of Dr. Abu Hayat's heinous acts led even farther into the past.

On July 14, 1988, *Susan Thompson* went to see Hayat at his office at 9 Avenue A. She, too, wanted to terminate her pregnancy, which was advanced to approximately the seventeenth week.

Three days later, on July 17, on the second floor of Hayat's Avenue A office, Hayat performed an abortion on Susan Thompson. But it didn't go so well.

After the procedure, Susan came downstairs and was hemorrhaging. Hayat told her that the bleeding was normal and that she should go home. "He did not tell her it was necessary to return for a follow-up examination," the State Medical Board later noted.

Hayat's reassurances to the contrary, Susan remained in extreme pain and returned to Hayat's office on July 19, accompanied by her girlfriend. Using the suction machine that is used in many abortions, Hayat resuctioned Susan. After the procedure, Susan was bleeding again. Despite that, Hayat told Susan's girlfriend that Susan could go home, that everything was going to be okay.

It was twelve hours after Hayat resuctioned Susan, when she started defecating fecal matter through her vagina.

Susan must have been frantic. This just couldn't be normal after an abortion. She spoke with a girlfriend about her medical problems and went to see her girlfriend's physician who sent her to North Central Bronx Hospital, where she was admitted at 9:13 A.M. on August 3, 1988.

The emergency room physicians found parts of a fetal skull in Susan's cervix.

Susan was diagnosed as having an uterocolic fistula, a [serious opening between uterus and the colon] and was operated on for that condition on August 5.

The following year, in an affidavit on November 29, 1989, Dr. Abu Hayat "denied that he ever examined or treated [Susan Thompson] and claimed that he had no medical records regarding this patient."

Once again, the State Medical Board found Dr. Hayat had lied through his teeth.

"During the course of performing a second trimester abortion . . . [Dr. Hayat] perforated [Thompson's] uterus in two places. These perforations caused a uterocolic fistula."

Following the pattern of his treatment with Celia McMurray, Hayat failed to transfer or arrange for the transfer of Susan Thompson to a hospital.

"[Dr. Hayat] failed to completely evacuate the fetal parts from [Susan Thompson's] uterus prior to sending her home from his office," the Board continued. And Hayat also failed to maintain a medical record which accurately reflected his evaluation and treatment of Susan.

After hearing all of the evidence, the Hearing Committee of the Board concluded unanimously "that the continued practice of medicine in the State of New York by [Dr. Abu Hayat] constitutes an imminent danger to the health of the people of the State and the Summary Order issued by the Commissioner of Health shall remain in effect.

"The Hearing Committee unanimously determines that [Dr. Abu Hayat's] license to practice medicine in the State of New York be REVOKED."

Dr. Abu Hayat's story does not end with his medical license being revoked on February 17, 1992. Even while the State Medical Board was investigating him, the District Attorney for the County of Manhattan was doing exactly the same thing.

Hayat had already been charged with knowingly attempting an abortion well past the state's legal limit of twenty-four weeks, as well as several other counts of assault and related charges.

Surprisingly, considering the plethora of abortion mills that flourish in the city, criminal charges of this type are rare. From 1987 through 1991, only four people were arrested in New York State for illegal abortions. None were prosecuted, as Hayat was about to be.

Amid the clacking of motor drives and camera flashes, and the blinding spotlights from video cameras, Dr. Abu Hayat's trial began on January 27, 1993, in the Foley Square courthouse in Lower Manhattan.

Ronald J. Veneziano, the attorney representing Dr. Hayat, chose the unusual tactic of not giving an opening statement. The opening statement usually gives the jury an idea of what the defense's version of events is, but without it, that remained a mystery.

On the second day of the trial, Rosa Rodriguez testified. Wearing a suit jacket that looked two sizes too big for her and hanging earrings, the petite blond woman identified Dr. Hayat as the man who had botched her abortion. Dr. Hayat sat impassively as she continued to recount her tale of horror.

During two days of testimony impressive for its stark detail, Rosa told of how she came to go to Hayat and the botched abortion, never sparing the gory details of what his office was like, what happened after she awoke with her clothing saturated with her own blood and her surprise when her daughter Ana Rosa was born without an arm.

Next came David Moise. Moise had to testify in Creole through an interpreter. He went on to describe, in harrowing detail, Dr. Hayat's attempt to get additional money for his wife's abortion while the doctor was in the middle of the procedure, and the offhanded way Hayat treated them when they could not pay the additional money Hayat demanded.

In the first few days of the trial, people all over the New York State region were talking about the case. The New York news media had a field day.

The tabloids, *Newsday,* the *New York Post,* and the *Daily News,* even that venerable broadsheet *The New York Times,* all gave the story prime coverage. The local news shows, which traditionally feed on people's suffering, all had reporters and camera crews covering the trial.

The verdict came in, on Monday, February 22, 1993.

The jury had been out for four and half days. The courtroom was tense and expectant as the jury foreman stood and read the verdicts.

"Guilty," the foreman intoned to the charge of performing an illegal third trimester abortion.

"Guilty," the foreman intoned to the charge of assault on Rosa Rodriguez.

"Guilty," the foreman intoned to the charge of assault on Ana Rosa Rodriguez.

"Guilty," the foreman intoned to the charge that he'd assaulted Marie Moise.

"Guilty," the foreman intoned again, to a second charge that he'd assaulted Ms. Moise.

Hayat had stood quietly, staring at the floor, as the verdicts were read. Justice Jeffrey M. Atlas, the presiding judge, dismissed one illegal abortion count and one assault count on which the jury deadlocked. He was acquitted of merely one additional count of assault on Rosa Rodriguez. For the crimes he'd been convicted of, Hayat was looking at a lengthy prison sentence.

When justice had run its course, the bailiff led him away like any common criminal. Ronald J. Veneziano, Hayat's lawyer, asked that Hayat be placed under a suicide watch. Later, he explained his request to newspeople by telling them that his client was depressed. The suicide watch was "an appropriate precaution."

"I think he's just shocked by the whole thing," Veneziano told *The New York Times* afterwards. "You don't really expect it [the guilty verdict] to happen."

The jurors, meanwhile, were taken out of the courthouse's back door to a waiting van and then driven by a court officer to a taxi stand near Union Square on 14th Street. They refused to discuss the case.

On Monday, June 14, 1993, Dr. Abu Hayat was sentenced to nine and two-thirds years to twenty-nine years in prison. He will not be eligible for parole until the year 2002.

Chapter Five

Dr. Irvin W. Gilmore

Did Dr. Irvin W. Gilmore murder his wife with a lethal dose of Demerol? Authorities in Berk County, Pennsylvania, had reason to wonder.

During their nine year marriage, Patricia Gilmore had been her husband's patient. Dr. Irvin W. Gilmore had frequently treated his wife for overindulging in the consumption of alcohol.

The treatment? Principally injections of meperidine, a powerful synthetic substitute for opiate narcotics, commonly known by the trade name Demerol.

When Patricia Gilmore died from an apparent overdose of meperidine in 1980, the District Attorney of Berk County had reason to suspect that it was Dr. Gilmore who'd administered the apparently lethal injection. Gilmore claimed she injected herself. Perhaps, Gilmore never meant to kill her, just miscalculated the dosage.

When Irvin Gilmore's wife died, the courts had to decide who administered the fatal dose, and, if it was Gilmore, whether he meant to kill her or not. Once those decisions were made, it would then be in the hands of the Pennsylvania State Board of Medicine to decide, based on the verdict, whether or not to revoke or suspend his license to practice medicine in the Commonwealth of Pennsylvania.

What finally happened is still being debated today.

The story began on a cold Thanksgiving Day, November 27, 1980, in rural Temple, Pennsylvania.

Irvin W. Gilmore had been practicing medicine in Pennsylvania since the state issued him a license on September 10, 1952, with nary a blemish on his record, until that Thanksgiving Day.

After a night of drinking and dining, Gilmore and his wife retired to their bed, although at different times. The next morning at 8:00 A.M., Gilmore awoke to discover his wife of nine years dead.

An autopsy revealed that Patricia Gilmore died of acute meperidine poisoning precipitated by her consumption of a prodigious amount of alcohol.

Meperidine is a drug that is commonly used to relieve severe pain. It acts to depress the central nervous system and can produce drowsiness, sleep, anesthesia, loss of consciousness and death.

In addition to fresh needle marks on her body, Mrs. Gilmore had apparent bruises on her face and hidden bruises on her scalp.

Authorities are often reluctant to charge a doctor with a serious crime unless they have strong evidence. After all, doctors are pillars of the community. In a sense, to attack them is to attack the sanctity of the community itself.

The District Attorney took almost a full year to investigate. On October 21, 1981, the District Attorney of Berk County, Pennsylvania, charged Gilmore with criminal homicide, aggravated assault, and recklessly endangering another person, in connection with the death of his wife, Patricia Gilmore.

The prosecution's theory of what occurred was very basic. It had happened like this.

On November 26, Gilmore's son and daughter-in-law arrived at their home for a visit. In the evening, all four attended a dinner party at a friend's home; several drinks were consumed by Gilmore and his wife before and during dinner.

It would be six more years of legal maneuvering before Irvin Gilmore came to trial in February of 1987. Like most cases involving a seemingly violent death between couples, their personal life gets paraded in public, and the Gilmores were no exception.

According to the report of the State Medical Board, that confirmed trial testimony, "During the marriage, Mrs. Gilmore would overindulge in the consumption of alcohol and Respondent [Gilmore] would undertake to treat the symptoms of overindulgence with various drugs, among them meperidine combined with Vitamin B complex and Stadol, each via injection."

The implication: Patricia Gilmore had a drinking problem, and her husband, acting as her physician, sought to assist her in alleviating the symptoms of "overindulgence."

When the Gilmore's returned home, Gilmore retired to bed sometime between 12:30 A.M. and 1:00 A.M., leaving his wife, son, and daughter-in-law in the kitchen.

Sometime in the early morning hours of November 27, 1980, Gilmore injected his wife Patricia with an unknown quantity of Demerol, which caused her death.

The state's evidence consisted of expert testimony as to the quantity of meperidine found in Mrs.

Gilmore's system at the time of death, based on autopsy and toxicology reports. Testimony was also given regarding the inability of Mrs. Gilmore to have injected herself with the lethal dose of meperidine at two of the injection sites found on the body.

The state also offered Gilmore's sworn statement to the District Attorney of Berks County shortly after his wife's death, made December 11, 1980. In it, he told the DA that his wife would not use meperidine because it made her ill. It was then that the state called its star witness, Pennsylvania State Trooper Barry Pease.

Trooper Pease testified that on December 14 or 15, 1980, Gilmore told him that his wife had been sick the night before she died and that he had given her several injections of Vitamin B and meperidine to treat vomiting and diarrhea.

The prosecution had raised a crucial question. If Patricia Gilmore was made sick by meperidine, then why did her husband, according to Pease, inject her with that same drug?

Continuing his testimony, Pease said later that same evening, he and Gilmore agreed that Pease would, and Pease did, take custody of a revolver in Gilmore's home because of Gilmore's state of mind.

A week later in another conversation with Pease, Gilmore stated that when he awoke on the morning of November 27, he found a stethoscope lying in the bed, a syringe and a bent needle in an ashtray on the nightstand, and a cotton ball with some blood on it. He told Pease that he threw the cotton ball and syringe away, moved the ashtray to the hallway, and put the stethoscope in his bag.

In other words, he removed what might have been evidence of the injection of a drug from their bedroom when he discovered the body the next morning.

To counter the prosecution's case, Gilmore's defense was that his wife injected herself. His evidence consisted of his own testimony in which he denied administering any drug to his wife that evening or early morning. He also presented the testimony of a patient and friends of the couple who testified that, on previous occasions, each observed Mrs. Gilmore inject herself with drugs from Gilmore's medical bag or office cabinet, and two other witnesses who testified that Mrs. Gilmore "represented to each of them that she administered drugs to herself via injection." Finally, Gilmore presented testimony from his own expert witnesses that contradicted the conclusions of the Commonwealth's experts on this issue.

On February 20, 1987, the jury found Gilmore guilty of recklessly endangering another person, his wife, by injecting an unknown, but under the circumstances, a potentially life-threatening dosage of meperidine; he was acquitted of the charges of aggravated assault and criminal homicide.

In Pennsylvania, the crime of recklessly endangering another person is a misdemeanor. On February 4, 1988, Dr. Irvin Gilmore was sentenced to two years probation, two hundred hours of community service, and the costs of the prosecution plus a $2,000 fee.

In formal hearings held before the Hearing Examiner of the Pennsylvania State Board of Medicine on November 22-23, 1988, January 12, 1989, and January 13, 1989, the question of whether Gilmore violated the terms of his medical license and, if so, what sanctions might result, was considered.

Here are what the Board calls FINDINGS OF FACT, beginning with the results of Patricia Gilmore's autopsy.

•The autopsy of Patricia Gilmore revealed four

needle marks, made up to twelve hours before death, in groups of two each, on her right buttock, approximately one inch in length.

●The trajectory of two of the needle punctures were toward the head. The trajectory of the other needle marks were not examined.

●The deceased's underpants contained four small blood splotches about a quarter inch in diameter corresponding approximately over the right buttock.

●A normal therapeutic dosage of meperidine is fifty milligrams for a non-chronically ill, not-habituated patient; one hundred milligrams for a person who has been given repeated dosages for chronic pain; and 150 milligrams for a person who is habituated to the drug.

●The deceased's body contained as much as six hundred milligrams of meperidine, *a potentially life-endangering dose*.

●Decedent was injected with about six hundred milligrams of meperidine within four hours prior to her death.

●Decedent's blood alcohol level was two times the legal limit at the time of her death.

●The concentration of meperidine, even without the concentration of alcohol, was high enough to be an *independent cause of death by arresting respiration*.

●Patricia Gilmore died no more than three hours after the last injection of meperidine.

●The alcohol which the decedent ingested affected the *speed of death, not the cause of death*.

●Within a reasonable degree of medical and scientific certainty, *it was not possible for the decedent to have injected herself with meperidine in the early hours of November 27, in the particular location of the fresh needle marks on the buttock of decedent*.

After completion of the hearings and the submission of post-hearing briefs, the Hearing Examiner, Norman M. Yoffe, ordered Dr. Irvin Gilmore be reprimanded for the immoral and unprofessional conduct and assessed a civil penalty in the amount of $1,000.

So, despite the fact that the state had proven in a court of law that Gilmore had recklessly endangered the life of his wife, he would still be allowed to practice medicine in the state.

Clearly not satisfied with the Board's verdict, the Commonwealth of Pennsylvania immediately filed an Application for Review with the Board on August 21, 1989. The Commonwealth contended that "The hearing examiner [Mr. Yoffe] gave no weight to the Respondent's [Gilmore's] conviction," and that "The sanction imposed by the hearing examiner is too lenient, inconsistent with the evidence, and constitutes an abuse of discretion.

"The Commonwealth prayed that the Board review the evidence presented at the hearing and revoke the Respondent's license."

The State Board of Medicine reconvened. They found that "All of the evidence taken together leads to the conclusion that on the fateful night and early morning hours of November 26-27, 1980, Respondent [Dr. Gilmore] attempted to treat his wife with an injection or injections of meperidine. Treatment of human ailments by the use of drugs is a medical act and when a physician performs a medical act so as to recklessly endanger the life of another, his conviction for that offense is a conviction related to the health profession."

But the Board wasn't finished. They were just getting warmed up. They said that Gilmore's act "in injecting meperidine as charged is an act of moral turpitude as an act 'contrary to justice, honesty and good morals.' "

And then the Board took a shot at Norman M. Yoffe, the Hearing Examiner.

"We do not understand the hearing examiner's reasoning," the Board continued. "By the Respondent's own testimony he had treated his wife on a continuing basis for the ill-effects of over-consumption of alcohol. As a practicing physician he either knew or should have known of the potential effect of his treatment. On the night in question, he knew that his wife had drunk a substantial quantity of alcohol which he characterized as 'her usual amount.' As a practicing physician, he knew or should have known of the combined potentiating effect of alcohol and meperidine on the central nervous system. Thus, as a practicing physician, he knew or should have known that the administration of meperidine placed his wife in serious risk of grave injury."

The Board concluded that they could just not understand the conclusion of Yoffe that Gilmore's actions merited a mere reprimand. And so they acted differently . . .

The Pennsylvania State Board of Medicine ordered on July 23, 1991 Dr. Irvin W. Gilmore's medical license "SUSPENDED for two years," and directed that he complete a course in continuing education in the dispensing, administration, and prescription of controlled substances as a condition of reinstatement.

After the period of his suspension, Dr. Irvin Gilmore was eligible to seek reinstatement of his license but instead retired.

Chapter Six

Dr. James Burt

When Coney Mitchell moved to Dayton, Ohio, in 1967, she was seeking a doctor to deliver her baby. She considered herself fortunate when Dr. James Burt, one of the city's most respected gynecologists, agreed to become her physician.

Coney Mitchell believed what all of Dr. Burt's patients did: Here was a compassionate, practiced healer who treated women with thought and respect. A hometown boy who had made good, Dr. Burt, with his thick beard and cherubic cheeks, looked like folksinger Burl Ives in a white coat.

Instead, he was a medical monster, a doctor who turned the pleasure of sensual and sexual experience into a nightmare of pain and degradation for many of his patients.

The delivery of Coney's baby should have been routine. There was nothing unusual about the pregnancy and the child was healthy. But instead of recovering in a few hours, she did not regain consciousness for two and half days.

When she finally awakened, it was to incontinence, pain, and bleeding. She would later learn that intercourse would be painful or impossible for her as well.

"I asked him, 'What have you done to me?' " Coney later told *People* magazine.

Burt's reply: " 'Oh, I just patched you up,' " Coney recalls him saying. "He told me by fixing me like he did, it would be just like being a virgin again."

She'd had two other children without complications. What had Burt done to her that left her feeling like she'd been raped, in excruciating pain, and without a sex life?

In 1973, Burt was Joy Martin's obstetrician in the birth of her son. Subsequent to his birth, Martin began experiencing recurring, nearly constant bladder and vaginal infections. And intercourse was too painful to even attempt.

In addition, "The opening to the vagina and urethra were covered, so when I urinated, it was backing up," Joy Martin later discovered.

The same year, Anna Mitchell came to Burt to have her child delivered. When the baby was born on December 24, 1973, she didn't learn until she was in the recovery room that Burt had performed what he called "love surgery" without her consent.

Mitchell would later discover that Burt had sewn her vagina from "end to end and beyond. It was a feeling of being violated and raped and nobody would say a word," she recalled.

Gerry Harness knew nothing of the controversy surrounding Burt. The vibrant, thirty-two-year-old woman sought out Burt in the early 1970s for advice about her problem, urine leakage and unusually heavy menstrual periods.

She strolled into his office like a lamb to the slaughter. Harness remembers feeling that the bewhiskered gynecologist seemed like a warm, caring man who was deeply committed to his patients.

Burt took her into his examination room, told her to put her feet up in the stirrups on the examining table. He began his internal, probing gently with his instruments, examining, looking, until he was finally done.

Stripping off his surgical gloves, he told Harness that only a partial hysterectomy, in which he would remove the uterus, would stop the bleeding. Burt also told her she needed corrective surgery on her bladder, which had dropped as a result of her three pregnancies and deliveries, causing her to leak a little urine at times.

The 1970s were a time when women were just beginning to take control of their bodies. Most women rarely questioned their doctors. If Dr. Burt said that she, a healthy thirty-two-year-old woman, needed to have part of her reproductive system removed to stem the flow of blood from a heavy menstrual cycle, who was Gerry Harness to disagree?

Besides, Burt was the best, the absolute best.

Harness's surgery was performed on October 17, 1972, at St. Elizabeth Hospital. The operation lasted twelve hours.

Afterwards, Harness was in terrible pain. When Burt came to visit her that night, he explained that he had discovered that her ovaries were diseased, and he'd had to remove them as well. He had performed the second procedure *without getting written consent* because he didn't want to put Harness through a painful second operation. Grateful she had avoided a second operation, she accepted his next piece of news placidly: she would have to take artificial hormones for the rest of her life.

In the weeks after the operation, Harness experienced

91

bladder control problems that were worse now than before, severe migraines, and, worst of all, excruciating pain whenever she and her husband William attempted intercourse.

At her six-week postoperative checkup, she told Burt about her problems. He assured her they were all psychological. As for the pain experienced during intercourse, Harness recalls, "Dr. Burt said that moving my bladder had necessitated repositioning my vagina as well."

Like Coney Mitchell and the other pregnant women who had "love surgery" under Dr. Burt's scalpel, Anna Mitchell was left with bladder, urinary, and vaginal problems and excruciating pain upon intercourse after Burt had performed his unauthorized procedure.

In fact, Burt had a penchant for operating without proper authorization.

Nancy T. Goodman was an obstetrics nurse who assisted Burt with many of his deliveries at St. Elizabeth, the hospital Burt was affiliated with. She became convinced that his procedures to repair episiotomies—the surgical cut to facilitate the delivery of a child—should have required an additional consent form signed by their patients or representatives. But something else was wrong. Burt's episiotomies would take one and one half to two hours, about twice as long as it took other doctors to do this simple procedure.

Goodman repeatedly warned St. Elizabeth officials about Burt's surgical techniques but was told by one of the hospital's top administrators that nothing could be done.

"His (the administrator's) response to me was that there had been many hours spent by him dealing with the issues around Dr. Burt," she would say in later court testimony. "Because Burt lacked privileges at any other Dayton hospital, he could sue St. Elizabeth for restraint of trade if they barred him."

Another nurse backed up Goodman's story. Monica Barrow, who worked with Burt at the same time as Goodman, recalled a staff nurses' meeting about Burt called by Sister Ellen Durso, who was then Director of Nursing Services at St. Elizabeth.

"All of us were upset," Barrow said. "And her response was 'As long as he isn't killing patients, we have to put up with him.' " Subsequently, Durso denied ever making that statement.

Barrow pointed out to Durso and to the hospital's Chief of Staff that Burt was altering the vaginas of new mothers. Her complaints fell on deaf ears. After all, she was a lowly nurse accusing the city's biggest gynecologist of malpractice.

Burt had an ego the size of the Empire State Building and a flair for self-publicity that matched P.T. Barnum's. So, to those who knew him, it came as no surprise that it was Burt himself who would answer the questions.

In his 1975 self-published book, *The Surgery of Love,* Burt explained that what he did in his surgery was to re-align the vagina and remove the skin around the clitoris, leaving it exposed, a so-called female circumcision. Burt claimed that his improvements on nature would bring about a startling metamorphosis, that a woman would be transformed from "A scared, reluctant little house mouse into a *horny* little house mouse."

But what Burt did not say in his book was that his "improvements on nature" included stitching the vagina tighter, making intercourse painfully impossible, and altering the walls separating the rectum and vagina. He also neglected to report that bowel movements through altered vaginas, bleeding and vaginal and urinary infections were often some of the results of his "innovations."

The sexual revolution that had begun in the 1960s reached its zenith during the mid-seventies, and Burt was riding the tail of the comet. *The Surgery of Love* was a literary and medical sensation.

Burt appeared on "Donahue" and received media attention that any author, let alone a doctor championing controversial surgery, would envy. Numerous articles were written about him. Overnight, he became a media star.

On September 3, 1975, the hometown newspaper jumped on the hometown boy's bandwagon. *The Dayton Daily News* published an article complimentary of Burt and his love surgery. Burt had become Dayton's favorite son.

Sitting at home, gynecologist Dr. Konrad Kircher read the story. He would later recall that the newspaper story "horrified" local gynecologists who knew that Burt's surgery was the medical profession's version of Barnum's flimflam, but with devastating physical, not to mention psychological, results. They pressed for a meeting of the ethics committee of the Montgomery County Medical Society (of which Dayton was a part).

No meeting ever took place and despite a law that had been passed in 1975 requiring doctors to report to the Ohio State Medical Board any colleagues they believe are practicing substandard medicine, not one gynecologist came forward to accuse Burt.

Clearly, the Dayton medical practitioners who were aware of what Burt was doing had a legal and moral responsibility to bring him to justice. In addition, doctors in Cincinnati, Cleveland, and Columbus, to whom some of Burt's victims had gone to for relief, were well aware of the extent of Burt's "love surgery" mutilations and did not report him either.

In fact, when Anna Mitchell actually tried to sue Burt

for malpractice, she could not get one doctor to support her claim. She had to settle for a mere $5,000 which didn't even cover her medical bills.

The Burt case was proving a time-honored maxim in the medical profession: When a doctor commits malpractice, the ranks frequently close.

As for the State Medical Board, it was woefully understaffed. Even if a colleague had broken the code of silence and accused Burt of wrongdoing, only twelve investigators are charged with examining complaints against the state's twenty-two thousand licensed and practicing physicians. Only two of those twelve are responsible for the densely populated southwest region, of which Dayton is a part.

Sanctioned by his own profession, supported and defied by the media, and, like any good actor, believing his own publicity, Dr. James Burt continued on his one-man quest to bring "virginal love" back to his patients.

One former patient recalled, "He was very high-priced and you had the best when you went to see Dr. Burt. He had a big *name*."

Burt's star continued to rise, and his patient list continued to increase. Anxious for his "love surgery," women flocked to his office.

In November 1976, under Burt's steady hand, Ruby Moore had "love surgery" at St. Elizabeth. She had a follow-up procedure for complications six days later and a third surgery on November 28. Still, Dr. Burt wasn't through.

On January 23, 1978, Ruby Moore had what Burt described as a "vaginal revision." She would be operated on six more times in February and March — all for complications stemming from her "love surgery."

In June 1978, having heard of the love doctor and his

national reputation, Judith Romer flew into Dayton from her New Jersey home to have "love surgery."

Six days later, she headed home heavily sedated on Percodan, a pain killer, and Quaaludes, a muscle relaxer.

On June 1, she returned to Dayton to have follow-up surgery for "complications." She went home, once again in pain.

Despite a ground swell of complaints that were beginning to be heard from some of Burt's formerly silent patients, the administration of St. Elizabeth decided to allow Dr. Burt to continue practicing at their hospital. In fact, they made it easy for him.

According to Lee Sambol, the attorney for a number of Burt's victims, Burt was allowed to practice surgery at St. Elizabeth without the hospital requiring him to obtain malpractice insurance.

In 1979, St. Elizabeth decided it was time to protect itself. They began requiring Burt's patients to sign forms saying the hospital's medical staff considered the surgery "an unproven, nonstandard practice of gynecology." Now, they wouldn't have to worry about liability in malpractice suits against Burt and the hospital. Their wisdom soon paid off.

In 1980, Judith Romer sued Burt, and Burt alone, alleging that "love surgery" left her unable to have intercourse. The case was subsequently dismissed when she failed to appear at trial.

Clearly, Burt led a charmed life. He sailed on into the 1980s. Even some of those he'd already maimed came back.

Coney Mitchell returned to Burt's office, still displaying the same symptoms as years before. She was desperate to alleviate her pain. Burt's diagnosis: She needed her reproductive system eliminated.

Burt performed a hysterectomy, and Coney went home in tears. Soon, she would discover that she could no longer have sexual intercourse with her husband.

In 1981, Janet Phillips came to Burt complaining of cramps. Burt's prescription for wellness was to perform a hysterectomy and, his "love surgery."

"You're raised to trust your minister, your policeman and your doctor. He (Burt) was the one with the degree on the wall. He knew medicine better than I did. I didn't think he would hurt me," Phillips would later say.

In 1984, Cheryl Sexton of New Lebanon, Ohio, went to Burt for bladder problems. Burt told her she needed a complete hysterectomy and that during the operation her vagina would be repositioned to support her bladder better.

That seemed to make sense. But he did not tell me everything he was going to do," said Sexton.

What he did not tell her, of course, was that he would disfigure her like he had already done to dozens of women. The procedure often included the removal of the hood of the clitoris (external tissue that responds to sexual stimulation), repositioning the vagina and urethra and altering the walls between the rectum and the vagina.

Doctors, who Sexton later visited for the ailments that invariably followed Burt's postoperative patients, were shocked by what they found.

"They would ask, 'Have you always been like this?' And I would say, 'Like what?' " Sexton said.

"Like a filleted fish," one of the doctors told her.

In 1986, Janet Phillips filed a suit against Burt and St. Elizabeth's for $30 million. She charged Burt with malpractice and the hospital with allowing Burt to operate, despite having full knowledge of what he was doing.

In her legal papers, Phillips claimed that Burt mutilated her genitals and caused her permanent injury with his surgery, which she said he did without her knowledge. Then, in 1987, Cheryl Sexton also filed for malpractice against Burt and St. Elizabeth's.

"West 57th Street," the now defunct CBS News magazine TV Show, heard about the suits and began interviewing some of Burt's former patients. On October 29, 1988, Joy Martin and many of Burt's other victims went on "West 57th Street" to tell their story, in a segment entitled *Dr. Love*.

Karen Burns, the correspondent who narrated the report, said during the program, "Burt says he does 'love surgery' to make women better sexual partners. But some women call him a butcher. He (Burt) remains convinced that women are born with their sexual organs in the wrong place."

The broadcast allowed ample time for Burt to defend his surgical procedure, or, some might say, rationalize it. During "love surgery," he told Burns, "The axis is rotated so that organs that can't stand trauma are no longer hit."

Burt was hardly a trauma specialist, except in creating it, as his former patients then told in one harrowing account after another.

Burt's response to the broadcast was to state that CBS engaged in "a conspiracy of lies." Burt charged that "West 57th Street" personnel "totally disregarded scientific documentation given them and suppressed the truth."

"Patients who know me are not canceling," he added confidently.

Burt's privileges at St. Elizabeth Hospital continued in full.

James B. Makos, then acting president of St. Elizabeth, tried to get off the hook by stating that the hospital "investigated the surgery for many years" and then required patients to sign forms saying the medical staff considered the surgery "an unproven, nonstandard practice of gynecology."

Finally, the medical profession, after a long silence, began speaking out. "Any of these groups (of physicians) could have easily turned off this guy fifteen or twenty years ago. Burt is a butcher," said Dr. Sidney Wolfe, director of the Health Research Group based in Washington. As for the hospital's explanation of the consent form, Wolfe added, that it was an "incredible ploy" to excuse itself from any liability in malpractice suits against Burt and the hospital.

"It's a sad state of affairs when our own doctors can't clean up a profession that really needs it," added Dr. Gilman Kirk, the retired professor emeritus at the Ohio State University School of Medicine and a surgeon with fifty years of experience.

Women's rights organizations also expressed their outrage.

"We feel that his actions were comparable to what the Nazi doctors did at concentration camps," said Donna Oblinger, then head of the Dayton chapter of NOW. "He was using women for his guinea pigs, his research, and all of St. Elizabeth was aware of it and let it go on," she told the *Cleveland Plain Dealer*.

With the glare of the national spotlight suddenly turned on the Dayton medical community, the system suddenly, miraculously, took up the cause of Burt's victims.

After years of inaction, only three days after the "West 57th Street" broadcast, the Ohio State Medical Board announced that it was investigating Burt. Two days later, the Board's president, Timothy Stevens, declared in a letter to the governor that the Board would also investigate Dayton's medical community amid charges that some local physicians may have violated the "snitch" law by not reporting Burt to the Board.

Burt knew he was in trouble. Whatever happened with the Board would not be nearly as costly as a judgment against him. Without malpractice insurance, he'd be ruined. He had to protect himself and his assets.

Burt filed for federal bankruptcy protection. Sexton and Phillips's lawsuits were immediately dismissed because, according to the court, bankruptcy proceedings were likely to delay the cases indefinitely. The cases, however, could be reopened at a later date.

Regardless, if Burt subsequently succeeded in bankruptcy court, all his debts, including potential judgments from future lawsuits, would be wiped out. Eventually, the court would grant his request. But he still had another storm to weather.

On December 8, 1988, the Ohio State Medical Board formally charged James Burt with "Gross immorality" and "Grossly unprofessional conduct," alleging he performed medically unnecessary operations, failed to meet the minimum standards of care, and did not have the consent of over thirty patients discovered by Board investigators to have complications.

The Board restricted his medical practice to nonsurgical procedures and decided to begin proceedings to suspend Burt's license to practice medicine.

If the lawsuits against him were a signal to circle the wagons, the Board's findings showed Burt that he was just about out of ammunition. They were about to revoke his license. It was time to get out of town.

Burt's attorney, Earl Moore, made a deal with the Ohio State Medical Board that in return for dropping all future proceedings against Burt, he would surrender his license. The Board, to their credit, took the deal a step further.

On January 25, 1989, Burt affixed his scrawl of a signature to the agreement that stated the following:

"I, James C. Burt, voluntarily, knowingly and intelligently surrender all rights to practice medicine and surgery in Ohio and hereby state that I shall not apply for a certificate to practice medicine or surgery *in any other state of the United States*."

Burt left town. In his wake, over forty lawsuits were filed by former patients including a woman named Janet Phillips.

On May 6, 1991, after a seven week trial, Phillips won a $5 million judgment against Burt. With Burt in bankruptcy, it was a victory in name only.

The jury also said it believed St. Elizabeth guilty of negligence but assessed no damages, saying Phillips's suit was not filed before the statute of limitations ran out.

Burt had protected himself well. With the protection of bankruptcy, former patients who had filed against him realized they would get nothing and instead turning their efforts toward St. E with mixed results.

Subsequent lower court rulings dismissed thirty suits by former patients against St. E, on the grounds that the statute of limitations for filing such suits had run out in each of the cases. But on January 17, 1993, the Ohio Supreme Court agreed to reexamine the lower court rulings.

"I'm absolutely delighted that the Supreme Court will be looking at the statute of limitations issues and clarifying the law," responded Frank Woodside, III, St. Elizabeth Hospital's attorney.

To date, not one former patient has collected a penny against St. E or Burt as a result of these law suits.

James Burt presently lives in Florida.

All efforts to contact him were unsuccessful. His son, James Burt, Jr., is the former doctor's spokesman. "My father's surgery has had hundreds of successful procedures," he claims. He asserts that because of the private nature of his father's treatment even those patients who had successful experiences are reluctant to speak up.

Sexual Abusers

Chapter Seven

Dr. William Dudley

Located halfway between Tennessee and the Gulf Coast, within thirty miles of the Alabama border, Meridian is not what many ignorant Northerners think of when they think of the South. While there are several mills that surround it, Meridian is not a rural town filled with hicks congregating around the general store. Anything but. Many of the residents are well-educated, financially secure, and wield powerful political influence in the state.

Meridian is a town of culture. It has a wonderful arts program, including two arts museums, two theaters, and a standing symphony orchestra.

While the town proper numbers forty-five thousand residents — many of whom can trace their ancestry back four centuries — it serves a huge section of eastern Mississippi and western Alabama, numbering 350,000 people. It's the place you go to when you need to entertain the services of a *professional*.

Meridian is made up of professionals: lawyers, accountants, and, especially, doctors. There are three hospitals in Meridian and one private, inpatient psychiatric facility. It was at the latter, Laurelwood Center, that Dr. William Dudley practiced psychiatry.

In fact Dudley, along with many of the health care professionals he worked with, owned the facility, considered one of the finest freestanding psychiatric facilities in the South. Dudley also had his own private practice that attracted wealthy women with self-image problems. His patients relied on his expertise for help.

Instead Dudley committed the cardinal sin of any medical professional: he betrayed the trust of his patients by sexually abusing them.

Carol Seymour was having trouble with her marriage. She and *Donald,* her husband of twenty years, just weren't getting along anymore. They began seeing a psychotherapist for individual psychotherapy and marriage counseling.

Sometimes marriage counseling works and people get better. However in Carol's case, she continued a spiral into depression. Carol eventually realized that she needed medication to help cope with her depression. A recovering alcoholic, she was referred by her therapist to Dr. William Dudley in June, 1987.

William Dudley was a man who most in Meridian would describe as gifted. A former University of Mississippi professor who came to Meridian in 1976, William Dudley quickly developed a solid reputation as an outstanding professional and a brilliant diagnostician.

His peers grew to like and respect him; his patients knew him to be a compassionate healer of their psyches. He rose to become the Chief of Staff at Laurelwood Center, and maintained a busy private practice.

His family, a beautiful wife over ten years his junior and a daughter who would eventually become a psychiatrist, loved and respected him. In short, Dr. Dudley was a pillar of the community. But it was a pillar rotting from the inside.

There was a dark, secret side to William Dudley. The man Meridian welcomed with open arms had been sexually abusing his patients for years.

While the building he was located in was modern, the decor of the office where he maintained his private practice was more eclectic, ranging from new, glass-lined bookcases, to an old-fashioned oak chair. Across from him was a rocking chair, where many of his patients chose to sit, including Carol Seymour.

Like many psychiatrists, part of Dudley's practice was psychopharmacology, prescribing drugs to help patients deal with a variety of emotional problems. Carol needed medication to help her cope with her problems.

At first, Carol's visits were infrequent, usually once a month, in order for Dudley to monitor the effects of the medication he'd prescribed to treat her depression. But, even within that brief period of time, the doctor got to know his patient. And they had something in common.

Carol was close friends with a woman who'd committed suicide, who also just happened to be one of Dr. Dudley's acquaintances.

Ordinarily, Carol would have gone to her psychotherapist to discuss the feelings she felt over her friend's loss. Unfortunately, the psychotherapist had taken ill and couldn't see patients. Carol looked around for professional help. Logically, she chose Dr. Dudley. He was there, she was already his patient; most importantly, he, too, was suffering from the loss of their mutual friend. Surely he could understand her feelings. After all, they had something tragic in common.

One thing common to many doctors that sexually abuse patients is they pick on the ones that, because of time and circumstance, are most vulnerable. With a long-time marriage falling apart, suffering from clinical depression, Carol was a prime target.

It was very subtle at first. After seeing Carol for awhile, Dudley ". . . asked me to [move from the rocking chair] and sit on the sofa. He sat down beside me and put his feet up on the footstool," Carol recalled. Not long after that, he motioned for her to put her feet next to his.

A woman who was actively dating, who was more aware of the methods of seduction, might have known what would happen next. But a woman like Carol, who was in a marriage that was dying, had forgotten about the ways men try to ingratiate themselves with women. She wasn't sure how to interpret his actions. Perhaps Dudley was simply trying to relax.

Feeling more comfortable, Carol kicked back, relaxed, and put her feet up as suggested.

The seduction continued.

Dudley began putting his hands around Carol's neck. Then in other places.

"He was touching me inappropriately," she says simply.

Carol is understandably shy when describing what happened to her.

In fact, what her psychiatrist did was kiss her on the lips. Then Dudley took off her clothing. His hands fondled her breasts. In utter shock, Carol sat stiffly as his hands moved down her body, settling on her genitals, which he manipulated.

Session after session, Dudley sexually abused Carol.

Carol was confused. With her regular therapist still ill, she had no one to talk to, not to mention she relied on the medication Dr. Dudley prescribed for her just to get through the day. "I was in a real crisis," she says. "I was [also] afraid of my husband. I really thought I was going crazy."

Carol did have problems, but she coped. In fact if anyone was disturbed, it was her husband Donald. She discovered that he was a pedophile. The way she found out about it was in a suicide note he'd written.

"It was Dr. Dudley who helped me do all of the things that were necessary to get Don treatment in Atlanta and to really get him out of my home. Dr. Dudley really validated my feelings and I had no idea [Donald] was so disturbed," Carol says, in a barely audible voice. So disturbed, in fact, that "he'd molested my daughter," Carol recalls, "and exposed himself in town."

Carol was completely devastated. She felt like crying like a baby. And Dr. Dudley ". . . got me in his arms to do that. It got worse after that.

"There was never actual intercourse, but there was a lot of what you would call heavy petting. The part about being held and letting go was actually stated. But the other stuff [that the heavy petting was part of the therapy] was implied."

"You've come a long way from being that person that couldn't touch anything," Dudley would tell her while he was sexually abusing her.

Dudley kept it up for approximately six months.

"Normally, when I went in to see him, he would kiss me right on the mouth," during a typical therapy session, Carol recalls. Dudley would then talk to her therapeutically for awhile, before the heavy petting began.

Carol was confused. What was her psychiatrist doing? Was his sexual interaction really part of the therapy? Or was she just being taken advantage of?

Carol had only told a few friends what was going on, including *Sally Reynolds* who was also seeing Dr. Dudley. But Sally claimed that Dudley kept his hands off her. "Sally was married to a doctor and I really feel like that was her protection."

These were upper middle-class, attractive, well dressed, well-to-do *ladies*. Because of the emotional crises they were going through when they visited Dudley, they were very fragile.

Experts say that sometimes women are reluctant to come forward when they've been sexually abused for fear of being branded as "loose women," a fear especially prevalent in a small town like Meridian.

Eventually, Carol's psychotherapist recovered from her medical problems, and she began seeing her again. Then Carol read an article, "Sex and the Forbidden Zone" in *Psychology Today* in 1989 which she says condemned "shrinks" who had sexual relationships with their patients. She hadn't even told her therapist yet what had happened.

After she did, the therapist told her that, one of these days, she was going to need to confront Dudley for herself. Carol agreed and made an appointment to confront her abuser.

Even though he wasn't physically imposing, Carol was afraid of Dr. Dudley. Dudley could easily say that nothing had happened. If it was her word against his, she would lose.

Carol managed to muster up her courage anyway. In she went to the office and handed the article to Dudley. He slapped it down on his footstool.

"Have you read it?" Carol asked.

"No, but I get the jist of it," Dudley replied, looking fairly calm.

Without acknowledging that any abuse had taken place, Dudley smoothly turned the conversation around to her husband, whom they discussed for awhile.

"I detect a note of forgiveness in what you said [toward your husband], and I believe you'll be able to forgive me, too," Carol recalls Dudley as saying.

Carol walked out feeling like she'd beaten around the bush and gotten little satisfaction.

Meanwhile, *Selma Tibbons,* one of Dudley's other victims, had moved out of Meridian to Jackson. In Jackson, Selma began therapy with a new therapist. When the new therapist found out about Dudley, the therapist immediately urged Selma to write a letter to the Licensing Board. She did, citing Dudley's abusive behavior. That opened a Pandora's box.

Meanwhile, Dudley's lack of response gnawed at Carol, until she found out that someone from the State Licensing Board, in response to Selma's letter, had gone to the director of the Laurelwood Center, where Dudley was Chief of Staff in psychiatry. Purportedly, someone on the Board told Laurelwood they would have to do something about Dr. Dudley or they would.

Dudley then went off for treatment for alcoholism.

"That just infuriated me," Carol says. "A whitewashing job, a smoke screen. It seemed like a cover-up. I felt there was a whole lot more to his problem than that."

Carol was even more suspicious than most. Carol Seymour is a recovering alcoholic. If anyone could spot the signs of alcohol abuse, she could, and she never saw anything during their sessions that indicated Dudley had a problem.

"I'm sort of an expert [on alcoholism]," she says wryly. "He couldn't get anything by me. If he'd ever been drinking when I was in there, I would have known," Carol says firmly.

What Carol did not know was that some of the staff at Laurelwood knew that Dr. Dudley drank to excess, *but never while he was working*. That would explain why alcohol didn't impair his medical abilities. Still, they could not condone Dudley's drinking nor his allegedly sober actions toward his patients.

"I couldn't stand that he would be sent off for treatment for alcoholism and then just let him come back and plug back into the system," Carol told her.

At first, because of the embarrassment it would personally cause her, she didn't want to come forward and publicly accuse Dudley. But over time, Carol began to change her mind and finally wrote the Mississippi State Board of Medical Licensure with her specific complaint about Dudley's sexually abusing her.

The Board of Directors of Laurelwood found out

about her complaint and called Carol in for a meeting. According to Carol, one of the Board members said if Dr. Dudley's license was revoked, it would destroy him. Then, "They asked me what I wanted."

Carol told them she didn't want Dudley seeing female patients, period. They had a stack of prepared papers, including a plan to keep Dr. Dudley in practice by putting a window in his door so his patient sessions could be monitored. That plan, however, was rejected.

On March 21, 1991, the Mississippi State Board of Medical Licensure met to consider Dr. William C. Dudley's fate. The Board cited two instances specifically where Dr. Dudley ". . . while maintaining a therapeutic, doctor/patient relationship . . . did engage in sexual activity" with his patients.

The Board noted that Dudley had been admitted for the treatment of alcohol abuse to the Brawner Psychiatric Institute in Atlanta, Georgia, and that he then entered another facility, the Metro Atlanta Recovery Residences, Inc., for additional treatment.

Most importantly, as part of the therapeutic process, Dudley "was referred to The Behavioral Medicine Institute of Atlanta under the care of Gene G. Abel, MD. During this treatment [Dr. Dudley] acknowledged inappropriate sexual conduct with approximately (12) patients between 1970 and 1989."

The local newspaper, the *Meridian Star,* would later report that Dudley expressed remorse for sexually harassing more than twenty women who were his patients since 1970.

Dudley was treated by Dr. Abel "regarding his inappropriate sexual behavior with patients," and discharged during January 1991. Dr. Abel laid out a " 'Treatment and Practice Plan' aimed at reducing the future chances of any inappropriate behavior toward female patients" if

Dr. Dudley were allowed to practice once again.

On March 21, 1991, the Mississippi State Board of Medical Licensure revoked his license. But there was an important clause contained in the revocation order.

"If [Dr. Dudley] chooses to petition for reinstatement, it is the strong recommendation of this board that Licensee attach to his Petition the written results of a complete and comprehensive psychiatric evaluation performed by Gene G. Abel, MD." He would be eligible to reapply for his license the following year.

Commenting on the Board's decision, Dudley told the *Meridian Star,* "Yes, I'm surprised by the outcome. I'm not surprised at the findings of guilt. I didn't contest that . . . I only wish I had stopped practicing long enough to get treatment earlier. I could have prevented all this."

Dudley claimed that the sexual advances he evinced toward his patients took place during psychotherapy sessions when he was under the influence of alcohol. According to the *Star,* Dudley had earlier stated that he'd been drinking between a half-fifth and a fifth of whiskey every night for a number of years.

Meanwhile, he was following through on the Board's recommendations for treatment for his problem.

"I'm doing all of that as rapidly as possible. I am complying with everything they want me to do," he said. "The circumstances of not being able to make a living are difficult. We will suffer greatly financially."

No comment was made as to how the patients he had sexually abused were suffering because of his actions.

Dudley, though, held out hope that he could, some place down the road, return to the practice of medicine. "I feel about as damaged as I can get. I accept the consequences of my alcoholism and I have remorse.

". . . And that remorse also extends, to a great extent, to the people who I have treated perfectly okay, patients

113

who may now be totally embarrassed by the way I've treated the others. They may now be humiliated just by their association with me, and for that, well, what can I say?"

The community as a whole was horrified about Dudley's behavior and believed that what had occurred was wrong.

These women abused by Dudley were affected in many ways. Many had problems making love after being sexually abused by Dr. Dudley. Marriages were strained. Others suffered from sleep deprivation, and still others lapsed into clinical depression that could only be treated through drugs and psychotherapy. But there were those who stood shoulder to shoulder in support of Dudley.

After the hearing, there was a tremendous, well financed campaign by his supporters to have Dudley relicensed. While this campaign to have Dr. Dudley reinstated was going on, some of Dudley's friends called and harassed Carol Seymour.

And then there were the Alcoholics Anonymous meetings. After Dudley entered recovery, he began going to AA meetings. The town has only one place where meetings are held, three times a day. By coincidence, Carol and Dudley would sometimes go to the same meeting. It made Carol feel terrible. After awhile, when Carol saw Dr. Dudley's van in the parking lot, she'd turn around and go home.

In May of 1992, William Dudley attempted to get his medical license reinstated. His intention was to form a limited practice, where he would only treat male patients. Dr. Abel, one of the country's foremost authorities on the treatment of people with sexual problems, was brought in to help with his defense. Dudley was under Abel's treatment and remains under his care. The Board, however, took a hard line.

They were concerned about emergency situations [involving women] that might come up and require his presence. Another compromise, that Dudley use a chaperone or that he hold sessions behind an observation window, was again rejected.

Dudley's response to the Board's rejection of his application was disappointment.

"I don't really know what I'm going to do now," Dudley was quoted at the time as saying. "But I've got to find a way to make some income. I don't know how because I've practiced medicine, and that's all I've done for twenty years."

Dudley said that he had the utmost respect for the Board, so much, in fact, that he was definitely going to refile again in 1993.

In early 1993, William Dudley made good on his promise. He reapplied for the second time to practice medicine in the State of Mississippi. The plan this time was for him to work at a state mental hospital that had problems attracting good doctors. He would not have one-on-one contact with patients without someone being present.

Dudley was subsequently relicensed to work at the East Mississippi State Hospital.

"In some ways, I feel like I have forgiven him," says Carol. "I don't have a lot of respect for the medical community here but I do have a lot of respect for the members and staff of the licensing board that I met and what they did."

Many of Dudley's victims felt that he was a very good doctor outside of his problem. In some ways he should be required to use his gifts. Working in a state mental hospital was a way to do that.

They took the position he should work but only under great supervision and restraint, that it should be done in a way where the public was protected and he was protected from himself. One businessman in the community had a different point of view.

"If he stays in a protected place, where he can do good and not harm, it will be okay. If he's the camel who's got his nose in the tent, then we're gonna have the whole camel in the tent, I think it's gonna be pretty serious, pretty dangerous."

One question, though, remained. How many mistakes should a doctor be allowed before his license is lifted *permanently?*

That's a complex question because as human beings we tend to err on the side of justice, giving people the opportunity to make mistakes and then be redeemed because, after all, we all make mistakes.

But the medical profession is different, or at least it should be. A doctor's error can result in the death of a patient or severe psychological scars.

A psychiatrist has as much of a sacred trust as a surgeon. While the surgeon holds the patient's life in his hands, balanced at the point of his scalpel, the psychiatrist is entrusted with the health of his patient's mind.

Psychotherapy involves uncommon trust between doctor and patient. The patient is willing to bare her soul in order to rid herself of her demons. In return, the therapist enters a sacred covenant, that he will in no way perform any action that could, in any way, violate this trust.

And, when a psychiatrist sexually abuses his patients, any trust that once existed between doctor and patient is ruined. Therapeutic gains are lost because of this betrayal of trust.

The patient has to live for the rest of her life knowing she was betrayed, perhaps as she was by so many other individuals in her life.

Just ask Carol Seymour and the other women that Dr. William Dudley hurt.

Chapter Eight

Dr. Gary Cohen

It was a Thanksgiving Dinner not unlike any other. There were serving plates piled high with turkey and stuffing, roast beef and sweet potatoes.

Around the table were a family, again not unlike any other.

Two of the men at the table, cousins *Mark Greenberg* and *Steven Schecter,* fourteen and twenty-two respectively, had something in common besides blood. They had been patients of pediatrician Dr. Gary Cohen.

They were the lucky ones. They had not been the victims of Cohen's sexual abuse.

All through Long Island on that day were children who had been sexually abused by the pediatrician. Those young men have nights filled with nightmares. They may never fully recover from the turmoil Cohen caused them.

"He was a good doctor, a real professional," Mark's father, *David,* recalls. "You never would have suspected."

When Gary Cohen was rejected from the American medical schools to which he'd applied, his wife Leona convinced him that it might be better to accept the offer of the medical school in Bologna, Italy. Convinced she was right, Gary agreed; Leona quit her job at the Internal Revenue Service, they packed their bags and headed for Italy in the late sixties.

It was not easy leaving home and family behind. But it was a new country to explore, a new people to meet, and lots of scrumptious food to eat. They lived, to a large extent, on the trust fund Leona's father had left her. They planned that Gary would graduate, they'd return to the States, and he'd form a successful and lucrative practice.

Gary Cohen, though, had other things on his mind.

"An American with glasses," the kids had told the cops.

Cohen was identified as the American who had shown several young boys pornography. Local police arrested him.

Accompanied by her landlord, Leona went down to the police station to get Gary out of jail. Whatever the landlord told his countrymen must have worked because Cohen was released. He successfully completed his courses without any other incidents.

Cohen came back to the States and a residency at Nassau Hospital on Long Island, now Winthrop-University Hospital. There was a thirteen-year-old boy, *Michael Fireman,* in the hospital at the time who had had very serious, life-threatening abdominal surgery.

During the course of Michael's recovery, Gary Cohen, who wasn't even assigned to the case, started to pay him nightly visits. They talked about boats, but Cohen turned every conversation around toward sex. He asked Michael if he ever masturbated.

Cohen came in one night to examine Michael's sutures. After telling Cohen he was in a bit of pain, Cohen administered a sedative. Before Michael lapsed into unconsciousness, Cohen took off Michael's surgical gown and masturbated the boy.

When his parents came to visit him, the boy was hysterical. He told his parents what had taken place. His parents reported Cohen to the authorities. Instead of dismissing Cohen, the hospital said, "What we'll do is assure you that Gary Cohen will never see your son any more. What we will do is allow you to stay twenty-four hours a day with your son." Cohen wasn't charged.

Cohen left and went to Long Island Jewish Hospital, joining their pediatric residency program. He was sent to Queens Hospital to do his actual residency though he remained under the overall supervision of Long Island Jewish Hospital.

At Queens, his impulses pushed him into sexually abusing a boy in the emergency room. This time he was arrested. Leona accompanied her husband to a closed courtroom for a hearing before a judge.

"I saw the mother of the child [making the charges]," Leona recalls. "I could have torn her apart for allowing her kid to lie." She pauses. "Over the years, I've come to feel guilty over feeling that."

Cohen was acquitted of the charge against him in January 1973.

He moved over to North Shore University Hospital in Manhasset, New York to complete the last year of his pediatric residency and to do an additional year of residency in psychiatry. North Shore would later say that they were never informed of Cohen's arrest.

After finishing his residency, he went into private practice, opening an office in Smithtown, on Long Island's moneyed North Shore. For the next fifteen years, he built a reputation as one of the leading pediatricians in the area.

Leona and Gary Cohen adopted a very traditional marriage. Leona kept house and the primary day-to-day responsibility for raising their three kids, *Rachel, Jona-*

than, and *Aaron*.

Over time, she became aware that Gary always seemed to be helping kids out, if not medically then counseling them.

One night, the phone rang and Gary answered it. After listening, he told Leona that it was a kid he'd been helping, a boy who, Gary said, immediately needed his help.

When Leona awoke the next morning, Gary told her that the child he'd helped out was asleep in his office. Would she give him a ride home? He had to go to the office. She agreed.

Gary would always be running to help some child. They'd even go to temple on the High Holy Days in separate cars because Gary always seemed to get calls, which, Leona assumed, were from kids with medical problems. "To me, it was perfectly logical that someone who liked kids would want to help them," Leona says.

Over and over again, similar scenarios would be played out over the years. But something kept nagging at Leona, an idea in the corner of her mind, something she just refused to accept. For Leona, it was like trying to solve a puzzle but without the board on which to fit the pieces.

Sexually, they didn't have a relationship, and it had been that way for quite some time. She couldn't seem to please him. She called up an old high school friend who had always lusted after her and they had an affair. After that, she realized that it wasn't her, and sought help from a therapist.

Then she started putting it together. The late night calls. His activities in the Boy Scouts. Gary wasn't tied to her sexually; he was turning to children.

Still, she refused to accept the truth. She would look for any way to believe that it just wasn't happening. She would rationalize that she didn't really see anything or hear of anything bad happening. Therefore nothing was happening.

The rationalizations could not make her believe that the marriage didn't work. By 1982, Leona had come to reluctantly accept that they could no longer live together. She talked it over with Gary, and they decided to separate. At first, Leona wanted Gary to move across the street, to a house being vacated by their neighbors. Instead, Gary chose to move twenty miles away.

The children, thinking their mother was to blame for the breakup, followed their father. Leona was devastated.

It became a bitter divorce contest. By the late 1980s, their divorce settlement still hadn't been determined. By that time, Gary had moved to a house in Long Island's Coram, New York, and opened a second office in nearby Medford. The practice was thriving.

On the third floor of a building in the middle of nowhere on Long Island is a squad room that looks like a movie set. Half-eaten Greek salads and empty McDonald's containers dot the trash cans throughout the long, rectangular room, made up of cluttered, institutionalized green desks and creaky swivel chairs. The drab green walls make the place look like the sun never shines in.

This is the office of the Sex Crimes Unit of the Suffolk County Police Department located in police headquarters in Yaphank, New York. The senior member of the squad is Detective Bill Quinn.

With his tousled brown hair that's going gray, brown pants, brown sleeveless sweater, patterned cranberry tie, and white shirt, he looks the epitome of the professional. He could be a banker or maybe a lawyer, until his gaze strikes you. Then you know you are dealing with a cop.

Quinn was working the day watch in April of 1989

when a psychologist friend, *Manny Wiseman,* called.

"Listen, Bill, I have a young man here who states that when he was in his early teens, he was sexually abused by his pediatrician."

The man was then in his early twenties. Quinn knew immediately that because the statute of limitations had expired, whoever the bad guy was, he couldn't be prosecuted for that case. He told his friend that.

"For what it's worth, you may want to look into this," said Manny.

At that time, the young man's family did not want to come forward publicly. What they did want to do was share information. They wanted something done. All they could give Quinn was the name of the doctor, a Dr. Gary Cohen, and that he was a pediatrician from the Smithtown area. Other than that, the parents just didn't want to get involved.

About ten days later, Manny called Quinn again.

"Come up with anything, Bill?"

"Just the name Gary Cohen."

"That's it. They told me that much in our session tonight and said I could share that with you."

Quinn was becoming intrigued. On a hunch, he started digging through the files of the Sex Crime Unit and came up with a case that was a year and a half old where Gary Cohen was a suspect in the sexual abuse of a fourteen-year-old boy.

Bill Quinn began looking into the case. He found that it had a lot of flaws. It had been put together by one of the general service squads that are not specialists in investigating sex crimes.

Quinn himself has an Associate's degree in Criminal Justice from the State University of New York at Farmingdale and a Bachelor's degree in Behavioral Science from the New York Institute of Technology. His approach to his work is decidedly psychological. Empathy is his stock and trade.

Quinn called the mother of the boy, *Kevin Copeland,* who Cohen had been accused of abusing.

"Mr. Quinn, that incident was so distressing to Kevin that he's gone to Florida to live with his father," said *Mrs. Copeland* in an anxious, tense voice.

"Would you be interested in prosecuting the case and have the boy come back and talk to me?"

"Well, I'll talk to him and find out what he thinks about it," she said.

That was June of 1989. By the end of August, she still hadn't contacted him so Quinn called Mrs. Copeland again.

"Have you talked to your son?"

"Yes," said Mrs. Copeland. "And he would be willing to talk to you. He'll come up after Labor Day."

When they finally spoke face-to-face, there was more detail to the incident of sexual abuse between Kevin and Cohen than he'd originally told the investigating officer. Based on that, Quinn contacted William Condon, an Assistant District Attorney in the Suffolk County District Attorney's Office, who specialized at the time in prosecuting sex abuse cases.

"Look, this is what I got," Quinn told Condon, and Quinn detailed his findings.

"Keep on digging," Condon replied.

At that point, Quinn was finally able to go back to his psychologist friend Manny who agreed to give him an introduction to the young man who said Cohen abused him as a child.

"It ruined my life up to now," said *Michael Creighton,* who was now in his early twenties. He had all kinds of psychological problems directly related to his abuse at Cohen's hands.

Astoundingly, Creighton knew of still other boys, including *Anthony Francesca, Steven Harmon,* and

Robert Wood who'd been abused by Cohen in their childhood. Quinn took down the names and interviewed them all.

"Don't tell my buddy that I gave you his name, but the same thing happened to him," a victim would tell Quinn.

Protecting the confidentiality of his source, Quinn would go to the friend's house and make up a story about how he got his name. Gradually, the sex crimes cop came up with a scenario that, at that time, Cohen would be abusing virtually every male patient who came into his office.

When the boys were abused as children, they did what kids often do in those circumstances: They kept their mouths shut. Children feel guilty, like they are in some way responsible for the assault. They told their parents nothing about the chamber of sexual horrors that was Gary Cohen's examining room.

As they got older, six of the victims got involved with the drug culture. Some smoked pot and hash; others went into more hard-core drugs.

These six boys used to gather beside an isolated, weed-strewn stretch of tracks of the Long Island Railroad in Smithtown. They started talking and realized that Dr. Gary Cohen had been their pediatrician. More talking and the truth dawned like a thunderbolt in the night sky: Gary Cohen had sexually abused them. *All* of them. Each story was the same, startling in its consistent detail.

When they were young boys, their parents brought them to Cohen for treatment. While their parents waited outside, kind, gentle Dr. Cohen would usher the boys into his examining room. Alone, he'd begin his examination. Inevitably, his hands would drift down to their genitals and he'd fondle them. As time went on and the list of Gary Cohen's victims piled up, the sexual abuse began to involve sodomy.

It got to the point where the smooth talking doctor

would convince the parents, many of whom had personal problems, to let him see their children away from the office. To take them out and away for awhile. He'd make arrangements to buy them stereo sets, guitars, whatever they happened to want at the time.

It was there, beside the tracks in Smithtown, that Cohen's victims would get together and share their pain while trying to suffocate the memories with drugs. One of those boys was *Sandy Myron*.

At the time, Sandy Myron's family was going through a crisis. His father had had a stroke, and Sandy was very upset about that. Cohen, always ready to help out a family in need, told Sandy's mother, *Melinda,* that he'd like to get to know Sandy a little better. He'd take the young man to dinner and then drop him off at home afterwards.

Sandy, like many of the other victims, was wined and dined in area restaurants. Cohen would be going up to a ski house he maintained in Vermont, and he would tell Sandy's parents that he would take Sandy up with his own children for a weekend of skiing fun.

Cohen's own children, who had chosen to live with their father after the breakup, slept in the next room, Sandy slept in Cohen's bed. In the privacy of his own home, Cohen was free to allegedly sexually abuse the boy at his whim.

Sandy, meanwhile, continued to see Cohen at his office in Smithtown. Sandy told his mother that she shouldn't keep on making him go to Dr. Cohen.

"If only you knew what he's doing to me," Sandy allegedly said.

His mother apparently kept insisting that Cohen was helping him.

Despite the abuse he was suffering from, Sandy was a model, straight "A" student and an Eagle Scout. By coincidence, Cohen was also active in the Boy Scouts.

In the summer of 1988, Sandy went away to Boy Scout camp. According to Quinn, Sandy's mother feels that Gary Cohen went up to the Boy Scout camp during that summer and met him on weekends and sexually abused Sandy. There is no evidence, though, to prove this happened.

However, after Sandy came home in the fall, he became a straight "F" student in high school. The school, noting the tremendous change, requested that an outside psychiatrist evaluate Sandy. A psychiatrist was then brought in and interviewed Sandy.

The psychiatrist's report, which Quinn read during the course of his investigation, "disclosed that Sandy was being abused by a pediatrician who was turning him into a homosexual and having him commit homosexual acts with other males," says Quinn.

Yet, Quinn goes on to say, "Based on that psychiatrist's [evaluation], no school authorities made a report" about what Sandy was being forced to endure, despite the fact that they are obligated by law to report alleged incidents of sexual abuse.

When Melinda Myron requested to see the report, the school told her it was confidential and she couldn't see it.

In a matter of months, Sandy placed a sixteen-gauge shotgun in his mouth and blew his head off. Sandy was only sixteen-years-old at the time. The days before his death, Sandy had been telling his mother that she shouldn't trust Gary Cohen, because he's not what she thinks he is.

"Let me tell you what Gary Cohen did, what kind of *chutzpah* he had," says Condon, the dynamic Assistant District Attorney. "When Myron killed himself, what Cohen told the other kids was, 'If you tell anybody what happened, the same thing's going to happen to you that happened to Sandy.' He represented it to them that

126

Sandy's death was not a suicide, that it was a murder or a hit of some kind. This is what they told me and Detective Quinn."

One of the group of boys was *Gerald Wyman,* a very intelligent kid, whose father was an attorney in Manhattan and his mother a schoolteacher in a local school. "As he said in my office, and he was trembling, he was legitimately afraid that if it got out to Cohen that he was in there talking to me that he would get shot like Sandy Myron," Condon continued.

Months later, Sandy's mother and brother were attending the taping of a local TV show, "The Joel Martin Show." The guest was psychic George Anderson, who made some shocking revelations on air.

". . . and I'm not saying anyone murdered him but possibly somebody very strongly cajoled him into killing himself. Maybe some of these people he was involved with, there was a falling out with this illegal business. And somebody said either you do it or we'll do it for you."

George Anderson seemed to be picking up emanations from Sandy beyond the grave.

"I feel somebody putting a gun to my head and telling me to make a decision because I'm gonna be dead one way or the other," said George, communicating what Sandy was apparently telling him. "Almost that he wanted to get out of something . . . it's local, something not in the city . . . he said it involved a ring but not the kind you wear . . . it's just not a drug ring, it's something else. You're not going to be able to prove what happened. It's over and done with. You have to let it go."

It would take some time to see just how prophetic Anderson's communication would be.

By December 1989, Quinn and Condon had interviewed the five victims who hung out at the Smithtown railroad tracks. Four out of the five didn't want to go public. One of the young men, *Neil Jasper,* in his early twenties, was starting a physical fitness business. Neil felt that if the allegations were made public, they might hurt his business, plus emotionally, he wasn't ready to go through with testifying at a court trial.

Nevertheless, Cohen was arrested and charged with sexual abuse.

Condon knew that he didn't have a strong case. The one young man that was willing to come forward, *Saul Bolting,* was, in Condon's words, ". . . a little slow. A very nervous kid. He didn't make a particularly good witness. I didn't know if he'd last through a trial in county court in front of a jury and a packed courtroom.

"In this business, you have to learn when you have a strong case and when you have a weak one. It was frustrating. I figured that if I went forward with the one kid I did have, I was not convinced that we would necessarily get a conviction and again we'd only be talking about a misdemeanor. But, our experience has been that with an individual like this where there's 1, there's 5, where there's 10 there's probably more."

A hearing was held in the chambers of Judge Alfred Tisch in Riverhead, New York. A deal was struck. Dr. Gary Cohen would plead guilty to one misdemeanor of sexual abuse in the second degree. In return, the District Attorney agreed not to charge Cohen with sexually abusing the other four boys. All the other charges on those boys would be dropped.

Cohen officially pleaded guilty on January 23, 1990. While the maximum allowable penalty under the law was one year in county jail for the misdemeanor sex charge, the deal called for Cohen to get three years probation. He was not to get jail time. Sentencing was put off to March 20.

Despite a weak hand, Condon had played aggressively.

Part of the plea bargain agreement was that Cohen cease practicing medicine immediately. This was important because rarely does the State's Health Department revoke a doctor's license before sentencing. Even when they're charged, doctors could still be practicing. Condon, however, had taken care of that contingency.

There were two other important conditions that Condon negotiated within the agreement.

The authorities were worried about Cohen fleeing the country. His passport had to be surrendered to the county. But according to Condon, Cohen had connections within Israel because he'd worked for a number of Jewish organizations. Through the Israeli government, he was able to secure another passport which is illegal.

When the DA's office contacted the Israelis, they acknowledged that they had, indeed, issued Cohen a second passport. They were embarrassed. This had never happened before because usually their security is airtight. Eventually, that second passport was surrendered, too.

The second important provision was that any charges that developed out of cases involving current victims would be part of a separate, valid indictment.

"I had no problem with that," Bill Quinn says quietly. "A leopard doesn't change its spots. Cohen is a pedophile. He's going to continue being a pedophile. It would only stand to reason there were current victims. I knew the publicity would flush them all out of the woodwork."

Quinn and Condon were right.

The press got a hold of the story. *Newsday* featured the case prominently. The local twenty-four hour news channel, News 12, gave the story in-depth coverage. The authorities gave out a phone number and said if there were any other people out there who'd been abused by Gary Cohen to call the sex abuse hotline.

129

The phones started ringing off the hook. People began calling up to report that Cohen had sexually abused them as far back as 1972. Others chronicled sexual abuses throughout the 1970s, 1980s, right up to the 1990 plea bargain.

Within two weeks, Detective Bill Quinn had received forty-four calls from other Cohen victims. Two of the calls were from attorneys who said they were sexually abused when they were kids. One was from a practicing medical doctor.

The tone of the calls was similar. Many of the victims stated they were willing to come forward and do whatever it took to make sure Cohen was punished.

But there was one big problem that Condon had to contend with in putting together his second indictment against Cohen.

The statute of limitations.

In New York State, the statute of limitations is five years on a felony, two on a misdemeanor. In too many cases, the statute of limitations had already lapsed.

Quinn narrowed the field down to eleven complainants, and then interviewed all the kids, as well as their parents. What they said Quinn knew was the truth. There were details that nobody knew except Quinn, because he was the only one on the case from the beginning. And everything the complainants said was consistent.

Cohen targeted kids aged nine to fifteen. According to Condon, Cohen would set up his victims in the following manner:

"He'd say, 'Mrs. Smith, your husband is ill and in the hospital. I see little Johnny is very nervous and withdrawn. I'm also a psychologist. I do have a limited practice in that area. Bring Johnny down after my office hours are over and let me spend time with Johnny. He seems very withdrawn.' And the parents would give their consent."

In cases where the parents had taken their child to the doctor for treatment, Cohen would find himself alone in his examination room with his victim. "He'd start talking about having sex with other boys. He'd ask, 'Are they going into the woods and doing it with a man? How'd they feel about going into the woods and doing it with a man?'"

While he was asking his puerile questions, Cohen would ". . . fondle them as he was talking to them," Quinn continued.

A lot of the kids told Quinn that they just accepted Cohen's questions as if they were standard medical procedure. There must be a reason Dr. Cohen is asking those questions. After all, he was the doctor.

"There was one kid who was being sent back there. His own mother was telling him 'You listen to everything Dr. Cohen tells you because everything he tells you is right.' Here's a kid who's twelve or thirteen and sexually, he doesn't know what the hell is going on," Condon recalls sadly.

Even the child who summoned the courage to complain that Cohen was deliberately touching his penis was not listened to.

"Well, Johnny, he has to check thing out," the parents would say.

"But for ten minutes he's got to stroke my penis?"

Condon recalls that the "special" kids Cohen saw away from his office were ". . . being approached for male prostitution. He would tell them, 'I'll introduce you to some friends of mine. If you go and cooperate, you'll get paid and rewarded.'"

Eventually, Condon made the decision to go forward with the prosecution of six boys and, curiously, one girl who alleged abuse at Cohen's hand. The girl, however, did not prove to be a good witness. Condon voluntarily dropped her from the indictment.

Of the six boys, Cohen had treated four medically. The other two had come to him for "psychological counseling."

The victims were *Clark, Ike, Tim, Rod, George,* and *Nathan.* At the time of the assaults, they ranged in age from ten to seventeen. Unlike the boys in the first group, none of them knew each other.

They were all good kids, but with problems.

Tim's mother got a neurological disease and was in a vegetative state. His father felt Cohen would be a good influence on him.

"Why don't you speak to Dr. Cohen," Tim's father suggested.

Tim went to see Cohen who allegedly told him, "You're a Boy Scout. You're looking to get your first aid merit badge."

Tim was.

"Great, I'll come and pick you up and I'll take you to my house and we'll work on your merit badge."

Tim went to Cohen's Coram home to gain his first aid merit badge. Allegedly, Cohen made him tie one bandage and then proceeded to discuss homosexuality with him.

With boys like Tim, Cohen would tell them it's okay to be homosexual. There's nothing wrong with it. If you have such feelings you should discuss them. And then Cohen would act on his feelings and the boys, confused and frightened, would have little if no choice but to acquiesce.

In the indictment the Grand Jury handed down, Cohen was charged with fondling Tim's penis on three separate occasions: at his Smithtown office, in the parking lot of a Japanese restaurant in Port Jefferson, and, in his house, where he made the young man disrobe and stand there naked in front of him.

132

"This poor kid is shaking violently and Cohen is saying 'Calm down,' " William Condon recalls.

Clark was one of the older kids. Intelligent, sensitive, and soft-spoken, he was a violinist. He was too embarrassed to say anything about what Cohen was doing to him. Cohen was charged with fondling Clark's penis in his office.

Ike was a very streetwise kid, a hockey player. He went to Cohen because he suffered a concussion playing hockey, and Cohen allegedly started massaging his penis. And he's, like, "Doc, I got a concussion, what's this all about?"

Rod, eleven-years-old, was a troubled kid. He was a hyperactive child referred to Cohen for counseling by a friendly rabbi. Rod had a twin brother *Vin* who would occasionally accompany Rod to Dr. Cohen's house and on outings. They went on skiing trips together. Cohen bought both boys gifts but he never abused Vin. Cohen was charged with touching Rod's penis.

George was the youngest, ten. Because of his age, it was tough for him to understand what happened, and he was very withdrawn, didn't want to say anything to anybody. In fact, the only time he said anything to anybody was when his parents confronted him after they saw that Cohen pled guilty to the original sex abuse charge, and they started wondering what Cohen had done to him.

Nathan was slightly older than George, eleven or twelve, at the time of the abuse.

George and Nathan were the ones Cohen sodomized. With George, there was contact between penis and anus and mouth and penis. With Nathan, it was penis to anus.

However, there are those in the Suffolk County law enforcement community who believe that there were still other children who Cohen sodomized that he was never charged with.

133

If the wheels of justice grind slowly, Leona Cohen felt she was underneath them.

Just about the time Gary was charged with abusing *Saul Bolting,* the divorce court allowed the pediatrician to move his children to his home in Vermont.

Despite the charges against their father, his kids still adamantly refused to accept the truth.

Cohen was now going to his assets and using a good portion of it for his defense. When the second indictment came down, on January 31, 1990, charging Cohen with seventy-five counts of sex abuse, sodomy, and endangering the welfare of a minor, Leona tried frantically to locate her children. She wasn't even sure what school her son was going to, and Gary had not been forthcoming with information.

Now, all Leona could do was watch helplessly as her husband's travails were being played out on the most public of stages, as she tried hopelessly to make some sense out of the whole thing.

"He always wanted his name in lights," Leona says. "When he was arrested, I said, now he's got his name in lights."

The trial opened on Tuesday, October 2, 1991, in the courtroom of Alfred Tisch in the county seat of Riverhead. Judge Tisch had a flowing black handlebar mustache and a steady penetrating gaze.

All of the boys testified at the trial.

"One little guy got up on the table at the trial doggie style and he demonstrated how Cohen got on top of him and pushed his penis against his rectum," recalls Quinn, who also testified at the trial.

Tim testified that when he went to Cohen's house to earn his first aid merit badge, Cohen took him to a darkened room where he talked to him about masturbation, and stroked his thighs and genitals.

134

Another of the victims testified that when he stayed overnight at the pediatrician's house, he slept in Cohen's bed and Cohen fondled him.

The Cohen children, loyal to the end, testified that one or more of them were at home when their father allegedly abused the boys, and that those boys were never there.

In the end, the jury believed the boys. Cohen was convicted on twenty-seven counts of sodomy, sexual abuse, and endangering the welfare of a minor on October 15, 1991.

At his sentencing on November 14, Cohen pleaded for mercy before the judge. Between sobs, he pleaded his innocence. He claimed that the children who testified against him "had lied and they have been deceitful. . . ."

In response, Tisch took out a dictionary. Turning to the "Bs," he read the definition of a beast: "a person who is not human, who has no moral integrity. . . . If Dr. Gary Cohen had such integrity the jury has found that it was wavering on a number of occurrences." Based on the conclusion of the jury, Tisch said Cohen's actions were "despicable."

Then Judge Tisch sentenced Dr. Gary Cohen to the maximum allowable penalty under law—91.2 to 274 years in prison.

Gary Cohen is now serving his sentence in Dannemora State Prison.

The trial might have been over, but the nightmare was still going on.

For the victims, it would be years of psychotherapy to get over their trauma.

Chapter Nine

Dr. John Story

For twenty-five years, Dr. John Story raped scores of women, most of them Mormons, in the small town of Lovell, Wyoming. While he was eventually prosecuted for his crimes, the damage Story inflicted by his perverse actions affected generations of women.

Story's rape extended to the town's very psyche itself. Once his crimes became known, the attendant publicity obliterated the town's reputation as a nice, quiet place to raise a family. Instead, it's been perceived as a hotbed of rape, fueled by the repressed sexuality of the women who suffered terribly at Story's hands.

John Story was born in Nebraska in 1926. He graduated from high school in Malcolm, Nebraska, not long after the Allies landed on the shores of Omaha Beach in June of 1944.

As an undergraduate, he attended two institutions of higher learning: Wheaton College and the University of Nebraska. It was at the latter that he met his future wife, Marilyn, who was there visiting a brother and a cousin. They fell in love and eventually married.

Story stayed to attend medical school at the University of Nebraska and graduated in 1955.

The young couple struggled. They didn't have rich parents paying the bills; they had to do it all themselves. Marilyn, who was raised on a ranch and could ride and rope with the best of them, was used to hard work. She worked full-time as a secretary to help support them. For relaxation, they would go walking on the overpass across the Omaha stockyards.

After graduation, Story did his internship in Omaha. With little money, the couple was forced to live in low-income public housing.

They moved to Ogden, Utah, for Story's surgical residency. Like most of the state, Ogden was dominated by Mormons.

The Mormons don't drink, smoke, or curse. Their highly regimented church structure rewards those who follow the rules and respect the elders.

Women in the Mormon community have traditionally been treated as second-class citizens. The men are dominant, the women subservient. Sexually, the women have tended to be discouraged from openly discussing or expressing their sexuality. How much Story learned about Mormons and their views on sex in Ogden is open for conjecture, but he was an intelligent man. Like most sexual predators, he was quick to pick up on signs of weakness.

Story and Marilyn had a child, Susan, during this period of time. After he completed his residency, Story moved his family to Crawford, a town in the Nebraska panhandle, where he assisted Dr. Ben Bishop on a salary of $1,000 a month.

Bishop's nurse, identified by the pseudonym *Rhea Jaffe* in Jack Olsen's memorable book *Doc* about the Story case, would later recall Story's method of examining the young women in Dr. Bishop's practice.

He would require them to get naked, and then, draped with a sheet, lay down on the examining table. After entering, Story would pull the sheet off, with the loose explanation that he could not do a conscientious examination with their bodies covered.

Information gathered from sources in Crawford indicated that Story gave his patients an unusually high number of pelvic examinations. The examinations lasted longer than was deemed necessary under routine conditions. Then, a nurse's aide at the Crawford Hospital complained to nurses about the way Story treated a senior citizen. The nurse's aide reported that during a purportedly routine exam, Story was "just playing with her."

Allegedly, Dr. Bishop confronted his junior protégé. At about this time Marilyn saw the newspaper ad, advertising for a doctor in Lovell, Wyoming.

With Marilyn pregnant with her second daughter Linda at the time, the Storys piled into the family car and took a ride to Lovell. What they found was a small, pleasant farming community in the middle of a parched desert. There was a sugar refinery at one end of the town that emitted a pungent smell from the beets that were being processed.

What they saw, they liked. For Story, it was a classic case of being in the right place at the right time.

The town needed a doctor desperately. William Watts Horsely, who'd previously been the town's principal medical man, had been forced into a limited practice because of scandal involving sexual relations that he had with young boys for years.

Clearly, what the town needed was someone to lift the town's spirits, to comfort and heal the sick of mind and heart and body. In John Story, the town thought they had their man.

Story and family took up residence in Lovell. From the word "go," Story's practice began to thrive. Story was the epitome of the country doctor: never too tired to help a patient, willing to trade his medical expertise for services or farm goods.

But he made money, enough to buy a Ritter "75" universal table, an examining table that, because of its multipositioning capabilities, was perfect for gynecological examinations.

Despite the fact that he was a Baptist and at least half of the town was Mormon, Story became the town's beloved family doctor.

If you were a resident of the town of Lovell from 1960 to 1985, it was John Story who probably brought you into the world, and it was John Story who signed your death certificate. He cared for young and old, rich and poor, and all the town's political heavy hitters.

Whether you went to him for medical care or just some sage advice, kindly Dr. Story was ready to oblige.

But the dark side to his character that had begun to emerge in Crawford found fertile field within the sexually naive Mormon community of Lovell.

For some reason, whenever the Mormon women of Lovell would come to Story with a complaint of a sore throat, an earache, or a cold, he'd ask them when was the last time they'd had a pelvic examination. He'd make them undress, run the water in his sink, make them lie down on his Ritter "75," get the table adjusted to the proper height; then with his patients draped from the waist down, he would insert the medical instruments into their vagina for the examination.

Logic might have said that there was no reason to examine a woman's genitalia when she was complaining about a sore throat, but logic seldom has anything to do with why doctors can get away with sexual abuse. Usually, the patient lets the doctor continue because they believe that since he's the doctor, he knows what's right. In Story's case, you have to add to this the sexual ignorance of the women he was examining.

After he was examining his Mormon patient for a few minutes, Story would say that she was "too tight" to continue, that he would have to dilate her. And then the women would feel something hard, but with a soft surface, entering her. However, the "tube" Story was inserting wasn't actually a medical instrument, but his penis.

Some of the married women perceived what was being done, but quickly pushed it out of their minds. It's much easier to cope that way, to make believe that the rape never happened, that Dr. Story really knew what he was doing and that they were simply imagining things.

Only a few of Story's patients ever got to raise themselves off the uncomfortable table to catch a glimpse of his penis. The rest didn't dare, for fear of upsetting the doctor.

After living with the lie for years, the women of Lovell began to believe it. Even after they returned to Story, even after he'd examined them and their insides felt sore for days, even after a very few of the women started complaining, no one really believed that John Story was doing anything wrong.

Like any hardened criminal, Story would eventually be tripped up, but it would take one family's courageous stand against almost an entire town to see that happen.

Alethea and *David Grant* were farmers and business people. Not only did they own their own 150 acres of land which they worked, they also leased off six hundred acres more. In town, they owned, at various times, small businesses, including a dry cleaning store.

Alethea and David had three daughters, *Mary*, *Michaela*, and *Marti*. Alethea and David formed a God-fearing family with old-fashioned values that they'd imbued in their children.

At first, when Story came to town, Alethea and he didn't get along, but, after awhile, they became friends.

Story became her family doctor.

Jack Olsen notes in *Doc* that Story's pelvic exams could last a half hour to forty-five minutes, which is unusually long. Alethea, herself, like most women, hated pelvics. She liked to imagine herself being someplace else when Story placed her in the stirrups.

Story made it a point to always have time for the Grants. When Marilyn and John Story lost their third child, Annette, in the late 1960s — she was run over by accident by a woman backing out of her driveway — it was Alethea who rushed to give Dr. Story comfort. When Marilyn wouldn't stop mourning, it was Alethea who urged "Doc" to help her get out of her shell.

It was a short time later that Alethea received a call from a friend named *Judith Lemmle*, who claimed that Story did something strange to her during a pelvic in his office. Alethea, though, refused to listen to anything negative about Story. He was always there when the Grants needed him, or anyone else in town for that matter. There was no way "Doc" had done anything wrong, that's how much trust Alethea had in Story.

Alethea's daughters would later tell their mother that Story was known as "Stud" Story because of the way he examined the young women of the Girls Athletic Association during their physicals. Supposedly, he made them undress, stared at them, made lewd comments about their developing bodies, and gave them pelvics that weren't even necessary.

Alethea and the rest of Lovell discounted such charges as idle gossip by children with too active an imagination.

Mary Grant had come to Story for a precollege physical. She had previously gone to him for a sports physical during which Story manipulated her breasts and put his hands down her underpants. Not knowing what a sports physical consisted of, Mary just sloughed the behavior off.

For this physical, Mary took off her clothes and got on the examining table. Story stretched a sheet taut across her upraised knees which screened off the lower half of her body. This way, she couldn't see what he was doing unless she craned her neck up and over the cloth barricade.

As he examined and manipulated her vaginal area, Mary felt a rocket of pain. She yelled. Story got angry and told her she'd have to keep coming back until he finished his exam.

Meanwhile, Story began counseling her sister Marti on her sex life after she got pregnant by a young man named *Sam Mellencamp,* whom she married during a tense ceremony. Conceiving a child out of wedlock was a cardinal sin in the Mormon community, and both Marti and Sam were put on probation by the church.

During her pregnancy, Marti visited Story every month. He'd make her wait for hours and then usher her into the examining room, where she'd have to lie down on the Ritter "75," while Story positioned it for the pelvics.

Story never wanted to be interrupted during one of his pelvic exams. He'd even had the contractor who'd built his office make sure that the door to the examining room could be locked from the inside by just turning the doorknob.

"I just can't seem to get it in far enough," Story would complain to Marti as he rooted around through her insides. Then he would make a request to "dilate" her, which would make it easier to insert the speculum, an examining instrument.

Like all of Story's patients, Marti never thought about questioning his methods. After all, John Story was the doctor, and doctors know best.

Later, she complained to her mother that Story performed a lot of pelvics. Alethea expressed her satisfaction in Story's expert treatment of her daughter.

In August 1976, Story delivered Marti's child, *Clark*, through a Cesarean section. She became pregnant again the next year. Story delivered *Wayne* on January 17, 1978, through another Cesarean.

A year later, she went to Story's office for treatment of a puncture wound. When the doctor noticed that she hadn't had a pelvic in awhile, he made her take off her clothes and get on the Ritter "75."

Like some astronaut's couch in takeoff position, Story adjusted the gears until Marti was back in the position that Story found comfortable for his "examination."

He began sticking and pulling; then, he was pushing something in that hurt. He asked her to help him guide it in. She said no, she wouldn't do that. As he stepped to the side of the table, something long and hard, but soft and warm, slipped through her fingers.

After a few moments of disbelief, she realized it was Dr. Story's penis. Story told her the exam was finished. He also told her she was pregnant.

She told her mother of Story's assault, who, apparently, made her realize that she must have been mistaken.

When her baby was almost due, Marti went back to Story for an exam. The same thing happened. Again, she told Alethea what had happened. Her mother tried to convince her that she was wrong. She *had* to be wrong.

Eventually, after a C-section with some complications, Marti gave birth to her third child, a girl, *Katherine Denise*.

A few years later, in 1981, Story delivered Mary's child. During the delivery, Story made a long incision through her anal sphincter and a facet of her rectal wall, that he sewed up with two hundred stitches. The incision did not heal well, so Mary went to Story for an exam.

She complained that sex with her husband hurt. He

143

told her that she needed to be dilated.

Story put Mary in a prone position on the table, her knees raised and legs in the stirrups, then was ready to proceed with the exam.

His fingers felt painfully around her insides. As he pushed, he'd ask if it hurt. It did, painfully so. Then he left.

When he returned, he positioned himself between her legs. He asked her to scoot down the table a bit. As Story began again, the pain intensified. She felt something being slid in. He kept asking her if it hurt.

It sure as heck did. What's more, whatever Story was probing her with, it made her feel like when her husband entered her with his penis.

Story kept going for an indefinite period of time. Eventually, he finished and told her to come back in a few weeks.

Four months later, she was back in Story's office because she was still having problems making love. It was just too painful.

During the first part of the exam, Story didn't run the water as he always did, and he didn't do the exam alone: he had a nurse present. After his finger probing, he left, then returned, alone. He told Mary that he was going to dilate her with a tube. He assured her that through his dilation treatment, she would be able to have pain-free sex with her husband.

Mary felt something brush against her pubic hair. His voice came softly. Would she like to guide it in?

Mary was trapped on the table, in stunned disbelief, knowing now what was happening to her. The tube moved in and out rhythmically. When he was done, he told her to get dressed.

Mary checked the examining room thoroughly. She couldn't find any tube.

When she returned home, she hesitated telling her husband what had happened. Instead, she told her sister Marti.

What she was really looking for was someone to validate her feelings. When Marti did not, she decided not to tell anyone else what had occurred.

It was like that with Story. He raped woman after woman. In disbelief, they wouldn't tell their loved ones. And so "Doc" continued.

Marti had a sore throat. In fact, the passage was so swollen, she couldn't ingest food. She was really reluctant to see Story. She made and cancelled one appointment after another until, finally, she acquiesced.

Story complimented her on her appearance, squeezed her breasts, then told her she needed a pelvic exam. The throat was okay. Nothing to worry about.

If it was okay, why was it so swollen? It just didn't make any sense, she'd thought.

Marti's legs were parted and in position on the Ritter "75." Story probed her and told her that dilation would help things go quicker. Marti acquiesced.

For Marti, that last pelvic made it clear what kind of a man Dr. John Story really was. Marti headed over to her parents' place to tell her mother what had happened.

When Marti arrived, Mary was there with their mother. By that time, Mary knew Marti was telling the truth. Story had done the same thing to her. But Alethea still refused to believe.

Mary accompanied her sister to inform *Leroy Sanders*, a Mormon bishop, of what was happening right under their collective noses. Astonishingly, Leroy told the sisters that he'd been hearing similar complaints for years.

Sanders claimed there was nothing anyone could do about it. What he'd been doing is telling the aggrieved parties to change doctors.

They phoned their mom and tried once again to convince her that Story had raped them. Finally, after her husband David checked it out with a medical friend of his, he told Alethea that doctors don't insert "tubes" into women during pelvics.

Alethea finally knew that Story was violating her daughters. At first, she felt shame and guilt for not having listened to her daughters' previous complaints. Then she remembered Judith Lemmle's complaint about Story from years ago.

The Mormon power structure controlled the town. If anyone could see to it that action was taken against Story, it was the bishop. But when Alethea complained, they threw their hands up in the air and said that since Story wasn't a Mormon, there was nothing he could do.

Regardless, like a mother bear protecting her brood, Alethea was determined to see that justice was done.

Meanwhile, Marti wrote a letter of complaint to the Wyoming Board of Medicine. The Executive Director of the Board, which licenses physicians in the State of Wyoming, did the follow-up himself. He called Marti, they chatted on the phone about Story and his pelvics and his dilation methods.

The Director, apparently evincing that stereotypical male attitude, put her on the defensive. But what Marti did not know was he had to act on the complaint. The State Board's obligation is to investigate complaints from patients, whether they believe them or not.

There are no secrets in a small town. By this time, Story knew that the Grants were speaking up against him. And he knew that unless he could quell the Grants' suspicions, the troubles in the pandora's box might be unleashed.

He called Alethea in for a chat. He denied everything. When she told him that the State Medical Board had been notified, he didn't bat an eyelash. He'd had some

146

trouble with them years ago, and he'd taken care of it.

Alethea was beside herself. She had to do something. If Story had raped her daughters, there was no telling how many other women in the community he had also violated.

The State Medical Board told her that to proceed with the complaint, she would need five victims to come forward. With Marti and Mary's complaints, the number came down to three. She was determined to move forward and find them.

She talked to three women she knew, ranging in age from nine when the alleged assault took place to a woman in her sixties. Eventually, they all wrote the Board with similar complaints, and the Board was forced to hold a hearing.

On July 22, 1983, the Wyoming Board of Medical Examiners took up the case of Dr. John Story of Lovell. When officially informed of the five complaints against him, Story countered that they were the product of a vendetta by an ex-employee who was a friend of Alethea Grant's. He attacked the character and credibility of the complainants and charged that they had psychological problems. Otherwise, why would they be attacking him this way?

Of course, he denied that any of the allegations made against him were true. He had not violated these women in any way, and he was insulted that such charges would have been brought against him in the first place.

The Board, though, had different ideas. There was no suspicion that the complainants were lying. Story himself had offered little evidence to counter their claims.

The Wyoming Board of Medical Examiners offered Story the following options: He could voluntarily surrender his license, in which case, the Board's investigation would cease, or, if he decided to fight the charges, the Board would proceed with a more formal investigation.

147

Being the egotist that he was, Story figured he could beat the charges and opted for a full hearing.

Dr. John Story was beloved in the Lovell community. In the period between his first and second hearings before the Medical Board, Story was honored for his twenty-five years of distinguished service to the local hospital. Many of the community's power brokers showed up to honor him. That force of strength clearly showed that the Lovell community was sharply divided on the issue of whether or not Story was a sexual abuser. More importantly, it showed the difficulties investigators would have to go through in order to build a substantial case against a man who could command such a powerful lot of support.

The Medical Board had depositions taken from all the women that had accused Story. Eventually, the Medical Board held full hearings. Typical of the testimony indicating Story's modus operandi was that of *Ilene Parsons*.

Under oath, she stated that when she was sixteen, she went to Story for a tonsillectomy. After the procedure and her throat was healing, she went back to his office for a checkup. And then, for some reason, Story decided to do a pelvic on her.

Ilene thought that something was wrong. After all, tonsils and the pelvis are a long distance from one another.

As for what it felt like to be examined by Story, *Chris Boland* testified that she was a twenty-one-year-old virgin when she went to Story for a premarital physical.

Story began the pelvic by putting some implement into her vagina. Then he examined her with one finger, followed by, he said, the insertion of two fingers, and he held the fingers up for Chris to see them.

After that, the examination started to become painful.

Chris told him she was hurting. "I know what you're doing down there, but you got to quit. That's hurting me bad," she told him.

Just a few more seconds he responded. After he'd finished, he told her that he hadn't realized, implying that he had no knowledge that she was a virgin.

Chris testified that she didn't know at the time what was happening, that it didn't dawn on her until after her marriage, when she told her husband, "That feels just exactly like that pelvic examination that Dr. Story gave me."

On March 24, 1984, the Board concluded its hearings. The word of its decision shook the town of Lovell to its foundations.

"State board revokes doctor's license" read the headline, curiously spelled out in lower case letters, in the June 7, 1984, edition of the *Lovell Chronicle*.

The lead stated that the revocation would become effective June 30. "The legal basis for the revocation was 'unprofessional and dishonorable conduct likely to deceive, harm or defraud the public,' " said Kathryn Karpan, the attorney for the Board, who was quoted in the article.

Story, who had not as yet been notified of the Board's decision, said that regardless of the decision, the damage to him was "irrevocable."

Story, of course, decided to appeal the Board's ruling. After all, he didn't seem to believe that he'd done anything wrong. Neither did his supporters.

Almost immediately, there was a public outpouring of sympathy in Story's favor. The *Chronicle* was filled with letters from Story's longtime supporters. The paper ran a special column, with the headline, "Cards of Thanks," where Story supporters could voice their support for the man they assumed was the defender of the weak and the comforter of the afflicted.

One month later, on July 5, District Judge John T.

Dixon stayed the license revocation. "He can practice through the appeal," Dixon told the *Chronicle*.

Despite still being able to practice, Story called in some political favors from *Jay Fallion,* the town's big shot politico, who also happened to be his patient. Fallion figured he could use his influence to get the governor to intervene on Story's behalf.

The appeal itself would take months and, in all that time, Story would still be allowed to practice. If Story decided to appeal the case as high as the federal courts, and he appeared to have the resources to do just that, it could take years before it was finally adjudicated.

Alethea was frustrated. Not only was Story free to conduct his pelvics exactly as if nothing had happened, she and her daughters, not to mention the women who'd testified against Story, were having to face up to almost continuous hostility from Story's supporters. There had to be something else that could be done and, of course, there was.

Criminal charges.

What Story had done to the women of Lovell was criminal. Why not prosecute him as a criminal?

Alethea met with Terrill R. Tharp, the County Attorney for Big Horn County, and the man whose job it was to bring criminal charges against malefactors. He told Alethea that in order for him to proceed, he needed a stronger case. He needed twenty more victims to come forward.

A doctor with as powerful a patient and political base as Story would be hard to prosecute successfully.

Despite her frustration, once again, through her contacts in the town and particularly in the Mormon church, Alethea began to round up the names of more Mormon women who would testify against Story, this time in court.

For his part, Tharp called in Lovell Police Chief Dave Wilcox and asked for his help. The idea was for Wilcox to interview the victims Alethea was able to find and to develop any leads on his own if he could.

It was difficult work. There were spies everywhere, ready to tip Story off just when Wilcox was developing a new lead. Still, Wilcox moved patiently forward, interviewing complainants, until he hit a wall. They still didn't have enough witnesses to make a convincing case. That's when Tharp imported a hired gun.

Judi Cashel was a sergeant on the police force in Casper, Wyoming, a specialist in sexual assault charges. Figuring that the victims might respond better to a woman questioning them than a man, Tharp brought her in on special assignment.

Cashel was able to interview the victims and elicit more details than the men had. She put the pattern together and discovered that Story did an unusually high number of pelvics for ailments having nothing to do with the female reproductive system; also that the examinations were on the Ritter "75," a sophisticated piece of machinery not usually seen in a small-town practice.

Cashel, Wilcox, and Tharp, working sometimes with Alethea's leads and sometimes with their own, put together enough plausible evidence to go for an indictment and bring Story down once and for all.

Interestingly, the detectives developed a demographic analysis of Story's victims, which, it turned out, included non-Mormon women, though the Mormons were still in the vast majority.

Story was arrested at 3:00 P.M. on October 31, 1984. As he was driven off to jail to be booked, he refused to sign a statement saying he was read his Miranda rights. Story was brought up on seventeen charges of sexual assault involving fifteen women.

Meanwhile, Marti and Mary Grant filed civil charges

151

against Story, claiming that Story sexually assaulted them on a number of occasions when administering his pelvics.

A few weeks later, Story filed a $10 million counter-claim against Marti and Mary Grant, based on slander, intentional infliction of emotional distress, and tortuous interference with business.

But the civil case took a decided backseat to the criminal one. Now, finally, Story's victims would have their say in court.

All through the resulting trial in April 1985, the victims paraded to the witness stand, as one by one, they told of their sexual assaults at the hands of the beloved doctor. The *Lovell Chronicle* noted, "As the women described the alleged attacks to the court in vivid detail, there was general agreement over such specifics as the layout of the examination rooms of the doctor's old and new offices, and that no violence, restraints or threats were used in any of the claimed attacks."

That was true. Story hadn't forcibly restrained or threatened them. He didn't have to. They had voluntarily consented to be examined.

They had not voluntarily consented to be raped.

Story and his supporters were convinced that he would beat the charges. The supporters really did not believe he had done what the women had testified, and they prayed for his exoneration. Despite the overwhelming weight of the testimony against him, they still could not believe that "Doc" had abused those women.

On the third day of jury deliberations, April 25, 1985, the jury sent a note to the judge telling him that they had a verdict. They came back into a courtroom crowded to the rafters with Story's supporters. County deputies were armed and about in case the crowd reacted violently to the verdict.

On the first count in the indictment, the rape of *Francine Whitmore*, Story was found "Not guilty."

The spirits of Story's supporters soared, but not for long.

The guilty verdicts rang out over and over again.

In total, Story was found guilty on one count of second degree sexual assault, two counts of forcible rape, and three counts of assault and battery with intent to commit forcible rape. He was acquitted on two counts of second degree sexual assault and one count of forcible rape.

Even as Story was being led away by a sheriff's deputy, his supporters vowed to pray for and stand by their doctor.

"I'm satisfied. I think justice was done. It took twelve courageous people to do it, and I think it shows the system works," Tharp told the *Lovell Chronicle* afterwards.

The defense lawyers, for their part, said they would appeal. His supporters would organize a Defense Committee to help pay for his legal expenses. But first up was the sentencing.

"Wearing white armbands in a show of unity and chanting 'We love Doc,' more than 100 supporters . . . crowded the courtroom to hear five members of Story's family, including his 85-year-old mother, ask the court's lenience . . ." was the way the *Lovell Chronicle* reported on the proceedings.

On June 20, Story was sentenced to fifteen to twenty years in the state penitentiary in Rawlins.

Story would eventually be granted bond while his case was appealed. "60 Minutes" would come to Lovell to film a report about the Story case and the controversy surrounding it.

In June 1986, the Wyoming Supreme Court upheld Dr. John Story's conviction. He is now serving his time in prison.

Chapter Ten

Dr. Pravin D. Thakkar

Frankton, Indiana, was a rural town, population two thousand, with a real problem. The town's only physician, Dr. Harry A. Bishop, had died in 1979. After his passing, patients had to drive to far away Elwood or Anderson for a doctor. The local Lions Club proposed to remedy all that.

In 1981, they set a up search committee to find Bishop's replacement. The man that rode to the rescue and was subsequently hired was Dr. Pravin D. Thakkar, a native of India.

Practicing general medicine, Dr. Thakkar was much liked and respected by the townsfolk. His practice grew and he became very successful.

On January 13, 1982, Carmen Brutchen Hertzinger visited Dr. Pravin D. Thakkar seeking treatment for a simple sore throat.

During her office visit, she told Thakkar that her four-year-old daughter had died four or five weeks earlier and that she was very upset about the loss. Thakkar was sympathetic. He gave Ms. Hertzinger his business card which listed his home phone num-

Dr. Abu Hayat was convicted of violating a New York State law that prohibits abortion after the twenty-fourth week of pregnancy. (*Photo: Rob Tanenbaum*)

The former office of Dr. Abu Hayat was located at 9 Avenue A in Manhattan's infamous "Alphabet City". (*Photo: Fred Rosen*)

Dr. William H.C. Dudley.

Dr. John H. Story before his conviction for rape.
(*Courtesy of The Lovell Chronicle*)

Dr. Gary Cohen after his first arrest in 1989 for
the sexual abuse of a child.

Assistant D.A. Bill Condon led the prosecution of Dr. Gary Cohen. (*Photo: Fred Rosen*)

The former home of Dr. Gary Cohen in Coram, New York was the site of some of the sexual misconduct for which he was convicted in 1991.

Dr. Pravin Thakkar leaving the Madison County Courthouse after being sentenced to twenty-four years in prison for performing illegal abortions on two of his former lovers and attempting an illegal abortion on another lover. (*Courtesy of Jeff Evans/Herald Bulletin*)

Former doctor and convicted pedophile Alan Horowitz. (*Courtesy of Harry Buffardi, Undersheriff, Schenectady County, New York*)

Dr. Cecil B. Jacobson leaving the U.S. Courthouse in Virginia for lunch, followed by the media. (*Photo: Mark Wilson, Courtesy of The Connection Newspaper*)

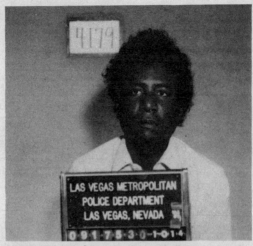

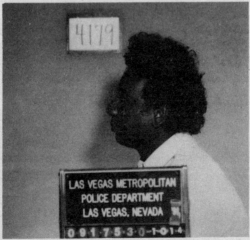

Dr. Kimble McNair upon his arrest in
1991 for sexual misconduct.

Dr. Kimble McNair accompanied by his attorney, Don Campbell, during his trial in Las Vegas in January, 1989. (*Photo: Jim Laurie, Courtesy of the Las Vegas Review-Journal*)

Mississippi's "Fat Doctor" Dr. George Camatsos.

ber on the reverse side. He also asked her to have a PAP test, which he scheduled for the following Saturday.

Within a day, Thakkar called Ms. Hertzinger and asked her to meet him, which she did. He invited Ms. Hertzinger into his home. They made love, and she stayed the night.

Ms. Hertzinger was excited to have found someone who cared about her, especially considering her recent tragedy, and to that extent, she relied upon Dr. Thakkar in the position that he held then as a licensed physician in the State of Indiana.

Thakkar continued to have an intimate sexual relationship with Ms. Hertzinger approximately once a week, although at times, the regularity of their lovemaking varied. But what was to prove troublesome to Thakkar, ironically, were the times they used no contraception.

In February 1983, Ms. Hertzinger became pregnant with Thakkar's child. She went to him and informed him of the situation.

"You cannot have this baby; you must have an abortion," Dr. Thakkar reportedly told Ms. Hertzinger curtly.

"But I want this baby," Ms. Hertzinger said. "I can't kill this baby because it's part of me, as well as you. I'm going to have it with or without your help."

Ms. Hertzinger's position was clear. At no time did she consent or acquiesce to have an abortion. She wanted their child to be born.

Dr. Pravin D. Thakkar had other ideas.

October 30, 1983, was the Friday before Halloween. On that date, Thakkar went to Ms. Hertzinger's residence to bring her money, which he had been doing for a period of time on a regular basis. The baby at that time was moving and could be felt by Ms. Hertzinger. It is estimated that she was pregnant by at least thirty-two weeks.

"Would you like to go for a drive?" Thakkar asked Ms. Hertzinger.

Ms. Hertzinger agreed and Thakkar took Ms. Hertzinger, then approximately eight months pregnant, to his home. While at his home, Thakkar informed Ms. Hertzinger that he could not hear the baby's heartbeat.

"The baby's dead," he said.

"No, no, it's fine," Ms. Hertzinger responded a little anxiously.

Dr. Pravin D. Thakkar, utilizing his position as a physician, convinced Ms. Hertzinger to take medications to calm her down.

"They were two or three round, blue pills," she would later recall.

Relying upon Thakkar's advice and suggestions, she did, indeed, take the mysterious medication, as a result of which, she became very drowsy.

Thakkar then escorted Ms. Hertzinger upstairs to a bedroom in his house, helped remove her clothes, and then, without her consent, induced labor.

The fetus was delivered by Thakkar, but Ms. Hertzinger never saw it. "The baby was stillborn," Thakkar told Ms. Hertzinger.

Yet, Ms. Hertzinger was sure she'd heard a baby cry. Unable to move or get up due to the medications administered to her by Thakkar, Ms. Hertzinger was helpless to check out his story.

Subsequently, Thakkar threatened her with a gun, saying that he would use the six bullets to kill her, himself, her son, the minister, her father and her ex-husband, thus accounting for each of the six bullets

156

in the gun.

Carmen Brutchen Hertzinger had had enough. She subsequently sought counseling at the Koala Center, including that for drug dependency, because of the medications that Dr. Thakkar had provided to her over the period of their relationship.

She also sought counseling at the Center for Mental Health in Anderson, Indiana. There, she told Gregory Richardson, a psychiatrist, and Brenda Turnbloom, a psychologist, that Thakkar had performed the abortion.

And she tried to get on with her life.

On February 12, 1982, during the time Pravin D. Thakkar was having a relationship with Ms. Hertzinger, Marsha Toppin came to his office. By coincidence, she also came for treatment of a sore throat, as well as a urinary tract infection.

He suggested to Ms. Toppin that she needed a PAP smear. But Ms. Toppin declined. Still, Thakkar kept getting personal.

During the course of his examination, he asked Ms. Toppin about birth control, and put his hand down her chest, sliding it from the shoulder down to her breast. Marsha Toppin would have none of that, and slapped his hand away.

Still Thakkar didn't give up.

He informed Ms. Toppin that he wanted a urine sample and she went to the bathroom to provide one. While she was in the bathroom, Thakkar, somehow, got in.

"Get the hell out!" Ms. Toppin exclaimed.

"I'm just trying to calm you down," Dr. Thakkar answered evenly.

Ms. Toppin left his office and later promptly returned with the urine sample. She was subsequently given the results of her tests showing that she did, indeed, have a urinary infection. But when Thakkar asked her if he could give her a pelvic examination, she declined.

Kathy Collins was not so lucky.

Kathy Collins, age forty-three, was next to fall into Dr. Pravin D. Thakkar's web of deceit.

In March of 1984, Ms. Collins, who was divorced and childless, met Dr. Thakkar as a patient at his Frankton office for a gynecological examination.

"I've decided to date again and I want to go on the pill," she informed Dr. Thakkar.

At her request, Thakkar did a PAP smear and asked if he could call her at home to which she consented. Thakkar also gave her his phone number.

After that office visit, Thakkar called Ms. Collins and asked her out for dinner that Sunday afternoon. They met at his home, where they made love, leaving briefly to go out for dinner. After dinner, they returned to his abode and had sex for a second time. Ms. Collins stayed the night.

From March of 1984 through and including January of 1988, Ms. Collins and Thakkar continued to have a sexual relationship, during which time Dr. Thakkar was her treating physician. In fact, from October 1987 through mid-December 1987, Thakkar dated Ms. Collins on a regular basis.

In December, Ms. Collins first complained of dizziness and other symptoms. It could be any number of things, including pregnancy, but she wasn't sure what it was. Neither, apparently, was Thakkar.

In a phone conversation after New Year's Day of 1988, Ms. Collins telephoned Thakkar because she again had these uneasy feelings, and she was getting worried about her condition.

"I think I'm pregnant," she told Thakkar during their phone conversation. Since she'd never been pregnant, she couldn't be sure.

Thakkar asked her to come in and see him on Friday before the office opened. Although Ms. Collins went to his office, she did not enter because she just could not face him.

On Saturday, February 9, Thakkar was visited at his office by Ms. Collins, who went into the examining room, got undressed, put on a paper robe, and sat down on the examining table. She put her feet in the stirrups, the position where women feel the most vulnerable, where they have absolute trust in their doctor.

Examining her, Thakkar told Ms. Collins that she was not pregnant, but that he would help her start her period. Thakkar then inserted a metal instrument into her cervix, which she referred in her later testimony as "personal parts."

Suddenly, Ms. Collins was in excruciating pain, so much pain that she was forced to move from the lower part of the table to the upper part, at which point she exclaimed, "Pravin, take this out; take it out now."

An appropriate response was not forthcoming.

"Pravin, take this out; take this out now," she repeated.

Ms. Collins waited until the excruciating pain subsided and then rolled off the examination table. An instrument fell out. She went into the bathroom and cleaned herself. Thakkar handed her a sanitary napkin.

"What is this for?" Ms. Collins asked.

"Honey, you started your period," Thakkar replied.

At that point in time, light colored fluid was seeping from her vaginal area.

Thakkar provided her with pills to take without informing Ms. Collins what they were, the dosage, or frequency with which they should be taken.

Ms. Collins left. Later, she went to St. John's Hospital, where she stayed for approximately two hours, seeing only one nurse. She left and returned to her residence.

Later that night, Ms. Collins began to bleed. After talking to a friend, who advised her to go to Community Hospital and indicate to the doctors there that she thought she had a miscarriage, Ms. Collins did so.

At Community Hospital, a Dr. Newkirk performed an examination. She was released and returned home, at which time Ms. Collins was informed by hospital personnel that she was pregnant.

Subsequently, Ms. Collins complained of chilling, cramping, fever and, worst of all, continued bleeding, and informed Thakkar of all that she was experiencing.

Thakkar, in turn, suggested to Ms. Collins that she go to Mercy Hospital, which is located in Elwood, Indiana. Ms. Collins told Thakkar that she didn't have the insurance to pay for a hospital stay, but Dr. Thakkar arranged for Ms. Collins to go to Mercy in late January 1988.

Thakkar sought to reassure Ms. Collins that she was going to be at Mercy only for intravenous medications. It was therefore hard to explain why he wanted her to sign forms for a dilation and curettage

160

(D&C), a gynecological procedure sometimes used for abortions.

Without her knowledge, Ms. Collins went through a D&C at the hospital. After the procedure, Thakkar asked her how she was feeling about the abortion.

"Abortion, Pravin, is that what I had, an abortion?" she asked incredulously.

Thakkar changed the subject.

Thakkar subsequently paid for the costs of the procedure and gave Ms. Collins a check for $1,750 on February 27, 1988, followed thereafter by cash payments that amounted to $700.

In May 1987, while Thakkar was in the midst of having a sexual relationship with Ms. Collins, he met Bonnie Lynn Coffey-Myers. She had responded to a November 1986 advertisement which Thakkar had placed in the *Indianapolis Monthly* magazine.

They met at a McDonald's, at the intersection of the Interstate 69 bypass in Anderson, Indiana. Thakkar asked Ms. Coffey-Myers to go to his home and she agreed to. In his car.

They made love that night and developed a continuing, intimate sexual relationship that lasted from May through July of 1987, ending on July 13, 1987. During July, Dr. Thakkar provided professional medical services to her as his patient.

In late June or early July of that year, Thakkar became aware that his lover was pregnant and convinced her to permit him to conduct a medical examination, to which she agreed.

Ms. Coffey-Myers's examination was conducted in the privacy of Thakkar's office. Thakkar informed her that she was not pregnant, even though she suspected that she was pregnant at the time.

As with Ms. Collins, Thakkar told Ms. Coffey-Myers that he would help her start her period. Thakkar inserted a metal instrument into her cervix, causing her excruciating pain. But unlike Ms. Collins, the procedure did not achieve the results Thakkar desired.

Thakkar then changed his tune and urged Ms. Coffey-Myers to seek an abortion from the Indianapolis Women's Clinic. Thakkar would later deny making referrals for abortions, statements that would be contradicted by testimony given before the State Medical Board by Jane Stout, who was employed at the Women's Clinic for five and a half years.

Ms. Stout testified that Dr. Thakkar called to schedule appointments for his patients for abortions *on at least five or six occasions that she personally recalled*. No other physician insisted on making appointments for his patients other than Dr. Thakkar.

Thakkar gave Ms. Coffey-Myers $200 to cover the cost of the abortion, and she went to the Women's Clinic, where she was informed of the clinic's policy that she had to be at least six weeks pregnant before they could perform the procedure.

Ms. Coffey-Myers then went to Tipton County Hospital in Tipton, Indiana, where the State Medical Board later found that Dr. Thakkar falsified hospital records by stating that Ms. Coffey-Myers was having complications following an abortion.

It was at Tipton that Thakkar told Ms. Coffey-Myers he would perform a D&C and tubal ligation. He did both, terminating the pregnancy and effectively making Ms. Coffey-Myers sterile.

Up to now, Dr. Pravin D. Thakkar had been conducting his crimes in private. That was all about to change.

In November 1988, Kathy Collins filed a civil suit in Madison Circuit Court, claiming that Dr. Pravin D. Thakkar performed an abortion on her without telling her, and that Dr. Thakkar was the baby's father. Besides seeking punitive and compensatory damages, she also charged the doctor with assault and battery and intentional infliction of mental distress.

"I'm very concerned that something like this has been filed. I don't know of anything about it that's truthful," Michael Lacey, Thakkar's attorney, said in a published account.

Dr. Pravin D. Thakkar's troubles had just started.

Like an avenging angel, Carmen Brutchen Hertzinger came out of Pravin D. Thakkar's past. On February 2, 1989, Ms. Hertzinger filed a suit in Madison District Court, on behalf of "Baby Brutchen." In the suit, she alleged that Thakkar administered drugs to her and then delivered the eight-month fetus in his home. Hertzinger claimed that Thakkar told her the baby was stillborn and he had taken care of it.

Ms. Hertzinger also said that she heard the baby cry.

"I was very much conscious at the time I heard my baby cry," Ms. Hertzinger told WISH-TV in Indianapolis. "There were many times of unconsciousness, but this was a time I was very conscious, and there's something about a baby's cry you don't forget.

Thakkar denied all the allegations. He even swore in court that he had never made anyone, besides his wife, pregnant. He was not very convincing, though, because the Indiana attorney general's office began

163

investigating Thakkar's actions.

Pending disposition of the legal proceedings, the Indiana Medical Licensing Board moved promptly and issued a ninety-day suspension of Thakkar's medical license. Meanwhile, in Frankton, the townspeople were divided. Some, like Joyce A. Thompson, believed steadfastly in his innocence.

"He's taken care of my kids, my daughter and both of my boys," she told *The Indianapolis News*. "That's why I just will never believe anything about the abortions, even if they railroad and convict him, because I've seen him with kids."

Kids, though, were not who Thakkar was abusing, and there began to emerge a picture of Thakkar as a doctor who had been abusing his female patients for a very long time.

"This has been going on for years. Now the abortion part, I didn't know about that," a former female patient of Thakkar's told the same newspaper. "I've realized it [the sexual abuse] now that it's all blown up. I can look back and see where we should have stopped this years ago."

On March 10, 1989, a circuit court judge froze Thakkar's bank account, so he could not make any withdrawals or hide his assets while Hertzinger's and Collins's suits were being adjudicated.

Thakkar acknowledged in court testimony that he was negotiating a financial settlement with a Bloomington, Indiana, woman who is the mother of his two-year-old son.

Dr. Thakkar was quoted as saying that the mother had made a request of $150,000, and that negotiations were ongoing.

Plaintiff's Attorney Robert York reminded Thakkar that he had previously testified on January

9 that he had never made anyone, besides his wife, pregnant. He now had to acknowledge that he lied.

What could be worse than incurring the wrath of the court that would decide your fate? How about getting the IRS mad at you?

On Monday May 8, 1989, at 4:45 P.M., agents of the Internal Revenue Service arrested Thakkar on a complaint that he deliberately evaded federal reporting requirements in withdrawing about $125,000 from his bank account.

It seemed that Thakkar had made fourteen separate withdrawals from his account, from March 23 to May 4, in amounts slightly under $10,000. Apparently, he was trying to duck a federal regulation that requires taxpayers to report withdrawals of $10,000 or more to the federal government.

He was not out on bail longer than a month before he was indicted on May 31 by a Federal Grand Jury. Not to be outdone, Madison County Prosecutor William Lawler, Jr., said that he would convene a Grand Jury to look into possible charges of illegal abortion and battery.

However, on July 20, a judge dismissed Kathy Collins's wrongful abortion suit, claiming that the case should first be pursued as a medical malpractice claim. The lawsuit was scheduled to be tried on November 13.

"As a practical matter, what this means is that we will be deprived of a trial in November. It will delay the case by a year to eighteen months," said Attorney York, who also said that he'd filed a malpractice claim with the State Department of Insurance.

On November 1, Federal authorities dismissed their charges against him. But, that same day, a Madison County Grand Jury indicted Thakkar on

165

eight counts of performing two illegal abortions, battery, and criminal recklessness. Thakkar pleaded innocent and was released on $100,000 bond.

In April 1990, the Indiana Court of Appeals overturned the lower court's ruling and allowed Kathy Collins to sue Thakkar without first adjudicating the malpractice complaint.

At Dr. Pravin D. Thakkar's subsequent criminal trial, Thakkar's former housekeeper testified that she found an abortion consent decree in Thakkar's home in 1983 that contained the name of the woman he was dating. The housekeeper said that the name on the abortion consent certificate was Carmen Hertzinger.

To make matters worse, the prosecution paraded three witnesses before the jury who testified that they knew she was pregnant with Thakkar's child.

A friend of Hertzinger, Janice K. Busby of Alexandria, Indiana, testified that she informed her that she was dating Thakkar. Busby then said she'd had two phone conversations with the doctor.

During those conversations, Thakkar denied he was the father and, what's more, denied that he had relationships with his patients. Busby claimed that Thakkar was distraught during the second phone conversation and that he threatened to kill himself.

The testimony of Marie N. Fowler, also a friend of Hertzinger and a student at Anderson University in 1983, was very damaging. She testified that she overheard a phone call between Hertzinger and Thakkar when Thakkar apparently suggested an abortion.

"I remembered her saying she couldn't abort her child, that it would be like murder," Fowler testified on the stand.

Dr. Trivadrum Ramaswamy, an Anderson psychiatrist and friend of Thakkar's, said Thakkar told him in April or May of 1983 that Hertzinger was carrying his child.

Perhaps to avoid paying off the civil claims that had been made against him, Thakkar filed bankruptcy during the period April 24-30, 1992, in United States District Court, Indianapolis. He listed $171,171 as debits and $4,000 as assets.

In April 1991, the Indiana Medical Licensing Board held hearings to decide what disciplinary actions to impose on Dr. Pravin D. Thakkar. The complaint included the following charges: fraud or material deception in the course of professional services or activities; engaging in lewd or immoral conduct in connection with the delivery of services; prescribing or administering a drug for other than generally accepted therapeutic purposes; failure to keep abreast of current professional theory or practice; and continuing to practice although unfit due to professional incompetence.

Thakkar knew that what he was doing was wrong and admitted as much before the State Medical Board when it held a hearing to determine whether or not the Board should take disciplinary action against him.

"What's wrong with seeing a patient socially," the questioner representing the state asked him at the hearing.

"It's unethical," Thakkar replied.

"According to what code of ethics?"

"The medical ethics."

"So your understanding of your own medical ethics or of ethics generally, is that it is not ethical to see a patient in the sense of dating a patient; is that correct?"

"Correct."

On February 13, 1992, the Board revoked Dr. Pravin D. Thakkar's license to practice medicine.

Under Indiana law, however, he can reapply for it after seven years. Anticipating that possibility, Ronald E. Elberger, the Board's legal counsel, recommended that future boards ". . . carefully consider the despicable and unconscionable acts committed by" Dr. Thakkar.

However, Mr. Elberger need not have worried.

On June 12, 1991, the jury at Dr. Pravin D. Thakkar's criminal trial found him guilty of performing illegal abortions on his two former lovers and attempting an abortion on a third without her consent.

On Wednesday, July 31, 1991, Dr. Pravin D. Thakkar was sentenced to sixteen years in prison for his crimes. He is currently serving his sentence. He is currently appealing his convictions.

Chapter Eleven

Dr. Kimble McNair

The first time Anne Rivera walked into Dr. Kimble McNair's Las Vegas, Nevada, office, he raped her anally.

The second time she walked in, she was wired.

It was the only way, police reasoned. There'd been a delay between the time of the assault and when Rivera had reported it. There was no physical evidence to directly link McNair, a gynecologist, to the alleged crime. Corroboration would be needed to build a case against a man of McNair's distinguished reputation. What better way than to get him to make self-incriminating statements on tape?

What's more, McNair wouldn't suspect anything. Rivera seemed as harmless as many of the women who, because of the severe shame and trauma involved with sexual assault, refuse to fight back.

"He always picked people who were afraid to turn him in," says Daniel Polsenberg, Anne Rivera's attorney.

But in Anne Rivera's case, McNair had chosen his victim unwisely.

What he didn't know was that Anne Rivera had previously been the victim of another sexual assault. After that, she'd received counseling, and been told if she were ever raped again, she had to report it. She did, and now Anne Rivera was determined that McNair be punished.

"During the tape recording of the conversation that took place between them, McNair makes many admissions that were very incriminating. As a result, it was enough to arrest him and file charges," recalls John Lukens, Chief Deputy District Attorney in the Clark County Sex Assaults/Child Abuse Unit, the man who would later prosecute Dr. Kimble McNair.

McNair's arrest shocked his friends and business associates, let alone his numerous patients.

Dr. McNain was a successful, respected, African American, gynecologist. He had a loving wife and adoring children. At least publicly, there was no hint of the extent of his crimes.

After arraignment on charges that he'd assaulted and raped Rivera, law enforcement authorities began to put together a case against Kimble McNair, a case that stretched in space and time back eleven years, and, with it, a trail of impropriety that ultimately led to depravity. The result was one of the most shocking and celebrated prosecutions of a sexual felon in the history of Las Vegas.

The trail began at Stanford University School

of Medicine. While studying for his degree there, McNair took up with a young woman, *Renee Jenkins*. Jenkins would later testify that McNair told her he was single when, in fact, he was already married to his wife Rosa at the time. Jenkins would also testify to the following.

After graduating Stanford in 1977, McNair decided to do his residency at the University of Miami-affiliated hospital in Florida. He sent his wife and kids to the Sunshine State by plane, while he followed along by car. His traveling companion was Renee Jenkins.

Once in Florida, Renee took a job to be near Kimble. Eventually, they had a falling-out and she moved to Las Vegas, Nevada. But according to John Lukens, McNair managed to find some other things besides his family and career to pass the time while in Florida.

"I got a tip from several doctors, who called and said, 'I don't remember what it is but I heard something that . . . He had some problems in Florida.' So I began to check on that and [the] only thing I came up with first was there was a police report.

"He was arrested in an assault domestic violence type of situation because he was sleeping with another man's wife or fiancée and this man came home and caught them in bed together. That kind of thing. It's a matter of record."

Whatever McNair's legal or domestic problems, they didn't stop him from pursuing his career in medicine. And in fact, there's no evidence to indicate in Florida, Las Vegas, or anywhere else that he was anything less than a truly accomplished, if not brilliant, doctor when he stuck to the practice of medicine.

McNair left Florida for a position at Humana Hospital in Las Vegas. He moved with his family to set up practice. He was licensed to practice medicine in Nevada in July 1981.

"Again, they [McNair and Jenkins], start their relationship and it breaks off after a very short period of time," Lukens recalls.

Ostensibly, until the time McNair was arrested for Rivera's rape, he had a spotless record. But the DA's investigation before trial disclosed something entirely different than was reported at the time.

"We finally subpoenaed our [state] medical society's file on him. McNair hadn't been in town but two months that they got their first complaint of sexual impropriety against him. They didn't do anything about it.

"They got a second one about six months after that. They apprise him of this and he writes a response denying he did anything wrong. There is an indication in there that says that 'We [the state medical society] also discussed with Dr. McNair the problem that he had in Florida.' That problem he had in Florida was *not* the arrest. It was a problem at the hospital he worked in in Florida and the physicians there never put anything in writing. They [the state medical society] were aware, I believe, of the problem in Florida. He hit town here, they knew about it and they didn't do anything about it," Lukens says angrily.

Yet, until Anne Rivera made her charges in

172

1988, Kimble McNair, at least as far as the public was concerned, was the epitome of professionalism. All that began to change with McNair's arrest.

"Kimble McNair was presented essentially with a female smorgasbord of female potential victims that came through his office," says Lukens. In fact, once news of McNair's arrest hit the airwaves and the papers, the DA's office was inundated with numerous other complaints. Most, though, could not legally be prosecuted.

In Nevada, the statute of limitations on a felony like rape is four years. Therefore, regardless of the truthfulness of the charges, Lukens's office could only bring charges in those cases where McNair's alleged assaults had not passed the statute's time frame.

Perhaps even more importantly, the women making the charges would have to be excellent witnesses, those who could stand up to what would almost certainly be a tough grilling on the part of defense lawyers. And these would not be overworked, underpaid public defenders.

McNair's Las Vegas practice was prosperous. His income afforded him the luxury of the best legal counsel money could buy.

After a lengthy investigation, the Clark County District Attorney's Office decided to charge Dr. Kimble McNair with twelve felony counts, including eight sexual assault charges, two of attempted sexual assault, and two of gross lewdness. The indictment claimed that all the assault charges involved sodomy.

In addition, all of the patients were white, and

all of their stories were remarkably consistent: Quickly and wordlessly, in the middle of an examination, McNair sodomized them in his office.

With charges filed, McNair was now in danger not only of losing his practice and his reputation, but his freedom. Permanently.

In most states, the worst a man convicted of rape can look forward to is a lengthy prison sentence. Nevada, though, has some of the toughest sexual abuse laws in the country. If McNair was convicted of rape, the sentence was life.

Dr. Kimble McNair's trial began in late January 1989. Some of the most dramatic testimony came when the second victim to testify, *Samantha Collins,* a thirty-one-year-old former cocktail waitress, took the stand.

She testified that after an examination by him in 1984, which included a rectal exam, he turned her around and, without a word, sodomized her.

Collins said that McNair later called her and requested that she not reveal the incident. Reportedly, he offered to pay for her school training as a medical assistant and hire her after she graduated. Apparently, a *quid pro quo* agreement was struck instead.

Samantha was a cocaine user and in danger of losing her job because of her drug use. McNair offered to write a letter to her supervisor which would indicate that cocaine will show up in a drug test for a good period of time after the effects had worn off.

Samantha further testified that it was when she went to pick up the letter that McNair raped her a *second* time.

Believing his personal office would be safer than an examination room, she met him in the former. But he locked the door and, again without saying a word, pulled down her pants. McNair, she said, bent her over his desk, and sodomized her. Samantha admitted she did not say anything, move away, or push him away.

"I was unable to do anything," she said. "Incredible, isn't it?"

When McNair's attorney, Gary Logan, asked her why she didn't do anything, Samantha replied, "Nothing logical makes sense. My life was so wrecked."

"I shut down ... shut down ... felt trapped. ... It's not that it didn't matter. It's just more than I could deal with."

Logan wanted to know if there was any pain. Samantha answered in the negative, explaining she had had anal intercourse with her husband and "Dr. McNair is not very large."

Samantha summed up by saying that she had come forward only after reading a newspaper article about McNair's initial arrest.

Next to testify against McNair was a thirty-year-old woman *Neva Johnson,* who had been using Dr. McNair as her gynecologist since 1982. She testified that McNair was "a very good doctor," who was "always there for me." But she continued, following a routine exam in 1986, he put his fingers in her anus and "played with my vagina."

According to Neva, McNair told her he was fondling her vagina as a means of getting her mind off the rectal exam. Neva said she pushed him away and said, "You're done." McNair also told her at a later date that anal sex was a cure for constipation.

While she returned to McNair after that for gynecological care, she always brought someone with her. Like Samantha, she filed charges after reading of McNair's initial arrest on the sexual assault charge that Anne Rivera had leveled against him.

"What he did was wrong," she testified. "I might have been naive not to go to the police when this occurred, but I'm not now."

Next to testify for the prosecution was *Sandy Bernstein.*

Sandy, who was thirty-three years old, testified that after an examination, McNair, "pulled my jeans down really fast and put his hand down the back of my panty hose.

"I pushed him away as hard as I could," she said. "I told him, don't do that, it's wrong."

McNair looked at her "in disgust," and asked, "Are you afraid you'll like it?"

She, too, contacted police after reading of McNair's arrest.

Another striking similarity between Sandy and all the other victims was that they confided in McNair many of the details of their personal lives, trusting that the doctor would not use any of that information against them.

For instance, Neva Johnson testified that she told McNair everything about her life, including details of one of her divorces, which happened mere days before the alleged assault.

To help the jury understand why the victims did not initially report their assaults, the prosecution brought in Dr. Anne Wholbert Burgess, a professor at the University of Pennsylvania. As an expert witness, Dr. Burgess described for the jury what happens psychologically when a woman is assaulted by a health care professional.

Recalls Lukens of her testimony:

"As the assaults take place these women are thinking 'Wait, this isn't happening, it can't be happening.' When they get out and do believe it did happen, they wonder 'Who would believe me? If I tell my boyfriend, he'd say, what are you crazy, a doctor did that? What did you do, did you lead him on?'

"They suffer in silence. A couple of our victims even went back to see McNair *after* they'd been assaulted. And Dr. Burgess helped the jury understand this and they could understand why the victims went back."

The prosecution had now made their case and rested. It was the defense's turn, and they went about their task with both guns blazing.

In his opening statement, Defense Attorney Don Campbell, another one of McNair's legal battery, impugned the motives of McNair's victims. He claimed that they were attempting to retaliate against McNair for perceived wrongs, or that they were seeking money in civil damages.

Campbell said that McNair had been involved

with Anne Rivera, and that while it was "dumb" of McNair to become involved with a patient, he was innocent of all charges.

Campbell began his case dramatically, putting the one man on the stand who knew the most about the now-celebrated Las Vegas gynecologist. A man of small stature, impeccably dressed, the courtroom was hushed as Kimble McNair was sworn in.

"When McNair took the stand, he tried to present himself as someone who loved life, never played around on his wife, who was a wonderful family man," says Lukens.

Gradually, though, the upright image that McNair was trying to project to the jury began to unravel under Lukens's aggressive cross-examination.

McNair admitted having sex with Anne Rivera on several occasions. But he could not remember who initiated the anal sex.

"You're just having sex and you do it," he said. McNair further testified that he called her "dear or honey" during their "affair," but that she continued to call him Dr. McNair, "because I don't like to be called Kim."

Lukens queried the doctor as to whether or not the affair was a "significant event" in his life.

"The word 'significant' is a little strong in my opinion," he replied.

"He was supremely arrogant. His testimony was a large part of his undoing because of his arrogance," John Lukens recalls. "His arrogance brought him down on the witness stand. How dare I or anyone question him?"

McNair did score a telling point when he produced medical records that showed that one of the women who was accusing him had not been in his office during the month she claimed to have been assaulted.

Turning to another area, Lukens tried to get McNair to admit that he had performed an elective abortion on a former patient with whom he'd been having an affair, a charge McNair vehemently denied. McNair also denied that the woman had sued him, and he had given her money to keep her mouth shut.

Since McNair's wife ran their finances and signed the checks, it is more than possible that McNair knew nothing about this settlement. But, "part of the agreement of the settlement was that she [the woman who'd had the affair] wouldn't say anything," says Lukens. "That didn't insulate it from a subpoena."

Claiming that he needed her testimony and that of four others to refute statements McNair made to the jury, Lukens asked District Judge Thomas Foley, who was presiding over the trial, to allow the testimony of the surprise witnesses. Some of the five claimed to have been assaulted by McNair, but the dates of those alleged crimes were beyond the statutes of limitations.

"This is insanity," Defense Attorney Don Campbell vigorously argued. "I can't conceive of anything more improper," than allowing the testimony of alleged prior crimes not included in the

179

indictment. "Fairness demands you grant a mistrial," Campbell continued.

Judge Foley granted Lukens's request but did give the defense attorneys a day to prepare for the testimony of the new witnesses.

In the interim, Wanda Brown, McNair's longtime nurse, testified that she was with McNair virtually every time he examined the complainants. "My job was to be there and I feel I was there," Brown testified. "I have no reason to feel I left the examination room."

This bolstered McNair's testimony that he always had a nurse present when patients were examined. Further, if Brown was right, then all of the women who said McNair raped them were lying. And Lukens could not shake Brown on cross-examination.

Unless Lukens's surprise witnesses provided relevant testimony, there was a possibility now that Brown's statements would create "reasonable doubt" in the minds of the jurors. If that happened, McNair would be found innocent and, because of the double jeopardy clause in the Amendments to the Constitution, could never again be tried on the same charges. As Lukens well knew, all the other alleged assault cases were either beyond the statute of limitations or too weak to bring to trial.

The defense had scored points and had originally been planning on having Rosa McNair, the doctor's wife testify in support of her husband. However, despite the fact that in their opening statements to the jury they had indicated that Rosa McNair would appear as a witness for her

180

husband, they chose instead to rest their case the day after Brown's testimony.

Wouldn't Rosa McNair have helped her husband's case by testifying? Or did she have something to hide? According to Lukens, there were a number of reasons why Rosa McNair didn't testify.

"She didn't testify for a good reason. His wife was allegedly in the office on the morning that the assault on Rivera took place. She tried to make it [the trial] like it was a big racist deal. She made some really incriminating remarks during one encounter with the authorities. His wife sort of took the posture that 'Hey Kimble you can screw anything you want.' Her words about one of his prior affairs were 'He can have all the white pussy he wants but he comes home to me.'"

The prosecution's star rebuttal witness, identified by the *Las Vegas Sun* as Melinda Southall, supported much of what Lukens says.

A former patient of McNair's, Southall testified that she had a two and a half year affair with the gynecologist.

"I had to listen for two years how he hated his wife and how he didn't want anything to do with her," Southall testified.

Southall said that Rosa McNair knew of the affair because she telephoned her husband at Southall's apartment. "It would have been hard for her not to know," Melinda Southall continued.

She testified that she saw McNair two or three times a week at her apartment. While making love, McNair asked her to "have his son. I told him I didn't want another child," she said.

The relationship broke up in late 1986 when McNair suddenly told her his wife was pregnant. Southall was angry, confused, and threw him out. Eventually, Melinda Southall sued McNair and testified that she settled for a $75,000 check drawn by Rosa McNair.

After testimony from other former patients (not named in the indictment), who claimed McNair had sex with them against their will, the prosecution finally rested.

Closing arguments went quickly. "We refer to our doctor as my trusted physician. It is engrained in us that physicians are to be respected for they are the healers," said Valorie Vega, who did the closing arguments for the prosecution. "When you're in a doctor's office, he's the one who's totally in control. This is what these victims experienced when they saw Dr. McNair," Vega continued.

She argued that the McNair Eight were patients who placed their trust in their doctor and were betrayed when he sodomized them.

But Defense Attorney Gary Logan argued that several witnesses who testified against McNair had a monetary reason for doing so: They had filed civil suits seeking monetary damages against the gynecologist. He also argued that one of the witnesses never testified she was sexually assaulted by McNair, but rather that McNair only put his hand in the area of her buttocks.

"When you see a gynecologist, you give your consent to be touched," Logan told the jury. And if anything did happen, "they [the prosecution] never proved that what happened was without . . . consent."

In time-honored tradition, the Defense Attorney stared at the jury and argued that the burden of proof is on the prosecution — not the defense. "Dr. McNair doesn't have to do anything."

The case went to the jury. It was time for everyone involved to sweat.

In the jury room, the jurors were hard at work. They put the pictures of all the victims up on the wall and charts with relevant information underneath. Then they spent two and a half days sifting through the information, trying to come up with a just verdict. When the verdict came, it was not without a few surprises.

On February 25, 1989, Dr. Kimble McNair was convicted on six counts of sexual assault, but acquitted on five other counts.

McNair himself kept his cool but the same could not be said for his wife. Rosa McNair stormed out of the courtroom. Bystanders heard her ranting in the hallway for several minutes afterward. Spying Melinda Southall, she reportedly walked toward her and said, "I'm going to kill you, you lying bitch," at which point, a District Court bailiff had to step between them to prevent anything from happening.

Soon, Rosa McNair dramatically returned,

throwing open the door to the courtroom like Scarlett opening Tara's French doors, and exclaimed, "You lying bitches!" at the jury.

Later, after she'd recovered her composure, she told all who would listen that the verdict was delivered by an "old, white prejudiced jury." She fervently promised to "expose this court."

Curiously, the counts on which McNair was acquitted involved all of the victims—with the exception of Anne Rivera—who were suing him or were contemplating suing him for civil damages. Therefore, in the minds of the jury, they had a motive for making the charges.

But he had been found guilty of some of the most serious charges in the indictment, and McNair was taken into custody immediately.

In the parole and probation department report prepared before sentencing, details of the initial complaints filed against him with the State Medical Board, as early as 1982, were finally revealed.

According to published information, the report indicates that one complaint came from one of McNair's office assistants, who stated McNair "grabbed at my backside in between my legs, tried to kiss me and verbally expressed his desire to have a sexual affair with me."

Other complaints allegedly involved questionable rectal exams and fondling. Clearly, the report didn't help McNair's case.

On April 21, Judge Foley sentenced McNair to six life terms to run consecutively, which means he would have to serve at least twenty years before he was eligible for parole.

Motionless upon hearing the conviction, McNair broke down as bailiffs attempted to cuff him in the hallway behind the courtroom.

"I just want to go home, go to bed, and go to sleep," McNair sobbed as the officers of the court led him to jail.

Most cases would end there, with the bad guy going to jail in chains and justice being served. But the case of Dr. Kimble McNair which had already proven to have its Byzantine turns, still had a few more curveballs to throw.

McNair's attorneys petitioned for bail pending appeal, at which point, "The judge issues a rather strange written order, all the reasons why he shouldn't be released on bail pending appeal, and then grants him bail," Lukens recalls. $900,000 in cash or 1.8 million in property.

It would take six months for McNair, whose financial resources had been severely tried by his legal problems, to raise bail. In the meanwhile, Rosa McNair was convicted of threatening Melinda Southall's life and disturbing the peace, fined $500, and ordered to have no future contact with Southall.

Finally, when McNair made bail in January 1990, it looked like he was getting a break. He would be free as long as his case was in appeal, which could take years. And that's when Anne Rivera moved in for the kill.

Her attorney, Daniel Polsenberg, filed two actions. The first was a suit against McNair for malpractice, which she lost. The Nevada Supreme Court felt, says Polsenberg, that "an intentional rape is not covered under medical malpractice coverage," even though the rape was so closely intertwined with his practice.

The second action, though, struck gold or, rather, tin. John Lukens takes up the story.

"Anne Rivera sues and obtains a default judgment against him [McNair does not show up in court to contest the suit]. He thinks, I'm assuming, 'I don't have any assets left' and he doesn't worry about it.

"Well, the default judgment is for 5 million dollars and then they move against the collateral that was put up for his bail. That caused me to go back into court to seek to revoke his bail bond because if he's not going to get the property back if he doesn't show up anyway, he has no incentive to stick around. That also caused the bail bond company concern, so they surrendered him. He ended up going back into custody over it."

Once a wealthy, respected doctor, McNair filed for bankruptcy. All that was seemingly left was the house where his wife and his children still lived.

Undaunted, Anne Rivera wasn't through.

"We have a judgment lien against any property he gets for the next six years and we can renew it for another twelve," says Daniel Polsenberg.

"He thinks he's safe right now because he had a discharge in bankruptcy of his debt," Polsenberg continues. "I don't think he's been informed that that discharge won't affect our judgment lien since we already have our judgment recorded."

So while Rivera can attach any property McNair acquires while in prison for the next twelve years, "the likelihood of him getting any property in the next twelve years is so remote that I talked to Anne Rivera and we've just shelved the case," adds Polsenberg.

So, after being raped and suing him, Anne Rivera wound up with nothing except maybe that most valued of commodities: her self-respect intact.

"Anne had some priorities. She's the client. She calls the shots. We could have early on gone after his money but she wanted to make sure he couldn't do this to somebody else so she's a real hero in this case," says Polsenberg.

John Lukens, though, is not as philosophical.

"Consider this. There are two people. One you know and trust and the other is a stranger. Both of them steal from you. Who hurts you the worst? The one that you know and trusted," Lukens asserts.

"And when a position is created and we put a person in that position, and we say honor and trust this person, I think that person has a higher degree of responsibility than does a stranger. And that's why McNair could do a lot of the things he did, because he was in that position of trust.

"His peers who foster that position failed to safeguard it and failed to safeguard the public with reference to McNair. They compound the crime. Our Board of medical examiners . . . allowed him to practice the entire time the charges

187

were pending against him. Even after he was indicted."

In fact, even after McNair was convicted, the
Nevada State Board of Medical Licensing did
not revoke his license, but rather suspended it
pending his appeal. It was only then, after his
conviction, that the Board announced that it
would conduct its own investigation.

Three years passed. The Nevada Supreme
Court upheld McNair's conviction. Finally, the
Las Vegas Sun reported on February 28, 1992,
that the State Medical Board had finally revoked
his license.

"I was appalled that our state board allowed
McNair to practice after he was indicted. They
stood behind that shield of presumption of innocence until proven guilty," says Lukens.

"They are charged with protecting the public,
not determining guilt or innocence. That's why
we have special laws and licensing for. Their
standard is a preponderance of evidence. They
don't have to prove it beyond a reasonable
doubt. Why? Because they're charged with protecting the public and there are a lot of women
that would be better off if this board here had
protected the public before it got to the point
that it did. Kimble McNair would have been better off if this board had severely disciplined him
and jerked his license. Kimble McNair might be
a free man today had they done that."

Kimble McNair is currently serving his time in
Nevada State Prison.

Chapter Twelve

Dr. Donald L. Weissman

Plastic surgeon to the stars, Dr. Donald L. Weissman's fall from grace was very quiet. Scandals in the medical profession usually are. The item in the February 27, 1988, edition of *The Los Angeles Times* was succinct.

"State officials are trying to revoke the license of a West Hollywood plastic surgeon . . . for allegedly botching breast-augmentation operations, sexually abusing patients and filing false insurance claims," the paper said.

"The physician, Dr. Donald L. Weissman, has requested a hearing on the allegations in a 14-page document filed by the state Board of Medical Quality Assurance based on complaints of eight women," the *Times* continued.

Eventually, Weissman got his hearing. The February 4, 1988, report, number D-3739 of the California Board of Medical Quality Assurance, lists accusations by seven women who were Dr. Weissman's patients, that were aired at that hearing.

Those shocking complaints, which follow, form the heart of the Board's case against Dr. Weissman. As we will see, the medical profession has its own particular code of honor.

Around August 7, 1984, *Brenda Smith,* a twenty-three-year-old female, came to see Weissman, complaining of difficulty breathing through her nose. On September 11, 1984, Weissman performed nasal surgery, including reconstruction.

The operation resulted in distortion and irregularity of the dorsal graft, nasal stenosis, and airway obstruction. In layman's terms, Weissman had botched a nose job, one of the most common plastic surgery procedures performed in this country. But Weissman hurt her even more in other ways.

During her office visits, Weissman hugged Brenda, invited her out, invited her to move in with him, and suggested she break up with her boyfriend.

Brenda told Weissman that his asking her out wasn't ethical.

"What's ethical?" Weissman allegedly replied.

On April 29, 1985, a twenty-seven-year-old woman named *Denise Small* showed up in Weissman's office complaining of difficulty breathing through her nose. Strangely enough, while she may have shown up with nasal problems, she subsequently agreed to have breast augmentation surgery, which Weissman performed that June 19, while her nasal surgery was not performed until July 10.

Both surgeries appear to have been successful. But Weissman violated his patient's trust by taking photographs that showed her face and her bare breasts after promising not to do so and then showed those photographs to others.

Then there was the matter of the phony medical records.

One of the two operation records for the June surgery, which were submitted to the Screen Actors Guild-Producers Pension and Health Plan, in support of an insurance claim, stated that what Weissman had performed was a bilateral mastectomy—the procedure where cancerous breasts are removed—and that he then immediately reconstructed the breasts.

Of course, it was a lie, because what Weissman had actually done was elective breast-augmentation surgery for cosmetic purposes only. In addition, his office progress notes for April 29, 1985, state that Brenda, a month before she became a patient, had fallen down some stairs injuring her nose, when in fact such was not the case.

On the face of it, it appears that Weissman falsified records so that Brenda could put in an insurance claim for medically necessary procedures, when in fact the treatments he performed were elective.

Irene Roper, a thirty-one-year-old woman, came to see Dr. Weissman about breast augmentation on July 7, 1985. Weissman did indeed perform the cosmetic surgery on both her breasts. But he botched the operation.

Irene was left with asymmetrical breasts and nipples, deformity, and scarring of the left breast. Weissman tried one operation to correct the problem, then another, and then a third, the last to correct scarring of the left nipple.

After one of the operations that left her with an assortment of physical problems, Weissman told Irene that he would not correct the bad surgical results unless she had sexual intercourse with him.

During the course of her many visits with Weissman, he made sexual advances and innuendoes. He would tell Irene he would make her breasts look so good, she would "want to give them to me."

On another occasion when Irene came to Weissman's office with her boyfriend, Weissman had Irene lie facedown on the floor to demonstrate certain exercises. Weissman told the boyfriend that when Irene was in this position, he could "get her from behind."

During still another visit, Weissman pulled Irene toward him, tried to kiss her, and when she turned her head, he stuck his tongue in her ear and suggested they get down on the floor and have sexual intercourse.

On still another occasion, Weissman tried to kiss her on the lips. When she pushed him away, he took her hand and put it on his hard penis.

"See what you do to me," Weissman said.

During her many visits to his office, Weissman ruminated on his patient's sex life and asked her to see him after office hours.

This scurrilous behavior continued with his paperwork. His operation report for his August 15, 1985, surgery, which was submitted to the Teamsters Miscellaneous Security Fund in support of an insurance claim, stated that Irene was "complaining of lumps in both breasts and considerable pain," when in fact, she had not.

Weissman had the reputation of being one of the best plastic surgeons in southern California. If anyone, other than some of his patients, knew that Weissman was not living up to his billing, they weren't saying.

Dr. Donald L. Weissman was so well-known and respected, he was quoted as an expert source in a 1985 *Los Angeles Times* article about the upsurge in plastic surgeries. So the women who came to see him at "The Weissman Institute of Cosmetic Surgery," or "The Beverly Hills Institute of Cosmetic Surgery," the two businesses he advertised and practiced under, had no reason to suspect they'd get anything less than the best possible care.

Had they known that both of those names were fictitious, that neither entity existed, and that he was not allowed by law to use them, maybe then they would have been suspicious.

Twenty-six-year-old *Laura Powers* came to Dr. Weissman's office on Sunset Boulevard in Beverly Hills, California, anxiously anticipating her breast-augmentation surgery. And expecting nothing to go wrong.

Like so many other of Weissman's patients,

Laura was seeking to enlarge her breasts. On November 27, 1985, Weissman obliged, when he performed breast-augmentation surgery.

Once again Weissman botched the operation.

On December 4, 1985, January 15, 1986, and February 7, 1986, Weissman performed additional surgeries in an attempt to correct the unsatisfactory results that he had encountered after the initial surgery.

November 1985 was a busy month for Dr. Donald L. Weissman. On November 27, Weissman took as a patient *Marilyn Newman,* a forty-two-year-old woman, who was seeking to have breast surgery.

Under the care of another physician, Marilyn had previously undergone breast augmentation, which left her with drooping, abnormally shaped breasts.

In December, Weissman tried to alleviate her problems. He replaced both breast implants and performed a bilateral upper lid blepharoplasty to enhance her appearance. He also sexually abused her.

During the course of Marilyn's office visits, Weissman kissed her, sucked on her nipples, made her feel his erect penis, and asked her if she wanted to have sexual intercourse with him.

Adding insult to injury, Weissman once again signed false medical documents, in that his operation report for the December 12, 1985, surgery, which was submitted to the Massachusetts Mutual Life Insurance Company in support of an insurance claim, failed to report the bilateral upper lid blepharoplasty, that he also performed on Marilyn.

While Dr. Weissman was perhaps best known for his breast-augmentation surgery, he had a reputation also for successfully performing other types of plastic surgeries, especially the removal of fat from a patient's body to leave them with a taut and lean appearance. According to *The Los Angeles Times,* he had even written a book on fat suction surgery.

Fat surgery was one of the reasons *Julie Rhodes,* a thirty-four-year-old woman, came to see Weissman on April 3, 1986. She wanted to reduce the fat around her abdomen, as well as have a bump on her nose removed. Weissman obliged.

On May 14, 1986, he performed a surgical procedure on Julie's nose and abdomen. He followed that up on May 22 with an additional procedure to replace a skin graft on her nose *while the nose was infected from the May 14 surgery*.

Like many of his other patients, the postoperative problems Julie had were compounded by Weissman's sexual abuse.

During the course of her office visits, Weissman asked her if she could ever be in love with her surgeon. He told her, "I want to be a bad boy and jump on [you]."

As was becoming the pattern by now in these cases, Weissman falsified medical documents relating to Julie's case. His operation report for the May 14, 1986, surgery, which was submitted to the

Connecticut General Life Insurance Company in support of an insurance claim, stated that Julie "noticed and complained of an abdominal mass, which at times became painful, causing increasing disability," when in fact, no such mass existed.

Once again, Weissman had lied.

It was on April 17, 1986, that Weissman chose to undertake the care and treatment of *Linda Allen*. Thirty-five years old, Linda complained of encapsuled breasts and was also seeking a reduction of her chin size. Instead, she was sexually abused.

During the course of Linda's office visits, Weissman told her she had a beautiful body. In fact, she so turned him on, he wanted to jump on top of her.

Weissman said that she gave him an erection. Did she want to feel it? He was so turned on by Linda, he told her, that he had to wear his white coat because of his erection.

When examining Linda's breasts, Weissman told her he wanted to bite them. He attempted to suck one of her breasts.

When examining her chin, he stuck his tongue in Linda's ear and started rubbing her breast. When she finally protested, Weissman told her to be quiet because she could get him in trouble. Again he told her that she gave him an erection and that no one other than his wife made him feel that way.

And at the end of each visit, Weissman wanted her to give him a hug.

Around April 21, Weissman performed surgery on her. There is no record to indicate that it wasn't successful.

The final case contained in the Medical Board's list of accusations against Dr. Donald L. Weissman was also the worst. It concerned *Barbara Eagan* who came to Weissman on June 3, 1986. Twenty-four years old, she, too, sought breast-augmentation surgery.

During the course of her visits, Weissman placed Barbara's hand on his erect penis and attempted to massage her pubic area. Weissman kissed her on the lips and breasts, and had Barbara orally copulate him and have sexual intercourse with him.

On June 30, 1986, Weissman performed the breast-enlargement surgery she had requested, and also a rhinoplasty (nose job).

The operation report for the rhinoplasty, which was submitted to the Mutual Life Insurance Company in support of an insurance claim, and the office progress notes for June 3, 1986, stated that Barbara complained of an inability to breathe through her nose because of an accident, wherein she had fallen down stairs a month previously, injuring her nose.

In fact, Barbara made no such complaint and was concerned only with her nose's cosmetic appearance.

By 1989, Dr. Weissman was under the care of a

psychiatrist and claimed that he suffered from a
". . . psychological and emotional state that dis-
abled him from practice of his profession. . . ."

Regardless of the reasons for his aberrant
actions, on December 4, 1989, the California
Board of Medical Quality Assurance gave Dr.
Donald L. Weissman the privilege of voluntarily
surrendering his license.

Dr. Weissman agreed, but in exchange for surrendering his license, all allegations not specifically enumerated in the agreement between him
and the state would be dismissed with prejudice.

He further admitted that the Board could have
made a case against him on the charges contained
in the agreement and waived the right to a hearing, reconsideration, and appeal.

Weissman admitted to abusing Irene, Denise,
and Barbara only. And while the rest of the
charges by the other women were dropped "with
prejudice," Weissman, and the Board, too,
avoided a lengthy, drawn-out hearing that surely
would have attracted the attention of the public
and brought further shame down on him, as well
as the profession. In fact, besides the February
1988 article, *The Los Angeles Times* made no further mention of Dr. Weissman or his troubles.

As a result of the California proceeding, Weissman also agreed to surrender his license to practice medicine in New York, which he did on
January 14, 1992.

In requesting that he be allowed to surrender his
license, Weissman agreed to the stipulation "that I

surrendered my license after a disciplinary action was instituted by a duly authorized professional disciplinary agency of another state, where, the conduct resulting in the surrender of the license, if committed in New York State, would constitute professional misconduct under the laws of New York State."

The Board was only too happy to comply with Weissman's "request."

Chapter Thirteen

Dr. Dennis Kleinman

It was at Englewood Hospital in New Jersey. He was visiting a postoperative patient that he'd taken care of in the operating room.

"Would you please describe the procedure that she had undergone," asked Paul A. Polifrone, Senior Investigator, Bergen County Prosecutor's Office.

"I believe it was for breast augmentation. But I can't recall," replied Dr. Dennis Kleinman, a tall, thin, bearded anesthesiologist.

"And what if anything do you recall happened at that time?"

"I went to see her postoperatively and we engaged in kissing," Kleinman stated.

"Did the kissing result in fondling?"

"No."

"Did the kissing result in a sexually inappropriate activity?"

"I thought that kissing was inappropriate enough," Kleinman replied tersely.

"Doctor," Polifrone said, "I'd also like to afford you the opportunity to discuss—if it's pertinent—if there have been any other episodes of inappropriate behavior sexually or in any other dimension professionally?"

"No," Kleinman said assertively. "I try my best to maintain professional behavior and attitudes."

His best wasn't good enough. Kleinman was about to be charged with raping a patient. And as the interrogation of Kleinman finished on September 7, 1991, in Conference Room #2 in the Bergen County Prosecutor's Office in Hackensack, New Jersey, the odds continued to grow that Kleinman was about to face some heavy-duty jail time.

Sharon Epson, a short twenty-three-year-old black woman, with short straight hair, was a clerk typist with a problem.

Sharon had been in a car crash in October of 1990 that left her with pain-producing neck and back injuries. To treat it, she needed nerve block therapy. Her physician, Dr. Nancy Mueller, referred her to Dr. Dennis Kleinman. An anesthesiologist with the Englewood Anesthesiology Associates for eleven years, he practiced out of Englewood Hospital in Englewood, New Jersey.

On July 7, 1991, Sharon went to Englewood

201

Hospital for her first visit with Kleinman. Sharon was on her stomach, the usual positioning for the course of treatment, which involved the use of certain drugs to "block" the sensation of pain.

"You have a nice butt," Sharon would later recall Kleinman told her. "Then he pecked me on the lips."

Next, Kleinman touched her buttocks.

"Why did you do that?" Sharon inquired.

Kleinman said it was a mistake. Sharon must have believed him because she didn't immediately report it or discuss it with anyone. "Because I trusted him and he said it was a mistake," Sharon would say later.

Sharon went back to see Kleinman for nerve block therapy on a second occasion when nothing happened. Then came her third visit.

Her third visit was on September 6. Her appointment was at 2:30 P.M. but she had to be admitted into the hospital to do the procedure.

With her grandfather driving her, she arrived at the hospital at 1:45 P.M. She didn't have to wait long because at two o'clock, she was admitted to the Day Accommodation Room by a woman she assumed to be, like herself, a clerk-typist.

Once that was done, she was taken to the second floor, to an area called "Same Day Service." She was placed in a hospital room with two beds. Separating the beds was a curtain that acted as a partition. No one else was in the room. She was wearing a blouse and green pants.

The treatment required her to take off her top, which she did. Then she put on a hospital gown as directed.

Dr. Kleinman arrived, alone, to begin the procedure. He was wearing his green medical suit and a green-and-white medical hat.

The first step was to sedate her. This was done by placing an intravenous drip in her right arm. The drip combined sedative hypnotics and narcotics. As Kleinman adjusted the IV, the drugs flowed through the tube and into her vein, knocking Sharon out.

She wasn't sure how long she was asleep, but at some point, she awakened from the sedation to a great surprise.

Her green pants and white briefs had been partially pulled down. Kleinman was standing over her and his penis was inside her vagina.

"What are you doing? Why?" Sharon asked groggily.

"Your treatment isn't finished," Kleinman allegedly told her. And with that, he sedated her again, and she went unconscious.

When Sharon awoke again, Kleinman was helping her put on her pants, her underwear, and her sneakers. Sharon, who recalled what had occurred, didn't question Kleinman. She just wanted to leave.

Kleinman left first and Sharon called the nurse, who told her that Kleinman wanted to see her. He came in a minute later.

"I don't think you're ready to go," he allegedly said. "You're still under sedation. You should stay here and lay down just a little longer."

"I don't want to," Sharon said firmly. "I want to leave right now."

But not before she'd cleaned herself. She put the end of a towel into soap, rubbed it, put some water on it and then cleaned herself vaginally.

Finally, she left.

Rape is an act of violence, not sex. But some women in similar circumstances, because of the sexual nature of the crime, do not report it and try to go about their daily lives as if nothing had happened. Sharon Epson was not one of these women.

She made a complaint to the Englewood Police Department, which referred the matter to the Bergen County Prosecutor's Office. That night, between 12:03 A.M. and 12:23 A.M., she gave her statement at the Bergen County Prosecutor's Office.

Later that morning, Kleinman was summoned to Englewood Police Headquarters, where he met with Paul Polifrone, the Senior Investigator with the Bergen County Prosecutor's Office.

After Polifrone had apprised Kleinman of his Miranda rights, and Kleinman signed a form acknowledging that he'd been read his rights, they discussed the allegation that Sharon Epson had made against him.

By 1:41 P.M., the venue had shifted to Conference Room #2 in the Bergen County Prosecutor's Office, where Kleinman voluntarily offered to give his statement to Stephan C. Ford, a detective with the Englewood Police Department; Frederick C. Krenrich, Jr., an investigator with the Bergen County Prosecutor's Office; and his colleague Polifrone. Sitting unobtrusively off to the side was Barry Gold, the official court reporter, who took everything down.

Kleinman began innocently enough, by recounting Sharon's injuries and how he was treating her with "the injection of a mixture of local anesthetics and cortisone derivatives into her neck just outside of the spinal canal for treatment of this pain" that she suffered from her auto accident injuries.

Polifrone wondered if "anything unusual either in terms of conversation or physical contact" occurred during her first visit.

"Only that she complained of discomfort and pain during the injection," Kleinman readily responded.

Because of that complaint, Kleinman informed her that "in order to perform the procedure she would require intravenous sedation."

The drugs he subsequently used would loosen the patient's inhibition, he said, and produce a state of relaxation.

"Would that also include a degree of unconsciousness?" Polifrone asked.

"There's a possibility that that might happen. It is generally not sought."

205

"Would that individual then be rendered incapable of responding to general circumstances around them," Polifrone inquired.

No, Kleinman said coolly, the idea was to make the patient comfortable, but without them losing control.

Kleinman then claimed that during the second treatment, after Sharon was sedated, she "indicated to me a desire to see me outside of the hospital environment." He agreed with Polifrone who characterized Sharon's demeanor as "contextually sexual."

It was now obvious which way Kleinman was going with his defense: Sharon had consented to have sex with him while she was sedated. He hadn't forced himself on her; she'd *asked* for it. But he denied ever having kissed her or commenting on her figure.

Polifrone asked, if during their third therapy session together, "Were you assisted from the onset . . . by anyone? A nurse? A medical colleague?"

"Yes. I was in part."

"Might I ask for the identity of that person?"

"Let me strike that, if I could," Kleinman replied quickly. He'd been caught in a lie and needed to get out of it.

"So the procedure that subsequently occurred was an unassisted private procedure between you and Ms. Epson?"

"Yes, it was."

After Kleinman injected Sharon with the sedatives, she became calm and relaxed. "Shortly after sedation, Ms. Epson began to tell me that she wanted to see me outside of the hospital environment.

"I asked her, 'Why?'

"She said because she was attracted to me from the beginning of our procedure."

There followed, he claimed, questions about his marital status and whether he had kids.

"I told her that I was married and that I had one child. But I did not tell her where I lived."

After that, the conversation became sexually oriented.

". . . she and I began to discuss the situation regarding how much she wanted me and what she wanted to do with me."

"Can you be specific, please, Doctor?"

"She wanted to make love with me."

Kleinman initially resisted her advances, he said, but, since "she said that it would be just one time," he acquiesced.

He helped her remove her pants and her panties.

"She then asked me if I had some sort of protection?" Kleinman recalled. "And I said 'No.' "

"You don't have a condom? Or anything?" Kleinman alleged Sharon said to him.

When he said that he didn't, she responded, "Well, then maybe you can use a plastic bag or anything because I don't want anything bad to happen."

"There was a plastic bag in the garbage, the bottom of the garbage pail, which is used by the cleaning staff to replace those that have been dirtied. I then went ahead, and put it on myself in a protective fashion and proceeded to have vaginal intercourse."

Eventually, Kleinman ejaculated into the plastic bag.

"I took the plastic bag out of the room and threw it in the garbage with the rest of the procedural instruments," Kleinman claimed.

When it was all over, Sharon asked Kleinman "how she can get in touch with me." He told her that he would get in touch with her in his usual follow-up fashion and that his office would get in touch with her.

But Sharon wanted more. She wanted to call Kleinman at work, an idea he quickly rejected.

"Doctor, during the vaginal intercourse, was there a time, to your recollection, that Ms. Epson may have been or was unconscious?"

"No," Kleinman replied.

Polifrone then went back to the statement Kleinman had given him at Englewood Police Headquarters.

"You indicated to me [this morning] that you had been during the procedure in the company of a nurse, is that correct?"

"I indicated that to you. Yes."

"And in retrospect was that accurate and true?"

"No."

"In the preliminary statement you indicated to me also that no sexual contact occurred, is that correct?"

"Yes."

"And you further indicated to me that Ms. Epson made inappropriate sexual overtures to you, is that correct?"

"Yes."

"And that subsequent to those overtures you reported it to a nurse, do you recall that?"

"I recall saying that. Yes."

"Was that, in fact, true or untrue?"

"Untrue."

Despite that lie, Kleinman maintained that his current statement was true.

"I feel like a total fool," Kleinman continued. "I did the one thing that I thought I would never do. It was a terrible mistake, a horrible occurrence. It's something that I wish that I had never done."

In addition to New Jersey, Dr. Dennis Kleinman was also licensed to practice in New York. While Kleinman might have lied to police about what happened with Sharon Epson in November 1991, Kleinman himself informed the New York State Health Officials on his license renewal form that he had been accused of sexual assault. No action was taken against him and his license, apparently, was renewed. New Jersey was not as lenient.

Unlike some states like Nevada that allow a doctor to continue practicing medicine while he's under investigation for a sex crime, or after he's already been charged, New Jersey is decidedly different. Even before the state completed its investigation of Kleinman, the New Jersey State Board of Medical Examiners moved almost immediately to suspend Kleinman's license.

The Medical Board held a hearing, where they noted "that the credibility of Dr. Kleinman's statement [of innocence] is questionable at this juncture." They discovered "that the doctor wrote in the 24 hour chart (part of the patient record), that a nurse was present throughout the procedure in an apparent attempt to cover-up the events. Furthermore, utilizing our expertise as physicians, we do not accept Dr. Kleinman's contention that (Sharon Epson) made a voluntary consent to sexual activity, given the mood altering drugs that had been administered to her by Dr. Kleinman. As an anesthesiologist he knew or should have known that a patient given those hypnotics and narcotics could not give valid consent."

The Board then temporarily suspended his license to practice medicine and surgery in the State of New Jersey. Now it was the justice system's turn.

On January 17, 1992, Dr. Dennis Kleinman was indicted by the Bergen County Grand Jury for the criminal sexual assault of Sharon Epson. The trial took place later that year and on December 23, 1992, a jury in Superior Court returned a guilty verdict. Sentencing was postponed until a later date. Kleinman was freed on $2,500 bail.

A Bergen County Prosecutor telephoned New York the next day to tell them of the verdict.

"We called New York and told them he was working there and that they should look into revoking his license," John J. Fahy, the Bergen County Prosecutor, told the *Daily News*. "Their answer," Fahy continued, "was that they couldn't do anything until he was sentenced."

Dr. Kleinman had an arrangement with a podiatrist who maintained an office on the Upper East Side of Manhattan. On February 26, 1992, just three months and three days after his New Jersey conviction, Kleinman was assisting the podiatrist with a procedure. While the podiatrist performed the surgery, Kleinman handled the anesthesia.

The *New York Post* reported that a screen separated the two doctors, so the podiatrist could not see what Kleinman was doing. The patient was a thirty-year-old secretary from Queens.

"She woke up to feel something on her chest," Assistant District Attorney Raymond Marinaccio told the *Post*. "He was first fondling one breast and then fondling the other breast. His penis was up against her hand. . . .

"She said that she screamed out and moaned, but that he pushed her hand back onto his penis."

Linda Fairstein, Chief of the Sex Crimes Unit in the Manhattan District Attorney's Office, went on to say that when Kleinman realized the secretary was conscious, he "quickly reinjected her with an anesthetic, and she passed out."

It was the same modus operandi Kleinman had used against Sharon Epson.

Kleinman was arrested and charged on May 5, 1993, with a single count of sexual abuse at an arraignment in State Supreme Court in Manhattan. Kleinman entered a plea of not guilty and was remanded into custody without bail by Acting Justice Herbert Adlerberg.

Because he was a convicted felon who had slipped through a loophole in the system and was allowed to continue to practice, all the local newspapers and television stations gave the story prime coverage. The story appealed to the emotional core of everyone who'd ever been abused by a doctor or had problems with the criminal justice system.

Manhattan District Attorney Robert Morgenthau told the *Daily News* that the case "raises serious questions" about the state's medical licensing system. Morgenthau himself might have been guilty of understatement.

Linda Fairstein told *The New York Times,* "To say that I'm outraged by this is an understatement. It certainly seems to me that his license could have been suspended."

Against this onslaught of adverse publicity, all the State Health Department, whose Board of Professional Conduct licenses physicians, could do was state weakly that they themselves were paralyzed into inaction by their own regulations. Until he was sentenced, a spokesman said, the state was powerless to revoke Kleinman's license.

212

Regulations or no regulations, it is doubtful the state would let Kleinman practice medicine again in the immediate future.

Rather than subject himself to a lengthy hearing before New York's Board of Professional Conduct, the outcome of which was probably obvious to him, Kleinman voluntarily surrendered his New York State medical license in May 1993.

In July 1993, Kleinman was sentenced by a New Jersey court to 8 years incarceration, at the Ayenel Diagnostic Center, a prison specifically designed to treat sex offenders. And unlike most prisons, he would have to serve his *entire* sentence.

Reportedly, Kleinman was disappointed at the severity of his sentence. As of this writing, the criminal charges in New York are still pending.

Chapter Fourteen

Dr. Alan J. Horowitz

Dr. Alan J. Horowitz was a psychiatrist in Hagerstown, Maryland. He had been on the staff of Brook Lane Psychiatric Center for several years before he left to start his private practice in the early eighties.

He set up offices at 221 East Antitam Street, where he received patients with a host of emotional problems, like the type twelve-year-old *Robby Hudson* was suffering from.

Rebecca Salinger, Robby's natural mother, had separated from her husband. She was raising Robby and his younger brother *John* by herself. Separation for a young child from a parent is never any easy thing.

Robby began suffering from recurrent nightmares. Rebecca's family doctor recommended that he see Dr. Horowitz for treatment.

Robby began seeing Dr. Horowitz on a weekly basis, on June 8, 1982. At first, they only saw each other in his office, but, after awhile, Horowitz seemed to develop a personal relationship with the troubled youngster. He asked Rebecca if he could take Robby and John, who was only eight at the time, to a festival. Rebecca saw no problem with that and gave her permission.

Horowitz continued to see Robby through the remainder of the year, during which time, the boy got involved in scouting. Sometimes John would go along on the scouts' camping trips. Horowitz attended one of them.

Just about this time, Robby decided he didn't want to go to his sessions with Horowitz any more. He never told his mother why; he just said he didn't want to go.

Sensing something was wrong, Rebecca called a friend who was a police officer. That cop and another talked to Robby and John. Gradually, the story of what had really happened during the therapy sessions began to unfold.

On April 18, 1983, the Washington County Grand Jury indicted Horowitz on six counts of sexual offenses and two counts of assault involving the two boys, one of whom, of course, was his patient.

According to the indictment, the incidents involving Robby allegedly occurred between July 5, 1982, and January 25, 1983. The incidents involving John occurred between December 14, 1982, and February 22, 1983.

Horowitz knew that the cops had him. If it

went to court, both boys could testify, and if their evidence was even half as damning as the indictment, he would go to jail for a long, long time. In all, he would face up to eighty years in prison. There wasn't a damn thing he could do about it but plead guilty and negotiate a way out of prison.

In Maryland, if you plead guilty to a felony, you don't have to get up in court, as you do in some states, and carefully describe what crime it is that you have pleaded to committing. In Maryland, the prosecutor gets that unpleasant duty.

On August 31, at 9:00 A.M., Horowitz stood in the courtroom of Judge John P. Corderman, in the Circuit Court of Washington County, Maryland. Beside him were his attorneys, Charles G. Bernstein and M. Kenneth Mackley. Representing the people was State's Attorney M. Kenneth Long, Jr. In the courtroom as witnesses were Rebecca Salinger and her sons, Robby and John Hudson. The boys were about to see an example of American justice.

The proceedings began with a series of questions from Judge Corderman to the defendant.

Was Horowitz currently on parole or probation from any other court?

No.

Had he sufficient time to discuss his plea thoroughly with his attorneys?

Yes.

Was he satisfied with the services of his

216

attorneys?

Yes.

Was there anything about the proceedings he didn't understand?

No.

Was his plea of guilty completely voluntary?

Yes it was.

"The Court finds the plea of guilty by Defendant Horowitz is being made voluntarily and understandingly. Mr. Long, if you would please, would you state the facts upon which the State contends that this Defendant is guilty?" Corderman turned the proceedings over to Long, who was ready to take center stage.

"May it please the court," Long began. "If the matter were called to trial, the State would call a number of witnesses; these witnesses would testify that this matter came to the attention of the Hagerstown Department of Police mid-March 1983."

Detective Kim Barnes of the Hagerstown Police Department was assigned the case and conducted an investigation.

"That investigation," Long continued, "included contact with a woman by the name of Rebecca Salinger, who is the natural mother of the two young men, Robert Hudson and John Hudson. Robert Hudson is a twelve-year-old boy, and he was contacted by Detective Barnes, who talked with him.

"The testimony would show that Robby Hudson had been having some emotional difficulties and, as a result, was referred to Alan J, Horowitz, a psychiatrist, in mid-1982 for these problems. A doctor-patient relationship developed between Robby Hudson at that time and Dr. Horowitz, and Robby was seen by Dr. Horowitz on a weekly basis or thereabouts from June 8, 1982, through the end of January of 1983, his last visit being on February 1, 1983. The psychiatric sessions occurred primarily on Tuesday morning between the hours of eight o'clock and nine o'clock A.M., at Dr. Horowitz's office.

"The matter came to light, as I said, in March of 1983. In the course of his investigation, Detective Barnes took a statement from Robby Hudson; and if called to testify, would testify today that during the course of this doctor-patient relationship the Defendant, Alan J. Horowitz, performed oral sex on him a number of times. When asked if he knew what oral sex was, Robby Hudson would testify that this meant Dr. Horowitz sucked his penis. As I said, this occurred a number of times primarily during the therapy sessions at the Doctor's office at 221 East Antitam Street. The Defendant maintained offices at that location at that time. Robby Hudson was able to describe the offices themselves; and it would be corroborated, Detective Barnes having been in that office, that in fact that does describe Alan J. Horowitz's offices as of during the period between July 5, 1982, and January 25, 1983.

"Thank you, your honor."

218

After a few perfunctory exchanges with the defense lawyers, the court was ready to enter the plea.

"The Court finds there are sufficient facts to prove that the Defendant, Alan J. Horowitz, is guilty beyond a reasonable doubt and to a moral certainty of the crime of unnatural, perverted, sexual practices as set forth in the Fourth Count of the Indictment filed against him, and his plea of guilty to that charge will be accepted.

"This case has caused a sense of outrage by this community generally and the people involved specifically," Corderman said. He was acknowledging the presence of Robby, John, and their mother, Rebecca, in his courtroom.

"But that outrage," Corderman continued, "must be tempered by the fact that your life has been one of contribution. I am concerned that you not be destroyed by this incident."

Corderman went on to state that this incident was apparently an isolated one, adding, probably quite rightly, that the publicity surrounding the case "would have brought out any other incidents.

"This was a tragic occurrence," Corderman concluded with compassion. "I don't know what the future holds for you but I hope you can restructure your life and someday again render benefits to the community."

Corderman then imposed sentence: five years in prison, to be suspended. In suspending the sentence, and placing him on probation, Judge Corderman ordered Horowitz to submit to a long, árduous program of psychotherapy in Monsey, New York.

The program Horowitz was placed in was known as *Ohr Somayach*. Administered by Rabbi Abraham Braun, headmaster of the Monsey Yeshiva, *Ohr Somayach* is a sixteen-hour-a day intensive program of study, peer support, and psychotherapy directed at the behavior disorder known as pedophilia, where the individual has a sick and perverted need to have sex with a child.

As for the rest of the charges, they would cease to exist. All the parties to the case knew that the rest of the charges would be thrown out. That's what plea bargaining is all about.

In addition to Maryland, Alan J. Horowitz was also licensed to practice medicine in Georgia, Pennsylvania, and Iowa.

On September 13, 1984, the Board of Medical Examiners of the State of Iowa, noted in forthright, simple terms that Horowitz's victim was a twelve-year-old patient, that his action was a "breach of trust in the relationship between a patient and a psychiatrist," and "[Horowitz] performed the sex act for no legitimate medical or psychiatric purpose on his patient."

And then they revoked his license. Pennsylvania and Iowa followed suit. He voluntarily surrendered his license to practice medicine in Georgia.

Strangely enough, Maryland, where he'd committed the offense he'd pleaded guilty to, was the most liberal. The Board of Physician Quality Assurance of the State of Maryland only suspended, not revoked, Horowitz's license to practice medicine. The suspension would be for five years, from the date he entered his plea, August 31, 1983.

If Horowitz, in all that time, did not violate the conditions of his probation, he could then reapply to have his license restored.

But the story of Alan J. Horowitz doesn't end there. Not by a long shot.

Had Alan J. Horowitz taken the shot he'd been given and run with it, everything would have turned out all right. After all, everyone was giving him a break. The prosecutor argued for leniency; his attorneys argued for leniency; and the judge gave him leniency.

By 1984, Horowitz had broken the terms of his probation. Horowitz was hauled back into court and asked by Corderman to explain why he was not living on the grounds of the Monsey Yeshiva. Instead, he was residing off campus in a residence where children also lived. Corderman made it clear that Horowitz must live on the yeshiva's grounds to comply with the terms of his probation.

In 1985, Horowitz was back in Judge Corderman's court to explain why he had broken the terms of his probation . . . again. Without letting the court know, he'd left the Monsey, New York rehab program for pedophiles and enrolled at the Rabbinical Assembly College in Brooklyn, New York, where he was working on a five-year program of religious study.

Corderman admonished Horowitz. "I remember writing Rabbi Abraham Braun saying that any program would require advance approval from this court," Corderman stated.

Horowitz's defense was that he'd completed his studies at Monsey and had to leave. The rabbinical program kept him in almost constant study from early morning to late night. Ironically, his new program emphasized the morals and ethics of the *Talmud* (Jewish law).

"My skills and the use of them depends on this court and the medical examining board," the Hagerstown *Morning Herald* reported that Horowitz told Corderman. "But in my studies, I have found there is also a tremendous need for rabbis."

Ever the compassionate justice, Corderman decided to let Horowitz continue his rabbinical studies in Brooklyn.

As for Robby Hudson, in the aftermath of the assaults by Horowitz, he hurt someone during a violent temper outburst and was sent to a group home. "I once put my fist through a wall because of my temper. There was a lot of anger," he would later tell the Hagerstown *Herald Mail*.

Somehow, though, he would have to get beyond the incidents if he was to lead a normal life.

Cases come and cases go. The court system, always backlogged, perhaps cannot be blamed when it cannot keep track of an old case. So for the next five years, no one paid much attention to Alan J. Horowitz.

In fact, Horowitz was no longer in the United States. He had gone to Israel, apparently to study under a rabbi. He shared a residence with a woman and her small children.

Eventually, Israeli officials began investigating sexual molestation complaints against Horowitz in connection with his live-in lover's children. Before the investigation was completed, Horowitz hightailed it out of the country, and came back to Schenectady, New York, where he maintained a home.

After returning to the States, Horowitz could not control his pedophilia. In the summer of 1991, he was charged by the Schenectady Police Department with sodomy. Before police could effect an arrest, Horowitz went on the lam again.

"He has a habit of getting out of the area when things get hot," Schenectady Police Department Investigator Peter McGrath told the *Herald Mail*.

Horowitz sought refuge in his old stomping grounds in Iowa, but to no avail. Acting on information McGrath had supplied them with, Iowa police arrested him near Des Moines, and he was extradited back to New York.

Alan J. Horowitz was indicted in Schenectady on thirty-four counts of felony first degree sodomy for alleged contact with two boys, aged seven and nine. Also included in the indictment were two counts of second degree sodomy, alleging that Horowitz molested a twelve-year-old boy, a single count of third degree sexual abuse for his alleged fondling of a fourteen-year-old girl, and four counts of endangering the welfare of a minor.

All the incidents allegedly occurred in 1990 at Horowitz's home and at a home in nearby Niskayuna, a suburb of Schenectady.

On June 29, 1992, Alan J. Horowitz, once the staunch defender of the Hippocratic oath, suffered further ignominy when he pleaded guilty to one count of sodomy in exchange for the dismissal of the other charges. Almost one month later, on Monday afternoon, July 27, Horowitz was sentenced to serve a minimum of ten years in a New York State prison.

Rip-Off Artists

Chapter Fifteen

Dr. Cecil B. Jacobson

Con men trade on trust that their victims willingly deliver up, trust that is then destroyed like a lamb led to slaughter. But when the con is perpetrated by a doctor, that trust has been taken to greater heights, then sacrificed on the altar of the Hippocratic oath.

Middle-aged and rotund, Dr. Cecil B. Jacobson looked positively benevolent, in fact he believed himself to be so, even after being convicted on March 4, 1992, of fraud and perjury involving the use of his own sperm to artificially inseminate many of his patients.

The story begins in 1976 at Jacobson's Vienna Reproductive Genetics Clinic, in Vienna, Virginia. There, Jacobson specialized in helping loving couples whose one goal in life was simply to have a child of their own reach that goal through the powers of modern science. Whether through in-vitro fertilization or artificial insemination, with the husband's own sperm or that of an anonymous donor, Jacobson was determined to give his patients what they wanted: a loving child all their own.

On the surface, Jacobson's patients had one of the most respected infertility specialists in the world. In fact, it was Jacobson who was the first doctor in the United States to introduce amniocentesis, the now standard test in which fluid is extracted from the womb for the purpose of detecting birth defects.

USA Today reported that Jacobson told *Susan Hudson,* one of his duped patients, "God doesn't give you babies—I do."

The Virginia Board of Medicine would later find that Jacobson would inject some women who were desperate to conceive with hormonal doses so large that pregnancy would be simulated, when, in reality, they would still be infertile. He would subsequently convince them that their bodies had mysteriously and sometimes repeatedly "reabsorbed" the dead fetus.

"He pulled a very cruel joke on all these women," said *Marilyn Reynolds,* who was twice diagnosed as pregnant. "He deserves what he gets."

Jacobson might have continued abusing his patients were it not for a select group of over twenty former patients that sued him in civil court for damages, stemming from their claim that Jacobson had led them to believe they were pregnant when they were not. Allegedly, Jacobson later told the women that the fetuses had died.

All the cases were settled in 1988, and Jacobson was forced by the Federal Trade Commission to reimburse several defrauded patients. His medical license was also suspended indefinitely. However, under the terms of his agreement with the State Medical Board, Jacobson can ask for his license to be reinstated in 1994.

After interviewing some of these former patients, Federal prosecutors strongly suspected that Jacobson's scam was greater than they'd initially suspected, that he had secretly impregnated patients with his own sperm. The case might have died were it not for a dedicated group of federal prosecutors who felt that Jacobson's activities were criminal, that he should be made, in criminal rather than civil court, to answer for them.

But there was one problem.

Jacobson had committed no crime.

There are no laws on the books that prohibit a doctor from impregnating a woman with his own sperm, let alone not telling her.

Like the RICO statutes, which give federal prosecutors wide latitude in prosecuting mobsters for a variety of illegal acts, criminal fraud charges involving the United States mail and telephones are frequently used to get indictments in criminal cases that fall into this gray area.

Since Jacobson had used the mail and phones to make medical appointments with patients, whom he subsequently defrauded, prosecutors realized they had the statutes with which to charge him. But to do that, some of the patients he had conned would have to come forward and testify in open court, and that could prove to be a problem.

Who would want to go into open court and admit that Jacobson, a man they knew and trusted, had secretly fathered their child? Well aware of the uncertainty they would face, the government proceeded slowly but methodically.

During the spring of 1991, letters began arriving in the mailboxes of Jacobson's victims. The letters were all the same, rather innocuous, from the United States Attorney's Office. In actuality, those missives were the opening salvos in the government's attempt to obtain the evidence needed for criminal indictments against Jacobson.

Each letter was registered, which meant only the person it was addressed to could sign for it. Therefore, only the person it was meant for could open it. Worded quite carefully, the letter simply stated that the government wanted to talk to the addressee about Dr. Jacobson's infertility programs.

The letters were sent after months and months of meetings and hundreds of hours of discussion between government prosecutors, guided by medical ethicists, social workers, geneticists, and other health care professionals. The central question was how to approach Jacobson's victims with knowledge of the "sting." After all, this wasn't just someone being bilked out of mere money but rather parents, and children, whose lives could easily be shattered by knowledge of Jacobson's crimes.

Eventually, the government decided that no one would be forced to testify, that the best way to approach the former patients was to contact them by letter, request their presence at the U.S. Attorney's Office and then to proceed gingerly, essentially allowing the families to control what they learned and how involved they would become in the case.

This game plan brought parents and prosecutors together in stages, when information about Jacobson was distributed in piecemeal fashion, and the parents themselves had to digest each bit of news before deciding whether to go forward. In a highly unusual move, the government actually allowed material witnesses [the parents] in a criminal case the opportunity to bail out, an option that many of the parents took.

"My husband was out of town [when I got the letter]," one of the mothers, *Sally Rogers,* told *The New York Times*. "So the first time I went by myself. The lawyers started talking in general terms about why I went to Jacobson — and little by little, the wheels started turning in my head.

"My husband and I had chosen not to tell our child she was donor inseminated. It was a big secret in my head. Suddenly I realized, 'They know, they know, and I wished my husband wasn't out of town. I wished he were sitting there beside me."

At about the time Sally Rogers was receiving

her letter, *Mel* and *Connie Franklin,* parents of three, received theirs. "I remember a feeling of dread when we first got it," Franklin recalled. "My wife's first reaction was 'no way.' She felt we should not get involved in any way, shape or form. But I said let's hear them out because I never thought in my wildest dreams it would lead to something like [the prosecution of Jacobson]."

These parents' reactions came as no surprise. It was part of the government's game plan to take Jacobson down. The patients had to decide whether to help the government or not. At stake was a chilling scenario that only the parents had the power to prevent.

What if the various Jacobson children later met and married? That would be incest, which could have devastating effects. Even worse, what if Jacobson had passed on some genetic defect his unknown children could be protected against, but only if they had the knowledge of who their father really was?

Dozens of Jacobson's patients who were initially approached never called the prosecutors, but most did. Once they did, the government told them they had more information for them, but that it meant disclosing the identity of their formerly anonymous sperm donor.

Meanwhile, prosecutors, preparing for the final showdown with Jacobson in court, gave each family a pseudonym to protect their identities and a list of social workers they could consult for free counseling.

232

"At some point, they told us they would eventually file for an indictment," recalls Mel Franklin. Initially, Franklin and his wife were unrelentingly opposed to testifying in open court. But that was before they were requested by the government to go with their child for paternity DNA testing.

If the DNA tests of the children matched those of Jacobson, it would prove irrefutably that the doctor, and not some anonymous sperm donor as he had claimed, was the father.

"I took my daughter to the lab — it was summertime — and the technician kept calling me Mrs. Smith [her government-assigned pseudonym]," Connie Franklin told the *Times*. "My daughter kept saying, 'Mommy, why is he calling you that?'

"It was probably the hardest decision we had to make," Franklin continues. "There was a certain comfort in knowing for sure. My wife cried about it a lot. But in the end, I wanted to know, to be able to have it settled and deal with it."

During the DNA testing phase, many families decided against testifying. Eventually, only seven sets of parents remained. The couples were informed that while the DNA testing would not oblige them to testify against Jacobson, the results of the tests, should they prove positive, would be evidence and therefore might be disclosed publicly by Jacobson's defense tacticians.

The DNA tests indicated that Jacobson had fathered fifteen children. The prosecution then asked those parents to be listed in the indict-

233

ment.

While some were reluctant at first, all seven couples agreed to cooperate. They were permitted to use their pseudonyms in court.

After months of careful planning, the government finally acted. Jacobson was charged with thirty-two counts of mail fraud and ten counts of wire fraud for using the phone to make medical appointments and then deceiving these same patients.

The icing on the prosecutorial cake was an additional four counts of travel fraud because patients crossed state lines to reach the Vienna, Virginia clinic he operated until his civil liability problems in 1988.

The last counts in the indictment, sex perjury charges, had to do with testimony Jacobson gave to the Federal Trade Commission in a 1988 civil suit brought against him by a former patient for the bogus hormone injection treatments.

The trial of Dr. Cecil Jacobson opened to the deafening roar of worldwide publicity during February 1992. In the United States alone, it made the front pages of many of the major newspapers, and the front sections of others. TV ate it up, with updates on the national nightly newscasts as the trial progressed.

Since Judge James B. Cacheris had allowed the parents to use their pseudonyms, placards were taped to the witness stand so the attorneys for all sides would not utter their real names.

234

Still, the embarrassment of going public was too much for some of the parents, who took to disguising themselves for their court appearances with wigs and makeup. To further protect their identities, the judge would not allow questions about the sex, age, or general residence of the children.

Like a procession of the damned, the government paraded a total of eleven parents before the jury to expose Jacobson's scam. Witness after witness testified about Jacobson's con game, and about their shock, dismay, and anger when they learned that their fifteen children were not the product of anonymous sperm donors as Jacobson had said, but actually from his own loins. Others testified about Jacobson's practice of deliberately misdiagnosing pregnancies.

"It won't ever leave me," said *Nancy Cartwright*. She told a hushed courtroom how Jacobson had convinced her that she was pregnant when he pointed to a sonogram and said, "There's Junior."

But there was no Junior for Cartwright and many of the others who came to Jacobson to get pregnant.

Gwen Welles, a hospital radiation therapist, testified that she was given hormones that caused her body to mimic pregnancy and was told three times she had conceived. But Gwen was wary. She and her husband had not been having relations, though she told Jacobson they had.

The defense, for its part, claimed that Dr. Cecil Jacobson was a humanitarian, that he deceived women into believing they were pregnant out of a desire to help people. As for the deceit involving his secret parenting, they claimed he used his own sperm only when anonymous donors failed to show up at his clinic. Jacobson pointed out that for purposes of conception, fresh sperm was more effective than frozen sperm.

Unfortunately for Jacobson, that claim was repudiated by three former receptionists at his Vienna Clinic and a laboratory, all of whom worked for Jacobson and testified that there were never any anonymous sperm donors at the clinic.

As for Jacobson's final claim, that he desired to protect patients from the AIDS virus (which he apparently knew he himself didn't have), it strained all standards of credibility.

The verdict came on March 4, 1992. Cecil Jacobson sat impassively, his arms crossed across his chest in a protective gesture as jury foreman Daniel Richard read the verdict:

"Guilty." Richard intoned to forty-six of the fraud counts and six perjury counts stemming from his previous legal troubles. On the rest of the indictment, he was found "not guilty."

"We knew he was lying to those patients," said Richard afterwards in *USA Today*. "We gave him the benefit of the doubt," added juror Deborah Earman. "But when we saw a pattern. . . . He couldn't make the same mistake over and over. He's a professional."

Despite the crash he had just taken, Jacobson's ego was still operating on all eight cylinders.

"It's a shock to be found guilty of trying to help people. I didn't break any law. I spent my life trying to help women have children. If I felt I was a criminal or broke the law, I would never have done it," Jacobson said.

Defense lawyer, James B. Tate, echoed his client's sentiments.

"If Cecil made any mistakes, it was in losing his objectivity and trying so hard to get patients pregnant."

Countered Richard Cullen, United States Attorney for the Eastern District of Virginia, "It speaks loudly that doctors who lie to their patients for profit are going to be dealt with as criminals.

"We wanted to make sure that we did everything we could to protect the parents. In the final analysis, though, this was a case of classic, basic fraud. But it was an unusual case and we were faced with a situation where there was no precedent."

Willing herself not to cry, but barely succeeding, a patient who testified during the twelve-day trial that Jacobson was the natural father of her daughter later told *The Washington Post* that the sentence was "fair," but summed up the experience for all the parents when she said that "nothing will make up for the pain" she and her husband suffered. Still, "the satisfaction is he can't practice now. Nobody should ever have to go through this again."

"He should go to jail," said *Jean Thompson,* who had been told by Jacobson that she was pregnant and had then miscarried.

In a presentencing memo, Assistant U.S. Attorneys Randy I. Bellows and David G. Barger stated that Jacobson's conduct was "as callous and cruel as any," the court has witnessed and requested that Judge Cacheris put Jacobson in jail immediately upon sentencing, rather than letting him remain free on bond while Tate and the rest of his lawyers appeal. They also wanted Jacobson sentenced to at least ten years in prison, the maximum for any count on which he was convicted, and that he should remain in prison for the entire time.

There is much speculation about whether white-collar criminals like Jacobson, who can afford top legal talent, ever get the punishment they deserve, especially when compared to their less fortunate brethren who commit more violent crimes who are defended by court appointed attorneys. In Jacobson's case, the speculation died with the sentence.

On May 5, 1992, Jacobson was sentenced by United States District Judge James C. Cacheris to five rather than ten years in prison, but would remain free on bail until the appeal process ended.

At his sentencing hearing, Jacobson told Judge Cacheris:

"I was totally unaware of the anger, anguish and hate I have caused — until these proceedings." Speaking of his former patients and their families, he continued, "I ask for their forgiveness so that the healing process can start.

"But I helped a great deal of other people. [And] I did not wish to hurt these people. I wished to help," Jacobson added, as if this would release the burden of pain he had imposed on so many people.

Assistant U.S. Attorney Bellows was nevertheless satisfied with the sentence, which he described as harsh for a white-collar defendant. "Cacheris made it clear that when a doctor is found guilty of lying to his patients on matters of fundamental importance, there will be a severe sentence meted out.

But Jacobson still had his medical license. He was free, while on bond pending appeal, to continue practicing medicine. Clearly, it was time for the Virginia Board of Medicine to act.

The Board began an investigation that gave a heretofore unseen look as to how Jacobson had conned many of his patients into believing they were pregnant.

According to the Board, from May 29, 1987, through February 5, 1988, "Dr. Jacobson administered a treatment regimen for Patient A to include 44 intramuscular injections of Human Chorionic Gonadotropin ("HCG"), 4 urine pregnancy tests and 6 ultrasonic examinations.

"On July 6, 1987, he informed Patient A that she was pregnant based upon a positive urine pregnancy test when, in fact, said positive urine pregnancy test was the result of excessive HCG in Patient A's system.

"Further, on July 27, August 24, September 16 and September 21, 1987, he performed ultra-sonographic examinations on Patient A and reported a developing gestation sac-embryo. Upon being informed by consulting physician James Stafford, M.D. on September 16, 1987, that Patient A showed no sign of pregnancy, Dr. Jacobson informed said patient that the gestation sac-embryo was being reabsorbed by her body."

Thus, Jacobson convinced Patient A that she had suffered some form of a mysterious miscarriage. Whatever it was, if Patient A was like many expectant mothers, her grief and aggravation at losing her baby must have been intense. Still, Jacobson showed no mercy.

"On two later occasions, September 25, 1987 and December 11, 1987," the society's report continues, "he informed Patient A that she was pregnant only to later inform said patient that her pregnancies had terminated and the gestation sac-embryos were reabsorbed."

Between June 1983 and January 1988, the Medical Board found that Cecil Jacobson had perpetrated this same con on seven different patients. No one knows how many such cons went unreported.

While Jacobson did not admit the truth of these charges, he did not contest them. On May

28, 1992 the Board revoked his license and ordered him to pay a monetary penalty of $1,000 per patient cited in their findings.

Assuming his conviction is upheld on appeal with time off for good behavior, Jacobson will serve a minimum sentence of four years and five months. However, he will not be serving his time in one of the government's maximum security prisons like Leavenworth.

Acceding to a plea of the defense counsel, Judge Cacheris said that he would request that Jacobson be permitted to serve his sentence at the minimum-security federal prison at Nellis Air Force Base in Las Vegas, Nevada. The "prison," where "prisoners" live in dormitory-style rooms without bars and on occasion are permitted to work on the base, is one of the closest to a home that Jacobson maintains in Utah.

Regardless of his sentence or where he serves it, the anguish that Jacobson caused can never be undone.

Chapter Sixteen

Dr. Emanuel Revici

As war clouds loomed in Europe in 1936, Dr. Emanuel Revici left his native Romania and emigrated to Paris. Trouble followed him. When the Germans marched into Paris in 1940, Revici sailed to Mexico.

It was during the war years that he developed his theories of the cause and the treatment of disease. Eventually, he claimed to have developed a method of treating cancer.

In 1945, *The Journal of the American Medical Association,* in examining "the Revici Method," "noted unsatisfactory clinical records and concluded that there was little benefit from his treatment."

Rejection didn't stop Revici from persevering. He moved to the United States in 1947 to continue his researches and clinical work. He was licensed to practice medicine in the State of New York on February 6, 1947, and set up a practice in New York City.

Persistence pays off. According to *The Journal of the American Medical Association,* "It appears that over the years a sum in excess of $2 million has been expended" in pursuit of "the Revici Method."

Revici was making some pretty strong statements on the success of his method. To find out whether it worked or not, the American Medical Association formed a Clinical Appraisal Group in 1963. Its purpose was to evaluate "the treatment of cancer by the method of Emanuel Revici, MD."

The Group consisted of some of the most distinguished doctor/researchers of the time: David Lyall, Stephen Schwartz, and Jane C. Wright of New York University School of Medicine; Frederic P. Herter, Charles W. Findlay, C.D. Haagensen, and Arthur Purdy Scott of the Columbia University College of Physicians and Surgeons; John M. Galbraith of Community Hospital, Glen Cove, New York; Perry B. Hudson, Montefiore Hospital, Bronx, New York.

They soon discovered that Revici believed that the manifestations of diseases are due to one or the other of two categories of "fundamental chemical imbalance." According to Revici, these categories can be seen by clinical and analytical data which also indicate what is effected, be it cells, tissue, an organ, or the whole person.

The Clinical Appraisal Group summarized "the Revici Method" as "a blending of clinical observation, laboratory analyses, and chemotherapy, which is constantly evolving as additional evidence becomes available."

Treatment of a cancer patient begins with basics. "The Revici Method" starts with urine and blood samples taken from the patient at the same time on each of three successive days, and then subjected to

243

various analyses.

For normal individuals, the values shown by these analyses will move above and below the average. "The range above and below the average is not immediately important since it is the fluctuating movement above and below which is Revici's criterion of whether or not the analysis is normal," the Clinical Appraisal Group reported.

According to Revici, in disease the values of these analyses stay constantly above or below the average. "It is this fixation above or below the average which indicates an abnormal off-balance."

Depending upon the categories of the imbalance, Revici would treat it with different medications. Butyl alcohol, glycerol, heptyl alcohol — an ether extract from fatty acids — hexylamine lactate, sodium thiosulfate — a sulfurated vegetable oil — epichlorohydrin, selenium diethyldithiocarbamate, and ethylmercaptan.

None of these "medications" are revolutionary. In fact, most of them are old-fashioned remedies that have been replaced by more effective drug therapies.

Since Revici claimed he could arrest tumor development, the Group chose "cases not amenable to conventional therapy, i.e. surgery or radiation, or in which conventional methods had failed."

In other words, only terminal cases were selected for the study.

The Group set about their work. They chose thirty-three such cases, people suffering from cancer of the large intestine, tongue, stomach, esophagus, liver, mouth, vulva, peritoneum, lung, and cervix. The youngest patient was thirty-six, the oldest eighty-two. Eighteen women and fifteen men comprised the group, and the periods of treatment ranged from three weeks to fifteen months.

Photographs were taken to substantiate written descriptions and measurements whenever possible. In some cases, X rays were taken. Response to "the Revici Method" was measured "in terms of objective tumor regression or other clinical charges."

To make things even fairer, the work of the Clinical Appraisal Group was "directed by Dr. Revici or his appointed deputy. No attempt was made to influence or modify Dr. Revici's regimen or to have it carried out by others. The records of the numerous analyses on each patient and the variable dosage schedules and variety of substances used were photoduplicated from time to time and kept with our own clinical files on each patient."

By late 1965, after two years of clinical study, the Clinical Appraisal Group of the AMA was ready to report. If what Dr. Revici claimed was true, he had made a huge breakthrough in medicine, a viable treatment for cancer that would improve the lives of millions and perhaps even save the lives of millions more who took "the Revici Method."

On October 18, 1965, the Clinical Appraisal Group published their results in *The Journal of the American Medical Association*.

"Of the 33 patients investigated, 22 died of cancer or its complications while receiving therapy. None of these showed evidence of tumor alteration ascribable to [Revici] therapy. Thirteen necropsies [autopsies] were done and in each instance cancer was listed by the pathologist as the cause of death. *In no cases did the examiner find gross or microscopic evidence of tumor alteration as a result of therapy.*"

245

After all the claims by Revici to the contrary, it had been scientifically proven that his method didn't work.

The study went on to note that "eight patients left the study group in an unimproved condition following periods of therapy ranging from three weeks to seven months and averaging about three and one-half months. Four of those died elsewhere of advancing cancer.

At the close of the study, the group noted, three patients were still under Revici's care, ". . . all showing signs of tumor *progression.*"

The conclusions of the Clinical Appraisal Group were somber.

"Based on the above-mentioned cases the Clinical Appraisal Group is forced to conclude that the Revici method of treatment of cancer is without value."

In the fall of 1980, *Rose Tannen* had been diagnosed as having breast cancer. Her decision was what type of treatment would she endure. She chose "the Revici Method."

Though it could never be proved, her husband claimed that Revici said that he could cure her cancer. Revici certainly felt that he could treat it. He took Rose on as a patient, and she began "the Revici Method."

Despite the fact that she was suffering, Revici, on more than one occasion, dissuaded Rose from seeking other treatment at a hospital. The State Medical Board would later note that Dr. Posnett, a physician who treated Rose, was "most appalled" by "the fact that (Rose Tannen) was repeatedly advised [by Revici] not to go to any hospital to seek other treatment."

In November 1981, *Linda Dardo* went to Revici after being diagnosed with breast cancer.

In November 1981, Revici began treating her with his elusive compounds.

Linda would later testify before the State Medical Board that in response to a question concerning surgery, Revici said, "Don't go for a biopsy. It spreads the cancer."

Biopsies ascertain whether or not a tumor is malignant. Though in a vast minority of cases, biopsies have been known to spread cancer cells, the test is looked on by the medical establishment as a vital diagnostic tool which Revici apparently dismissed.

Linda further testified that Revici said, "Do not have an operation. It will spread the cancer."

While cancer cells can be spread throughout the body during an operation, surgeons will generally hold off on such procedures when such an event is likely. Otherwise, surgery is effectively used to cut out tumors so they *don't* spread.

Eventually, despite the method, Linda's cancer spread to her spine. Curiously, the Medical Board later accused Revici of treating the pain of her spinal cancer with vinegar. And, as in Rose's case, Revici also attempted to dissuade Linda from seeking other treatment at the hospital.

At least Linda was alive to testify against Revici.

Jeanine Franks had a previous diagnosis of rectal cancer when she began treatment with "the Revici Method" in March of 1982.

This was a particularly telling case because, while

many cancer patients cannot be helped with surgery, Jeanine was one of the few who just might have been. Revici didn't even bother to pursue the option of surgery. As the State Medical Board noted, "This patient was a definite candidate for that method of treatment."

Almost two years later, Jeanine Franks died as a result of her cancer on November 16, 1983.

These three cases were the ones cited when Dr. Emanuel Revici was charged on December 22, 1983, by the New York State Department of Health, State Board for Professional Conduct with the following: fraudulently practicing medicine; gross incompetence; gross negligence; failure to maintain a record for each patient which accurately reflects the evaluation and treatment of the patient; and a host of other charges.

Dr. Revici's reply was swift and cutting. On January 3, 1984, Revici denied all of the charges.

In his reply, Revici stated that "the treatment rendered to each patient can [be] effective for the treatment of their illness provided the patient followed the program of treatment."

He stated that "each patient was advised and acknowledged that no guarantees were made to them concerning the results of the treatment."

An undercover investigator, posing as a cancer patient, had gone to see Revici. Revici never claimed that he could cure any of his patients, but he also did not recognize the term "cure," because there is no way to determine whether there are any cancer cells in the entire body.

Revici went on to say that "the method of treatment was still investigatory awaiting further research."

Revici went on to claim that he never dissuaded any of the patients from receiving more traditional forms of therapy; perhaps most importantly, he got each patient or their representative to sign "an informed consent form acknowledging that the treatment provided was investigatory therapy and releasing Dr. Revici from all liability, claims and complaints."

"Since each patient signed an informed consent form with respect to the treatment received, and, since each patient has a constitutional right to receive the treatment of their choice, the State is without power to insert itself into the physician-patient relationship. . . ."

Revici went on to vigorously deny that he had ever dissuaded any of the patients from receiving traditional therapy.

His attorney told *The New York Times* that Revici's "methods of treatment are being used throughout the world today, and obviously, the charges against him we dispute. There are hundreds and hundreds of people that he has apparently saved who are now walking the streets."

After hearing the charges against him, the State Medical Board brought in its conclusions and recommendations on September 19, 1985. The Board said that the charge of making his patients believe he had a cancer cure was not valid.

The committee then concluded what the Clinical Appraisal Group had years before: that Revici's "method" for treating cancer was ineffective. It found him guilty of "failing to realize that his method was not effective for treating cancer and persuading [Rose Tannen and Linda Dardo] from seeking other treatment."

He was further found guilty of gross incompetence and gross negligence, negligence and incompetence on more than one occasion, unprofessional conduct as to willful violations of law, and unprofessional conduct as to inadequate record-keeping.

Their unanimous recommendation was to revoke Revici's license.

While Revici continued to practice, he and his attorneys appealed the ruling all through the state bureaucracy. In a sense, it was a battle of wills.

Revici tried to portray himself as the little guy on the frontiers of science, being silenced by the big, bad, powerful medical establishment. He believed the whole prosecution against him was "unfair and not objective."

Eventually, on advice of counsel, he dropped out of attending further proceedings. Revici said that "no valid purpose would be served by continuing or participating in hearings before the Office of Professional Medical Conduct (OPMC)."

The matter found its way onto the desk of the New York State Board of Regents, which at the time had the last word on whether a physician whose license was revoked could keep it or not.

The Regents noted that at the heart of Revici's defense was his contention that he was a "physician who was sui generis [unique] and without peer."

Through his attorney, Revici argued that his "professed distinct and unique practices cannot be judged by any researcher or physician unfamiliar with or untrained in his methods. By these contentions, [Dr.

Revici] argues in effect that, because of the needs of his cancer patients, no legal standards may be applied by the Board of Regents or anyone else to (Dr. Revici's) treatment of [Rose Tannen, Linda Dardo, or Jeanine Franks]."

The State Board of Regents took a dim view of Revici's claim. They sided with the Hearing Board and revoked his license with conditions.

His license to practice medicine would be revoked all right, but the revocation suspended. Instead, he was to be placed on probation for five years under special terms.

Those special terms included:

a) Not treating patients for cancer unless they'd been previously diagnosed by another doctor not associated with Revici.

b) Informing his patients who have been diagnosed as having cancer that they have been urged by him to consult board-certified oncologists [cancer specialists]; understand that Revici's treatment is "experimental"; understand that Revici cannot guarantee that the results of his treatment will be successful; have the right to seek other treatment elsewhere.

c) The patients have to acknowledge in writing prescribed by OPMC that they understand all of the foregoing.

d) Revici has to make available to the OPMC the records of all patients he treats for cancer.

e) Revici wasn't allowed to dissuade any patient from seeking treatment elsewhere.

f) Revici could not treat any patient with agents (medications) in violation of law.

Further provisions were attached but the message was clear: Revici would be allowed to continue practicing, despite the fact that he had foisted an unproven cancer treatment on the unsuspecting public.

By the end of 1991, the state legislature of New York had changed their laws, making the OPMC, aside from any court action, the final arbiters on whether a physician could keep his license or see it revoked. No longer could a physician appeal to the Board of Regents and expect or get mercy.

Revici's probation is scheduled to end in 1993. When it does, he'll have new problems to contend with.

The OPMC reports that new charges have been filed against him, that are currently in the hearing process.

Chapter Seventeen

Dr. Valentine Birds and Dr. Stephen Herman

Mark Snider lay dying in the bathtub of his Los Angeles home. He had been there for several days, immobile because he had not received proper medical care for the AIDS virus that was now waging all-out war on his immune system.

Already he was suffering from symptoms of meningitis, dehydration, and pneumonia.

Mark was powerless to reach a syringe of Viroxan. Had he been able to, he probably would have injected it through the Hickman catheter that had been implanted within his body. He would hope that it would be effective against the AIDS virus.

That was not to be.

All Mark could do was sit and wait and hope that the Viroxan already in his system would kick in or, at the very least, that someone would find him before he died.

Whether his thoughts turned to Dr. Valentine Birds of North Hollywood and Dr. Stephen Herman of Villa Park, no one knows. If they did, they could not, at that moment, be too complimentary.

Birds and Herman promoted the use of Viroxan as a treatment against AIDS. In a country where at least 120 phony AIDS drugs are advertised and promoted as effective at combating the AIDS virus, Viroxan is at or near the top of the list.

On June 24, 1978, Dr. Valentine Birds's license to practice medicine in the State of California had been revoked for "unprofessional conduct." But the California Medical Board had been generous.

They stayed the revocation and placed Birds on five-years probation. Thus given a second chance, his license was fully restored to unrestricted status on December 28, 1980.

Eight years later, on December 1, 1988, Mark Snider, a floral designer, became a patient of Dr. Valentine Birds. Snider had been infected with the HIV virus and was seeking some sort of effective treatment and had come to Birds for help. He was placing his very life in the doctor's hands.

Birds's idea of treatment was unorthodox. He gave Mark a "typhoid skin test."

Maybe Mark figured that he had nothing to lose. Maybe he was a student of medical history and knew that substances of use against one disease are sometimes effective against another. Regardless, while the typhus virus has not been linked to the AIDS virus, the following month Birds began Mark on a "therapeutic protocol using typhoid vaccine."

Mark kept approximately thirteen separate appointments with Birds during the next three months, during which time Mark received varying amounts of typhoid vaccine for treatment of his HIV infection.

But blood tests showed the infection getting worse.

Scientific studies have shown that effective treatment in the early stages of the disease can slow it down. That's why the staff at the Philip Mandelker AIDS Prevention Clinic of the Gay and Lesbian Services Center in Hollywood recommended that Mark consider using AZT, a drug that has been found effective in combating the symptoms of HIV and prolonging the life of the patient. They also recommended that he receive primary prophylaxis against the development of Pneumocystic Pneumonia, which asserts itself as the disease progresses.

Mark gave a copy of his latest blood tests to Birds. Ignoring the dire fate that the blood tests predicted if Mark did not immediately undergo more proper and conventional treatment, Birds administered still more typhoid vaccine and made no recommendation concerning the use of AZT or the other therapy that the Mandelker Clinic had recommended.

Rather, Birds's recommendation was to contact Dr. Stephen Herman, his colleague who had a home in Orange County. Mark did, and went to see Herman, hoping he could help him.

After noting that Mark's immune system was failing him, resulting in "moderate Lymphadenopathy, SIGI upset, fatigue, herpes recurrent and hair loss," Herman began Mark on Viroxan via intravenous injection.

Mark was not the first patient to receive Viroxan, nor the last. What Mark and all of Herman's patients did not know was that this miracle compound was made from plant sources in a primitive laboratory located in the kitchen of Herman's home.

The California Medical Board would later state unequivocally in its report on Birds and Herman,

"Viroxan had never received approval by the United States Food and Drug Administration (USFDA), or the Food and Drug Branch of the California Department of Health Services, or any other regulatory agency as being safe and efficacious for use against HIV infections."

The report would go on to state that both Herman and Birds were aware that Viroxan "was not proven safe for use in human beings or efficacious against AIDS infection HIV, infection or any bacterial, fungal, or viral infections. Nonetheless, prior to receiving even basic animal toxicity data," Birds and Herman began injecting human beings with Viroxan.

Conning people with a hopeless disease into believing they had discovered a proven agent against the AIDS virus, when they apparently knew otherwise, was bad enough. What made Birds's and Herman's actions worse was that they failed to heed the warnings of Dr. Herman's scientific consultant, identified in the report as Dr. K.

Dr. K. warned them that the rubber stoppers on the vials containing Viroxan, having been manufactured and bottled in Herman's kitchen, were not airtight. They leaked and were therefore subject to microscopic contamination.

Furthermore, Dr. K. told Herman that Viroxan had a "toxic effect on animals at doses greater than 1.9 mm (107 mg/kg). In fact doses greater than 1.9 mm killed all test mice and rats; and, rabbits experienced adverse reactions at the 'Viroxan' injection site."

If Viroxan killed some animals, and caused others to develop adverse reactions, what effect would the "drug" have on human beings? Mark Snider was about to find out.

Three days after he'd received his first injection of Viroxan at Herman's home, Birds recommended that Mark have a Hickman catheter surgically implanted in the chest. The catheter would allow further injections of Viroxan, which Herman would supply, through a plastic tube surgically implanted in the skin.

Both physicians should have known that with Mark's immune system already compromised because of his disease that surgically implanting the Hickman catheter had potentially lethal complications. They said nothing.

Without this knowledge, Mark went ahead anyway and was admitted to the Medical Center of North Hollywood. On October 17, 1989, the Hickman catheter was placed pursuant to Birds's order. Birds indicated the need for placement of it due to his professional diagnosis of "lymphoma."

Subsequently, on five dates in late October, Mark visited Birds, and, on each of the five, Birds supplied Mark with quantities of Viroxan. Mark also visited Herman again, who supplied him with an additional dosage of 4,000 mg IV of Viroxan.

By Halloween, Mark was experiencing severe breathing problems and was acutely ill. Birds noted that Mark had been nauseous and vomited for three days. Regardless of these symptoms, Birds failed to physically examine Mark, nor did he draw any blood for a laboratory analysis of his condition. Instead, Birds gave mark an injection of Viroxan through his catheter and gave him additional amounts of the wonder drug so Mark could self-infuse the Viroxan at home.

Mark continued to get worse.

By Sunday, November 5, Mark was back at Birds's office complaining of "total body numbness and pain." Once again, Birds did not perform a physical examination. Instead, he gave Mark some Cipro, an antibiotic used to treat a urinary tract infection, and recommended Mark to continue to take Viroxan.

It was on November 8, 1989, that Mark was found lying still in his bathtub at approximately 2:30 A.M. He'd been there for several days. Clearly, Viroxan had not helped his condition, and, if the animal studies that Dr. K. alluded to are to be believed, it may even have made his condition worse.

Paramedics called Birds. As the attending physician, they wanted his approval for transporting Mark to the hospital. But Birds would not agree. He also did not rouse himself out of bed and go to help his patient, who was going through tremendous suffering at that moment.

Two hours later, at approximately 4:30 A.M., Birds was called once again and told that Mark's condition was worsening. Again, Birds did not recommend that Mark be hospitalized. Instead, he indicated that Mark would be fine and to just keep an eye on him.

At approximately 7:00 A.M., Birds was called for the third time and told that Mark needed *immediate* medical attention. Birds promised to call an ambulance. But by 9:00 A.M., the ambulance hadn't arrived. Instead, Birds appeared, in person, and informed those present that he had *just* called for an ambulance. Shortly thereafter, paramedics arrived to transport Mark to Queen of Angels Hollywood Presbyterian Medical Center.

Mark was admitted to the hospital at approximately 10:10 A.M., with signs of septicemia (blood poisoning), meningitis, dehydration, pneumonia, and rhabdomylosis [muscle disorder] due to his prolonged immobilization in his bathtub.

His immune system was not strong enough to fight off disease. Desperately, doctors tried to help him, but Mark's condition continued to deteriorate. His lungs filled with fluid.

Mark Snider died from cardiac arrest at 6:13 A.M. on November 12, 1989. An autopsy revealed the widespread presence of a staphylococcal infection in Mark's organs, an infection that could easily have been gotten from the injection of the non-sterile Viroxan compound.

Doctors Birds and Herman went on about their work.

On June 1, 1989, *David P.* was admitted to LAC-USC Medical Center, Psychiatric Ward because of his suicidal tendencies. After he was discharged from the Psychiatric Unit, a chiropractor that he saw recommended him to Dr. Valentine Birds.

On June 21, David became one of Birds's patients. Birds took a medical history but, in what would develop as a pattern in his non-treatment of patients, didn't examine David physically. Inexplicably, Birds also did not include a psychiatric history and therefore failed to discover David's past psychiatric problems.

During three subsequent visits, Birds ordered lab tests to be performed on blood samples taken from David. The tests disclosed some anemia, but Birds failed to initiate any type of additional tests. But the lab tests also revealed the presence of herpes. Therefore, Birds started David on a "therapeutic protocol using typhoid vaccine." It may have been the first time ever in the annals of modern medicine that a victim of herpes was treated as if he was a victim of typhus.

Most topical and oral medicines are able to alleviate the herpes symptoms within weeks. Evidently, and not surprisingly, the typhoid vaccine did not work as well, which is probably why on November 6 Birds recommended that David visit Dr. Herman for help with his herpes infection.

Herman recommended regular injections of his miracle drug, Viroxan, but, in order to inject it on a regular basis, it would be useful to have a Hickman catheter implanted in his body.

A week later, around November 13, David returned to Birds for a medical history and a physical examination in preparation for insertion of a Hickman catheter, which was implanted the next day.

On November 15, David visited Birds, and Birds gave David his first treatment with Viroxan, which had been prescribed and provided by Herman. Birds showed David how he could self-administer the Viroxan via an IV drip.

David moved back home to San Antonio, Texas, in December. While in Texas, he talked with Birds and Herman over the phone, and they sent him Viroxan through the mail.

David continued to self-inject the wonder compound through the Hickman catheter until approximately January 17, 1989, when another physician advised him to discontinue using Viroxan. David complied.

Stanley H. began Viroxan treatment with Herman on June 21, 1989.

Stanley, who had HIV, injected Viroxan into his veins in various doses. Eventually, as the California Medical Board would later say in its report. "Stanley H. began having 'trouble with his veins' due to the 'Viroxan' injections."

The solution? Herman referred Stanley to Birds for placement of a Hickman catheter.

Like Mark, Stanley was admitted to the Medical Center of North Hollywood by Birds for insertion of the Hickman catheter. According to Birds, the catheter was necessary "to allow for IV therapy for the infection and the evidence of lymphocytic enlargement. Possible viral lymphoma type reaction to be considered as the cause."

That sounded like a good diagnosis except Birds failed to explain the nature of the problem. And if you fail to explain the nature of a problem, its root cause, how can you treat it?

On December 12, Stanley had the Hickman surgically implanted and was discharged from the hospital that same day. Then he began injecting Viroxan, which Herman supplied, through it. Herman, meanwhile, did not leave a paper trail; he kept no medical records concerning his evaluation or treatment of Stanley.

By the middle of January, Stanley was feeling awful. For the previous two weeks, he's been experiencing fever, shaking, chills, headaches, and increased respirations. On January 15, 1990, he was admitted to Fountain Valley Regional Hospital and Medical Center "for possible blood poisoning (septicemia) caused either by the Hickman catheter site or contaminated Viroxan."

Stanley H. was lucky. He didn't die from the treatment or lack of it. Soon after he was admitted to the hospital, he sought out other medical help.

Ronald M. was suffering from AIDS-related complex and AIDS dementia (encephalitis due to HIV) by the time he came to see Dr. Birds on August 14, 1989.

Without reviewing Ronald M.'s medical records, Birds began Ronald on a "therapeutic protocol using typhoid vaccine." These treatments continued until approximately November 1, 1989, when it was time for Viroxan.

Around November 3, Ronald had a Landmark catheter inserted into his left arm to facilitate Herman's treatment of Ronald with Viroxan.

Three days later, Ronald visited Herman's Orange County home, where Herman noted that Ronald was HIV positive. He also noted that Ronald had severe neurological damage, severe debilitation, and diarrhea. No further history was noted nor was a physical examination conducted. Nonetheless, Herman prescribed two thousand milligrams of Viroxan and noted that the dosage would increase to four thousand milligrams of his untested drug after a Hickman catheter was placed in Ronald.

The next day Ronald returned, and Herman administered another three thousand milligrams of Viroxan. The day after that, November 8, Birds admitted Ronald to the Medical Center of North Hollywood for insertion of a Hickman catheter so Ronald could "start a chemotherapy program that requires daily IV medication. . . ."

The State Medical Board would later cite Birds for "dishonesty or corruption in ordering a Hickman catheter inserted in Ronald M.'s chest without prior medical indication for the Hickman catheter when

. . . Birds knew, or should have known, that Ronald M. was severely immunocompromised; and, by failing to properly advise Ronald M. of the potential lethal complications of such a procedure and the extremely low likelihood of any benefit."

By late November, Ronald developed a cough and began experiencing difficulty swallowing. On December 5, Ronald saw Birds at his office, as indicated by a billing slip. But Birds, despite Ronald's deteriorating condition, failed to make any physician notations concerning the visit.

The next day, Ronald was taken to Kaiser Anaheim Emergency Room suffering from high fever, chills, and mental confusion. He was admitted to the hospital and treated with antibiotics for bacteria infection resulting from the Hickman catheter site and/or contamination due to self-injections with Viroxan.

Ronald M. did not have long to live.

On December 15, Ronald M. suffered cardiopulmonary arrest. On December 24, 1989, Ronald M. died.

Doctors Birds and Herman went about their work.

What could be lonelier than lying alone in bed with night sweats and chills knowing that you have a disease which is incurable?

Robert H. was in such a predicament when he went to see Dr. Valentine Birds on August 3, 1989. He was desperate for something that could combat the disease wracking his body, and Birds was only too happy to oblige.

He treated Robert H.'s HIV infection with "a therapeutic protocol using typhoid vaccine," an action that would later be cited for its "incompetency" by the

State Medical Board. From approximately August through October of 1989, Birds saw Robert on a regular basis. After his initial examination, he didn't bother to examine him physically nor even record his temperature on subsequent office visits.

But the vaccine did no good. The nights got longer, sweatier, colder. When Robert complained to his physician on October 3 about night sweats and chills, Birds attributed the problem to the typhoid vaccine. He failed to consider other diagnostic explanations for the symptoms Robert was evincing.

Because of the breakdown of the immune system, the most common illness, and one of the worst problems an HIV infected individual faces, is the development of a particular type of pneumonia, known by the acronym PCP. It's a particularly deadly form of the disease that requires immediate, therapeutically proven treatment.

When Robert's blood tests showed that he was at risk of developing PCP, rather than recommending medication to treat or prevent it, Birds instead recommended "Aloe Vera Juice."

Soon, Birds recommended that Robert go see Herman, which the latter did on October 17. Herman took a very brief medical history, noting that Robert was HIV positive. Like his partner, he did not perform a physical examination, formulate a treatment plan, nor recommend measures to prevent the deadly PCP from taking hold.

Robert began treatment with Viroxan, which Herman therapeutically prescribed on October 17. On October 24, Herman and Birds arranged the second step of their treatment, the surgical placement of the Hickman catheter inside Robert's body, to facilitate the injections.

On October 24, the catheter was implanted. Birds, of course, indicated the reason for the placement of the Hickman catheter was "for chemotherapy for his [Robert's] lymphoma [a form of cancer]."

Robert's condition continued to go downhill.

Robert visited Birds on October 30, complaining of flu-like symptoms which Birds believed may have been associated with Viroxan. Birds believed that Robert's cough, fever, night sweats, chills, and breathing problems might be due to PCP.

In early November, Robert had a chest X ray taken at San Pedro Peninsula Hospital. The X ray revealed "evidence of bilateral interstitial disease greater on the left than the right."

Robert needed to see his physician. But he was too ill to travel. House calls being a thing of the past, they communicated by telephone. By phone, Birds prescribed Bactrim to treat Robert's PCP. There were problems, though.

First, Robert was allergic to sulpha and Bactrim contained sulpha. Second, the dosage Birds described was too weak and inadequate. Third, he failed to monitor his patient's use of the drug. Four, most importantly, he failed to hospitalize his patient.

Robert had contracted PCP. His condition worsened. Around November 8, via telephone, Birds ordered Robert to get supplemental oxygen at home. Again, Birds couldn't be bothered to visit his patient, who was dying. He prescribed the oxygen over the phone.

On November 10, Robert became acutely short of breath. Due to lack of oxygen, he turned blue. Paramedics were called, and Robert was admitted to San Pedro Peninsula Hospital. On admission, his condition was grave and his survival "impossible."

On November 16, 1989, Robert H. died due to cardiopulmonary arrest. His heart and his lungs just ceased to function.

Doctors Birds and Herman went about their work.

On September 12, 1989, *Michael K.,* an HIV infected individual, had the misfortune to become a patient of Dr. Stephen Herman. Herman, who failed to physically examine his patient, started Michael on Viroxan, with injections directly into the gluteus maximus muscle.

Michael self-injected Viroxan daily until he developed a black scab at the injection site and began experiencing pain. Despite the very real possibility that the injections had caused some sort of infection, Birds ordered that Michael have the Hickman catheter implanted in his chest so he could inject Viroxan intravenously on a daily basis.

The Hickman catheter was installed. Afterwards, Michael continued experiencing pain in his right gluteal area, where he'd previously injected Viroxan.

Around November 13, Michael began undergoing a series of excisions of his right buttock. On December 7, ironically the anniversary of the Pearl Harbor bombing, Michael was admitted to Eisenhower Memorial Hospital for extensive debridement of a deep muscle abscess of his right buttock.

After the tissue that was removed was tested in the lab, it was found to be decayed, with the necrosis extending deep into the subcutaneous tissue and skeletal muscle. He was treated and released.

On January 15, 1990, Michael was again admitted to Eisenhower suffering from recurrent toxic shock; he was treated and released.

Michael was so desperate to alleviate his pain, he overdosed on an injection of methadone (a powerful synthetic substitute for heroin), and other drugs that had been mixed together. Unconscious, he was admitted again to Eisenhower on January 26.

Chest X rays revealed PCP, which he was treated for until his death on February 4, 1990.

An autopsy revealed Michael suffered from staphylococcal pneumonia, which he could have gotten from the non-sterile containers of Viroxan. The post-mortem also revealed a "massive ulceration of the right buttock." The State Medical Board later found that the latter "resulted from contamination due to regular intramuscular injection of Viroxan supplied by . . . Herman."

Colby S. was desperate. At least that's the way he sounded when he called Birds on December 27, 1989, and told him he had just tested HIV positive and was interested in receiving treatment.

Over the phone, Birds told Colby that he used typhoid therapy, and then referred him to Herman to discuss treatment. Birds gave Colby his colleague's phone number and made it clear to Colby that Herman had good results treating AIDS patients with Viroxan.

Dutifully, Colby called Herman and explained that he wanted to hear about Herman's AIDS treatment. Herman told Colby to come to his home the next day at 11:00 A.M.

On January 10, 1990, Colby and approximately five others attended a two-hour presentation conducted by Herman at his home. During the presentation, Herman told the desperate patients that other

AIDS treatments were ineffective, but his treatment with Viroxan had long-term effects in arresting the disease.

Herman claimed that treatment with Viroxan produced no side effects and that Viroxan had been tested and found nontoxic and effective against a wide spectrum of diseases. He recommended to the group that any of them receiving Viroxan be referred to Birds so Birds could arrange surgery for placement of the Hickman catheters.

Then he got down to the nitty-gritty.

Herman told his guests that Viroxan treatment required daily injections, and a thirty-day supply costs three hundred dollars. And, to make things easier all around, it would be unnecessary for them to return to see him except to pick up more Viroxan because they could self-inject the Viroxan, using the surgically implanted Hickman catheters.

Colby was convinced. He would get his money and come back and buy Viroxan.

That same day, January 10, Jeffrey Y. called Herman at home and arranged to attend a Viroxan presentation set to occur at 11:00 A.M.

The next day, Jeffrey attended a presentation on Viroxan at Herman's home. During the presentation, Herman depicted Viroxan to be a "breakthrough," "clearly demonstrated" to be effective in the nontoxic treatment of T-cell mediated diseases like AIDS, chronic long-term arthritis, and cancers such as Hodgkin's disease and leukemia.

After the presentation, Colby S. returned and purchased ten vials of Viroxan from Herman for three hundred dollars. As soon as the sale occurred, Herman was arrested by the authorities.

Colby S. was a Senior Special Investigator for the

Medical Board of California.

Jeffrey Y. was an investigator for the United States Food and Drug Administration.

And Dr. Stephen Herman and Dr. Valentine Birds were, to put it mildly, in a lot of trouble.

On May 17, 1991, the Medical Board of California issued a forty-two page document that listed the charges against Doctors Stephen Herman and Valentine Birds.

Slowly and carefully, they built their case. The way Herman and Birds treated their patients is referred to as their modus operandi.

"As a result of respondent Herman's and respondent Birds' custom and habit evidenced by their pattern and conduct in treating patients, and aiding and abetting each other in treating patient . . . [they] are subject to disciplinary action . . . for their gross negligence, repeated negligent acts, incompetence, and dishonesty and corruption in treating patients with 'Viroxan' and ordering Hickman catheters to be placed in the patients without proper medical indication notwithstanding the fact respondents knew, or should have known, the patients were at extremely high risk of infection because they were immunocompromised."

The Board was throwing the book at both doctors, but they were only getting warmed up.

"Respondents' conduct was exacerbated further by their continued neglect of patients as evidenced by their lack of proper medical records, and failure to monitor patients' home use (self-injection) and progress while using 'Viroxan,' a substance toxic to laboratory animals and unproven as effective in treating AIDS, HIV patients, arthritis, cancer, or any other ailment," the Board continued.

A request was then made for the full Board to hold a hearing, at which time it should consider revoking or suspending Birds's and Herman's licenses to practice medicine and surgery.

Stephen Herman was subsequently arrested and charged with sixteen criminal counts in Orange County, California, related to the advertising and sale of Viroxan.

After he was charged, Herman was quoted in *The Los Angeles Times*. He denounced the allegations as "mindless innuendoes and attacks."

He went on to say, "They [the charges] are purely minor harassment and the issues involved are far above the charges. Viroxan has been openly understood and accepted by the medical community outside the United States."

Herman even added that he had been giving himself Viroxan—though no mention was made if it was through a Hickman catheter he had implanted in *his* chest—for a lymphoma, a form of cancer. He also stated that his research on the drug began after his twenty-eight-year-old son Ken died from AIDS in 1987.

Herman's statements to the contrary, the treatment he and Birds gave their patients was publicly condemned.

"I think they took advantage of some people who were already desperately ill and dying and put them through a process that made them sicker," the *Times* quoted Kathleen L. Schmidt, a Senior Medical Board Investigator. ". . . I think they just essentially treated them like guinea pigs."

William T. Jarvis, Executive Director of the National Council Against Health Fraud, an organization based in Loma Linda, California, also told *The Los Angeles Times* that some researchers think "quackery is the standard of practice for AIDS — that's how bad it is."

And Dr. John H. Renner, Director of the Consumer Health Research Institute, a clearinghouse for information on medical products located in Missouri, estimated that the usual AIDS patient spends upward of $2000 a year on phony AIDS drugs. Herman's own figures for the wonder drug Viroxan were actually a little higher: $3200 for a full year's supply.

On December 19, 1991, the State of California revoked Dr. Valentine Birds's license to practice medicine and surgery.

On March 12, 1992, Dr. Stephen Herman voluntarily surrendered his physician and surgeon license to the Medical Board of California.

They are no longer practicing. But that is not the end of the story. Stephen Herman kept going.

In an extensive *L.A. Times* story dated October 9, 1992, reporter Jack Cheevers wrote that Herman "plans to sell his portion and spinoff products worldwide. He is negotiating marketing agreements in China, Thailand, Mexico, South Korea and various African nations. To help cinch a deal in China, he enlisted a nephew of Richard M. Nixon."

"I think I will be the wealthiest man in the world," Herman is quoted as saying in the article.

Chapter Eighteen

Dr. George Camatsos

Some people will do anything to lose weight.

In its most extreme form, the neurotic need to lose weight becomes anorexia, where the individual literally wastes away because of lack of nourishment. Then there are those who are bulimic. They'll eat then throw it up soon after. They, too, do not want to gain weight.

There's even a third category of people who exercise compulsively in order to keep the pounds off. This type of exercise disorder is frequently combined with bulimia or anorexia to produce both life- and soul-threatening problems requiring therapies for the mind and the body.

Most people, though, fight the battle of the bulge with fad diets. And when that doesn't work, when their sense of self-esteem is so tied up with their girth, they will take whatever radical measures are necessary to shape up. That's when they seek out so-called diet doctors.

Diet pills, as they are known in the trade, are usually amphetamines, powerfully addicting drugs with a host of adverse side effects.

Yet there are those unscrupulous operators of diet clinics, some of whom are medical doctors, who are willing to prescribe such controlled substances. Without even conducting a thorough physical of their clients, thereby putting them in even greater danger, and despite the fact that amphetamines can permanently destroy the health of their patients, diet doctors will frequently prescribe them.

Dr. George J. Camatsos was one such doctor, whose practice gave artificial hope of weight loss through chemical means. Camatsos was not some fly-by-night operator who was here today and gone tomorrow. He was well-established in both Tennessee and Mississippi. With seeming impunity, he operated a business that was successful by any standards.

Memphis is in the southwestern corner of the state of Tennessee, bordering on Mississippi. Further south and west, Biloxi, Mississippi, is on the gulf of Mexico. Not more than forty miles west as the crow flies is the city of Pass Christian, Mississippi. And Southhaven, Mississippi, is in DeSoto County, located in the northwest corner of the state.

What all these locations had in common was that they were home to Dr. George J. Camatsos's clinics. It was on a bright, early fall day, October 3, 1989, that Diane Collins went to Dr. Camatsos's clinic, at 520 Goodman Road East, in Southhaven to lose weight.

Like many people who make a decision to change their life, she was very vocal about it. She complained to the staff at the clinic that she needed to lose weight.

Diane was given, and partially completed, a "medical history questionnaire," and a statement pertaining to previous weight loss programs. The statement requested that the patient had made "a good faith effort to lose weight in a treatment program or programs utilizing a regimen of weight reduction based on caloric restriction, nutritional counseling, behavior modification and exercise without the utilization of controlled substances, with such treatment being ineffective."

Attorneys would probably interpret this as a release, freeing the doctor who does not do all of the above from any legal hassles. The patient has acknowledged they've done everything to lose weight and now this was their course of last resort. The doctor, presumably, was only giving the patient what she wanted.

Diane, who was anxious to lose the weight, was more than willing to state in writing that she "had not been in another program."

Before being given treatment for her weight loss problem, Diane had to fork over a fee of $140. After she did, but only after, Diane was given a neat folder containing a booklet and calorie guide. Then, she was examined by a nurse/employee.

Her weight was 160 pounds, her blood pressure was 120/70 — which is normal — and her neck area was also examined. Finally, presumably to make sure there was nothing wrong with her that hadn't shown up during the examination, blood was taken for the purposes of a complete blood count and thyroid profile.

Once her blood was drawn, the same nurse performed an electrocardiogram (ECG) and "body composition test." When all the tests were completed, Dr. George Camatsos came in to review Diane's present weight, her target weight, and other contents of her file in her presence, and in the presence of other patients going through the same program.

Camatsos described the six different medications he was prescribing for her, and Diane was directed to purchase the medication at the pharmacy across the road from his office. Diane, though, had other ideas.

Could she use her local pharmacy? she asked Camatsos. Camatsos's reply was firm. He refused to write her a prescription that was filled anywhere else besides the place across the street. All Diane could do was shrug her shoulders.

Diane left the clinic, and as Camatsos had requested, drove to the nearby pharmacy that Camatsos had identified, the Delta C. Pharmacy, at 579 Goodman Road East. There, she turned in her prescriptions for the following medications:

Prescription number	Medication	Quantity
31536	Lefcotabs	30
31537	Furosemide 40 mg	30
31538	Belladonna ALK/PB	83
31539	Kaon CL-10 mg	30
31540	Phendimetrazine 35 mg	83
31542	Trophemin	30
31543	Leptotabs	83

Phendimetrazine is an innocent-looking little pill, green on one side, yellow on the other, white in the middle. Manufactured by Carnrick Laboratories under the brand name Bontril, its nonoffensive appearance belies its effects.

275

Bontril is actually an addictive amphetamine, considered a schedule IV controlled substance in the State of Mississippi.

Strangely enough, according to the 1993 edition of the *Physician's Desk Reference,* Bontril, which increases blood pressure and stimulates the nervous system, has shown only limited success in brief clinical trials.

"The magnitude of increased weight loss of drug-treated patients over placebo-treated patients is only a fraction of a pound a week. . . . The amount of weight loss associated with the use of [diet pills] varies from trial to trial, and the increased weight loss appears to be related in part to *variable others than the drug prescribed, such as the physician investigator, the population treated and the diet prescribed,*" the *Physician's Desk Reference* says.

In other words, you could just as easily lose weight with a properly managed diet and a properly managed exercise program—instead of taking diet pills and not having to risk your health in the process.

As for Diane, she filled the prescriptions and left, presumably to go home and begin taking the medications.

On November 2, Jerry Robbins showed up at Camatsos's clinic at 381 John R. Junkin Drive, in Natchez, Mississippi. Robbins was vague about his complaints, but despite that, he was placed in the diet program after being given a "Medical History Questionnaire" and a preprinted statement pertaining to the previous weight loss programs he had considered.

Robbins was a little bit more wary than Diane was. He completed the questionnaire but did not complete the statement pertaining to previous weight loss programs, nor would he certify that he had previously tried to lose weight through all of the conventional means that Camatsos outlined in writing. Nevertheless, Robbins was never questioned by Camatsos or anyone else about his previous weight loss experiences.

Before treatment could begin, Robbins was required to pay $110 in cash, which he did. Then he received a booklet entitled "Advisory and Preventive Medical Centers," a "Delta-C Calorie Counter" that bore Camatsos's name and a directory of Camatsos's medical centers in Memphis, Tennessee, and the four in Mississippi. So, even if he was traveling and needed treatment, there'd be a Camatsos medical center that could meet his needs.

Just like with Diane, a nurse took a blood sample for the purposes of getting a Complete Blood Count (CBC) and a thyroid profile. After that came the ECG and "body composition test."

According to the nurse, his ECG was "borderline," with an "undetermined rhythm." That sounded serious and Robbins inquired if he could see Dr. Camatsos.

Camatsos was out. Robbins's case would be treated by Dr. Jesus Lemus-Parada. It seemed that Dr. Camatsos was frequently not available, and it fell to Dr. Lemus-Parada to conduct the counseling sessions with patients and to supervise the staff. But they operated the same way.

Upon completion of the tests, Dr. Lemus-Parada reviewed Robbins's file in his presence and in the presence of others going through the same program. He explained the seven medications being prescribed, all in the name of Dr. George Camatsos, and directed

Robbins, as well as the other patients, to purchase their medications up the street at First Pharmacy, located at 301 John R. Junkin Drive.

Before leaving, Robbins asked Dr. Lemus-Parada about his borderline ECG. He was told it was normal and not to worry.

Robbins left and drove to the First Pharmacy on Junkin Drive, turned in his scripts and received his medication, as follows:

Prescription number	Medication	Quantity
43468	Diethylpropion HCL 25 mg	83
43469	Furosemide 40 mg	30
43470	Belladonna ALK/PB	83
43471	Kaon CL-10 mg	30
43472	Leptotabs	83
43473	Trophemin	30
43474	Lefcotab 1250 mg	30

Furosemide is a fairly harmless diuretic that pulls water out of the body. But another of the prescription drugs, eighty-three tabs of 25 milligrams each of Diethylpropion HCL could be deadly.

Once again, it was a drug with an innocent appearance, this time pristine white. Manufactured under the brand name Tenuate by the Merrell Dow company, Tenuate is a schedule IV controlled substance in Mississippi.

Like its sister drug Bontril, which had been prescribed for Diane Collins, Tenuate is an addictive amphetamine, another type of diet pill. It, too, has limited capabilities as far as aiding in weight loss.

Meanwhile, Robbins's thyroid profile, which came

back on November 3, showed he was experiencing a moderate hyperthyroid condition. One of the other seven drugs Lemus-Parada prescribed, Leptotabs, *stimulates* the thyroid.

According to later testimony presented to the Mississippi State Board of Medical Licensure by Dr. William C. Nicholas, a specialist at the University Medical Center in Internal Medicine and Endocrinology, the prescribing of thyroid medications under these circumstances described can result in harm and even be life-threatening to the patient.

Did Dr. Lemus-Parada or Dr. Camatsos take Jerry Robbins off this "life-threatening" medication?

Someone from Dr. Camatsos's office needed to get to Robbins and tell him if he took the medication, his life was in danger. But according to the record, they made no attempt to modify or change the medication.

Jerry Robbins was on his own. So, too, were Sharon Evans and Margaret Jones.

On November 2, 1989, they, too, went to Camatsos's clinic and were put on a weight reduction program. They were examined by Camatsos's staff, under the direction of Dr. Lemus-Parada, after which Lemus-Parada issued orders for medications in the name of Dr. Camatsos.

Once again, in what was clearly a pattern, Lemus-Parada prescribed drugs in Camatsos's name, including the amphetamines phendimetrazine for Sharon Evans and diethylpropion HCL for Margaret Jones.

The day of November 9, a week later, was a busy

one for the Camatsos clinics. Tommy Strain, Hazel Wilson, Billy Vining, and Bob Smith all came for treatment. Strain, Wilson, and Vining all received the usual assortment of pills, including the amphetamines, diuretics, and thyroid pills, prescribed by Lemus-Parada in Camatsos's name. None appeared to have any extenuating medical problems. Smith's case, though, was more problematic.

Smith's examination revealed serious heart problems, including an erratic heartbeat and a pattern of pulmonary disease. Just to be sure, the ECG was repeated with the same results.

To Dr. Lemus-Parada, none of this made any difference. Smith would be treated like anyone else.

Dr. Lemus-Parada, prescribing once again in Dr. Camatsos's name, issued orders for a diet pill (amphetamine), diuretic, and thyroid medication.

Clearly, Camatsos, either through his own actions or his representatives/employees like Lemus-Parada was, in the words of Nicholas, putting his patients into "life-threatening" situations.

November 9 was also the day that Charles Moore came to the Natchez clinic run by Dr. Camatsos. Like Robbins the previous week, he, too, offered no specific complaint. Still, he was placed in the diet program and given the standard "Medical History Questionnaire" and preprinted statement pertaining to previous weight loss programs.

Moore completed the questionnaire. On the preprinted statement, he indicated that he had not participated in any weight loss program. But he did not execute the "Good faith" certificate.

Apparently, it made no difference to the clinic

whether the agreement was signed or not. Without any further questions being asked, Moore was going to be treated for weight loss. Prior to treatment, of course, he was requested to pay $110 in cash.

Once he'd paid, Moore was given the folder with the booklets containing a list of Camatsos's weight loss centers and the "Calorie Counter."

Blood was taken for the blood test, he was given the "body composition test," and, of course, an electrocardiogram.

Dr. Camatsos was a busy man. He wasn't there to treat Moore, so Dr. Lemus-Parada showed up. Lemus-Parada reviewed Moore's file in the presence of others going through the weight loss program.

Moore had a problem. The ECG indicated an abnormality in his heart. Lemus-Parada though told him that his ECG was normal. Worse, one of the seven medications Lemus-Parada prescribed was Tenuate.

In addition to its narcotic tendencies, Tenuate is not supposed to be prescribed for people, like Moore, with heart abnormalities, especially abnormalities that haven't been properly diagnosed or treated. "Caution is to be exercised in prescribing Tenuate for patients with . . . symptomatic cardiovascular disease," the *Physician's Desk Reference* states.

Moore, like Diane and Robbins, wondered if he could fill his scripts in a pharmacy of his own choosing. Lemus-Parada, again, declined to write such a prescription. It had to be filled at the First Pharmacy nearby.

And there'd be no argument about that. At least, that's what he thought.

What Dr. George J. Camatsos, Dr. Jesus Lemus-Parada, and company did not know was that Diane Collins, Jerry Robbins, and Charles Moore did not exist, at least in the way they'd presented themselves.

"Diane Collins" was actually Donna Conner, "Jerry Robbins" was Gerald W. Robbins, and "Charles Moore" was Charles A. Moore. All were undercover agents for the Mississippi State Bureau of Narcotics, who infiltrated Camatsos's clinics in order to gather information against him and his operation. And once the evidence was gathered, they were ready to move in for the "bust."

On November 9, 1989, investigators from the State Medical Board descended on Camatsos's Natchez clinic. There, they found the following:

●158 blank prescriptions. Written on each, either mechanically or photostatically, was a prescription for "Phenteramine 8 mg," a controlled substance.

●392 blank prescriptions. "Phendimetrazine 35 mg" was written on each of them, either mechanically or photostatically reproduced. Phendimetrazine is an amphetamine and a controlled substance.

●549 prescriptions. Each one had emblazoned on its surface "Diethylpropion 25 mg," either mechanically or photostatically reproduced. Again, another amphetamine and a controlled substance.

There was even more damning evidence.

The medical investigators found five presigned, blank prescriptions for Phenteramine 8 mg, and other medications; twelve presigned, blank prescriptions for Diethylpropion 25 mg and other medications.

All seventeen prescriptions bore the signature of Dr. George J. Camatsos, MD.

Nineteen days later, on November 28, 1989, agents of the Investigative Unit of the Mississippi State Board of Medical Licensure went to Dr. George's Camatsos's clinic in Southaven. Searching his office, they discovered the following:

• 47 blank prescriptions. On all of them were written, either mechanically or through copying methods, a prescription for Phenteramine 8 mg.

• 171 blank prescriptions. "Diethylpropion 25 mg" was written on each and every one of them, either mechanically or through copying methods.

• 154 blank prescriptions. Just to make sure there was equal time for another of the diet pills the clinic prescribed, on all of them were written, either mechanically or through copying methods, "Phendimetrazine 35 mg."

Camatsos was in a lot of trouble. At stake were his license and reputation. Instead of throwing himself on the mercy of the Board, or mounting a vigorous defense, he decided to ignore them.

The State Medical Board was set to hear the charges against Camatsos on January 18, 1990, but Camatsos managed to get three continuances, delaying the actual hearing until August 21, 1991.

The hearing was convened at one o'clock, despite Camatsos's failure to appear. He didn't even send his counsel, John M. Collette, to appear for him. Maybe he just figured the result would be a foregone conclusion.

Turning the language of his patient release against him, the Board found that ". . . as a result of [Camatsos's] failure to place patients on a weight program utilizing a regimen of weight reduction, behavior modification and exercise prior to utilization of controlled substances and making a determination that said treatment in the past has been ineffective," he was violating a Board rule "pertaining to prescribing, administering and dispensing of medication."

They also found that he prescribed "drugs having addiction-forming or addiction-sustaining liability otherwise than in the course of legitimate professional practice."

The list went on.

Camatsos was guilty of "unprofessional conduct, including dishonorable or unethical conduct likely to deceive, defraud or harm the public."

Camatsos was guilty of utilizing "a diuretic and thyroid medication for the sole purpose of weight loss."

Camatsos was guilty of refusing to honor a patient's request for a written prescription "so as to have the prescription filled at a pharmacy of the patient's choice."

Camatsos was guilty of using blank prescription pads or order forms "upon which the controlled substance prescribed had been mechanically or photostatically reproduced."

As for Dr. Jesus Lemus-Parada, the Board found that he wasn't a licensed physician. He had no license to practice medicine in Mississippi whatsoever. If Camatsos knew that "Dr." Lemus-Parada wasn't licensed, and allowed him to practice at his clinic, he therefore bore responsibility.

Camatsos was found guilty of the additional charge of "knowingly performing any act which in any way assists an unlicensed person to practice medicine," and "utilizing pre-signed blank prescription pads or order forms and making them available to non-physician employees or support personnel [Lemus-Parada] under any circumstances."

On August 22, 1991, the Mississippi State Board of Medical Licensure revoked the license of George J. Camatsos.

Afterward

What can you do to stop from being a victim of a doctor from Hell?

What I found in my research is that most doctors who do abuse patients have a history of doing just that. There's a paper trail. You don't have to be a detective, though. That's what the State Medical Boards are for.

It's their job to keep track of complaints, investigations, suspensions, and revocations against the medical doctors licensed to practice in their state.

If you want to check on a doctor and see if any sort of action has been taken against him, consult the list that follows of all the State Medical Boards in the country. Sometimes, with a simple phone call, they'll let you know if a physician is or was in trouble.

Sometimes, you may have to write for information, but under the law, you're entitled to that information. Likewise, if you want to make a complaint against a doctor, contact your State Medical Board.

Finally, bear this in mind: Just because someone has a medical certificate on his/her wall, it doesn't make them a responsible, caring healer.

The following list has been supplied by the Federation of State Medical Boards of the United States, Inc.

State Medical Boards

Alabama State Board of Medical Examiners
Larry D Dixon, Executive Director
P O Box 946 — *(848 Washington Ave, 36104)*
Montgomery, AL 36101-0946
(205) 242-4115
Fax: (205) 242-4155

Alaska State Medical Board
Caroline Stuart, Executive Secretary
3601 C Street, Suite 722
Anchorage, AK 99503
(907) 561-2871
Fax: (907) 561-5781

Arizona State Board of Medical Examiners
Douglas N Carf, Executive Director
2001 West Camelback Road, #300
Phoenix, AZ 85015
(602) 255-3751
Fax: (602) 255-1848

*Arizona Board of Osteopathic Examiners in
Medicine & Surgery*
Robert J Miller, PhD, Executive Director
1830 W Colter, Suite 104
Phoenix, AZ 85015
(602) 255-1747
Fax: (602) 255-1756

Arkansas State Medical Board
Peggy P Cryser, Executive Director
2100 Riverfront Drive, Suite 200
Little Rock, AR 72202
(501) 324-9410
Fax: (501) 324-9413

Medical Board of California
Dixon Arnett, Executive Director
1426 Howe Avenue, Suite 54
Sacramento, CA 95825
(916) 263-2333
Fax: (916) 920-6350

Osteopathic Medical Board of California
Linda J Benjamann, Executive Director
444 North Third Street, Suite A-200
Sacramento, CA 95814
(916) 322-4316
Fax: (916) 327-6119

Colorado State Board of Medical Examiners
Thomas J Beckett, Program Administrator
1560 Broadway, Suite 1300
Denver, CO 80202-5140
(303) 894-7690
Fax: (303) 894-7692

Connecticut Div. of Medical Quality Assurance
Stanley K Peck, JD, Director
Connecticut Department of Health Services

Division of Medical Quality Assurance
150 Washington Street
Hartford, CT 06106
(203) 566-7398
Fax: (203) 566-8401

Delaware Board of Medical Practice
Wayne Martz, MD, Medical Director
Margaret O'Neill Building, 2nd Floor
Federal & Court Streets
Dover, DE 19903
(302) 739-4522
Fax: (302) 739-2711

District of Columbia Board of Medicine
John P Hopkins, Executive Director
P O Box 37200
(605 G Street NW, Room 202, Lower Level, 20001)
Washington, DC 20013-7200
(202) 727-9794
Fax: (202) 727-4087

Florida Board of Medicine
Dorothy J Faircloth, Executive Director
Northwood Centre, #60
1940 North Monroe Street
Tallahassee, FL 32399-0750
(904) 488-0595
Fax: (904) 487-9622

Florida Board of Osteopathic Medical Examiners
Henry Dover, Executive Director
Northwood Centre, #60
1940 North Monroe Street
Tallahassee, FL 32399-0775
(904) 922-6725
Fax: (904) 922-3040

Georgia Composite State Board of Medical Examiners
Andrew Watry, Executive Director
166 Pryor Street, SW
Atlanta, GA 30303-3465
(404) 656-3913
Fax: (404) 651-9532

Guam Board of Medical Examiners
Teofila P Cruz, Administrator
Department of Public Health & Social Services
P O Box 2816
(Route 10, Mangilao 96923)
Agana, Guam 96910
(671) 734-7296
Fax: 011-671-734-2066

Hawaii Board of Medical Examiners
Christine Turkowsky, Executive Secretary
Department of Commerce & Consumer Affairs
P O Box 3469
(1010 Richards St, 96813)
Honolulu, HI 96801
(808) 586-2708
Fax: (808) 586-2689

Idaho State Board of Medicine
Donald L Delaski, Executive Director
State House Mall
280 North 8th, Suite 202
Boise, ID 83721
(208) 334-2821

Illinois Department of Professional Regulation
Nikki Zollar, Director
State of Illinois Center
100 West Randolph Street, #9-300

Chicago, IL 60501
(312) 814-4934
Fax: (312) 814-1837

Indiana Health Professions Service Bureau
Sarah B McCarty, Executive Director
402 West Washington Street, Room 041
Indianapolis, IN 46204
(317) 232-2961
Fax: (317) 233-4236

Iowa State Board of Medical Examiners
Ann M. Martino, PhD, Executive Director
State Capitol Complex, Executive Hills West
1209 East Court Avenue
Des Moines, IA 50319-0180
(515) 281-5171
Fax: (515) 241-5908

Kansas State Board of Healing Arts
Lawrence T Bemening, Jr, JD, Exec Dir
235 SW Topeka Boulevard
Topeka, KS 66603
(913) 296-7411
Fax: (913) 296-0852

Kentucky Board of Medical Licensure
C William Schmidt, Executive Director
The Hurstbourne Office Park
310 Whittington Parkway, Suite 1B
Louisville, KY 40222
(502) 429-8041
Fax: (502) 429-9923

Louisiana State Board of Medical Examiners
Mrs Delmar Rorison, Executive Director
830 Union Street, #100

291

New Orleans, LA 70112
(504) 524-6761
Fax: (504) 561-8893
Maine Board of Registration in Medicine
David R Hedrick, Executive Director
State House Station #137
Two Bangor Street
Augusta, ME 04333
(207) 287-3601

Maine Board of Osteopathic Examination & Registration
Susan E Strout, Executive Secretary
State House Station #142
Augusta, ME 04333
(207) 287-2480

Maryland Board of Physician Quality Assurance
J Michael Compton, Acting Exec Dir
P O Box 2571—*(4201 Patterson Ave, 3rd Flr, 21215-0095)*
Baltimore, MD 21215
(410) 764-4777
Fax: (410) 764-2478

Massachusetts Board of Registration in Medicine
Alexander F Fleming, JD, Exec Director
Ten West Street, 3rd Floor
Boston, MA 02111
(617) 727-3086
Fax: (617) 451-9568

Michigan Board of Medicine
Herman Fishman, Licensing Executive
P O Box 30192—*(611 West Ottawa St, 4th Floor, 48909)*
Lansing, MI 48909
(517) 373-6873
Fax: (517) 373-2179

Michigan Board of Osteopathic Medicine & Surgery
Herman Fishman, Licensing Executive

P O Box 30018—*(611 West Ottawa St, 4th Floor, 48933)*
Lansing, MI 48909
(517) 373-6873
Fax: (517) 373-2179

Minnesota Board of Medical Practice
H Leonard Boche, Executive Director
2700 University Avenue West, Suite 106
St Paul, MN 55144-1080
(612) 642-0538
Fax: (612) 642-0393

Mississippi State Board of Medical Licensure
Frank J Morgan Jr, MD, Exec Officer
2688-D Insurance Center Drive
Jackson, MS 39216
(601) 354-6645
Fax: (601) 987-4159

Missouri State Board of Registration for the Healing Arts
Tina Steinman, Acting Executive Director
P O Box 4—*(3523 North 10 Mile Drive, 65109)*
Jefferson City, MO 65102
(314) 751-4447 (direct line)
(314) 751-0098 (for public use)
Fax: (314) 751-3166

Montana Board of Medical Examiners
Patricia I England, JD, Exec Dir/Bd Atty
Arcade Building, Lower Level
111 North Jackson
Helena, MT 45620-0407
(406) 444-4234/4276
Fax: (406) 444-1667

Nebraska State Board of Examiners in Medicine & Surgery
Katherine A Brown, Associate Director
P O Box 9500X—*(301 Centennial Mall South, 68509)*
Lincoln, NE 18509-5007

(402) 471-2115
Fax: (402) 471-0383

Nevada State Board of Medical Examiners
Patricia R Perry, Executive Director
P O Box 7238 — *(1105 Terminal Way, Suite 301, 89502)*
Reno, NV 89110
(702) 688-2555
Fax: (702) 681-2321

Nevada State Board of Osteopathic Medicine
Larry J Tarro, DO, Executive Director
2121 East Flamingo Road, #204
Las Vegas, NV 89119
(702) 732-2147

New Hampshire Board of Registration in Medicine
Patrick J. Moehan, MD, Executive Secretary
Health & Welfare Building
6 Hazen Drive
Concord, NH 03301
(603) 271-4501
Board Office:
2 Industrial Park Dr
Concord, NH 03301
(603) 271-1203

New Jersey State Board of Medical Examiners
Charles A Janousek, Executive Director
28 West State Street
Room 602
Trenton, NJ 08608
(609) 292-4800
Fax: (609) 984-3930

New Mexico State Board of Medical Examiners
Dorothy L Welby, Executive Secretary
P O Box 20001 — *(491 Old Santa Fe Tr, Rm 134)*
Santa Fe, NM 87504

(505) 827-7373
Fax:(505) 827-7377

New Mexico Board of Osteopathic Medical Examiners
Michelle McGinnis, Administrator
P O Box 25101—*(725 St Michaels Dr, 87501)*
Sante Fe, NM 87504
(505) 827-7111
Fax: (505) 827-7095

New York State Board for Medicine
Thomas J Monahan, Executive Secretary
Cultural Education Center, Rm 3023
Empire State Plaza
Albany, NY 12230
(518) 474-3841
Fax: (518) 473-0578

New York Board for Professional Medical Conduct
Kathleen Tanner, Director
New York State Department of Health
Room 438, Corning Tower Building
Empire State Plaza
Albany, NY 12237-0614
(518) 474-8357
Fax: (518) 474-4471

North Carolina Board of Medical Examiners
Bryant D Paris, Jr, Executive Secretary
P O Box 26808—*(1203 Front St, 27609)*
Raleigh, NC 27611-6808
(919) 828-1212
Fax: (919) 828-1295

North Dakota State Board of Medical Examiners
Rolf P Sletten, Exec Secretary/Treasurer
City Center Plaza
418 East Broadway
Suite 12

Bismarck, ND 58501
(701) 223-9485
Fax: (701) 223-9756

Ohio State Medical Board
Ray Q Bumgarner, Executive Director
77 South High Street, 17th Floor
Columbia, OH 43266-3015
(614) 466-3934

Oklahoma State Board of Med Licensure & Supervision
Carole A Smith, Executive Director
P O Box 18256 — *(5104 North Francis, Suite C, 73118)*
Oklahoma City, OK 73154-0256
(405) 848-2189
Fax: (405) 848-8240

Oklahoma Board of Osteopathic Examiners
Gary R Clark, Executive Director
4848 North Lincoln Boulevard
Suite 100
Oklahoma City, OK 73105-3321
(405) 528-8625

Oregon Board of Medical Examiners
John J Ulwelling, Executive Director
620 Crown Plaza
1500 SW First Ave
Portland, OR 97201-5826
(503) 229-5770
Fax: (503) 229-6543

Pennsylvania State Board of Medicine
Linda D Wildross, Administrative Assistant
P O Box 2649 — *(Transportation & Safety Bldg, Rm 612, Commonwealth Avenue & Forster Street, 17120)*
Harrisburg, PA 17105-2649
(717) 787-2381

Pennsylvania State Board of Osteo Medicine
Jack Paruso, Administrative Assistant
P O Box 2649 — (*Transportation & Safety Bldg, Rm 612,*
Commonwealth Avenue & Forster Street, 17120)
Harrisburg, PA 17105-2649
(717) 783-4858

Puerto Rico Board of Medical Examiners
Pablo Velentio Torres, JD, Exec Director
Call Box 13969 — *(Kennedy Ave, ILA Building,*
Hogar del Obrero Portuario, Piso 8, Puerto Nuevo 00920)
Santurce, PR 00908
(809) 782-8982
Fax: (809) 783-8733

Rhode Island Board of Licensure & Discipline
Milton W Hamolsky, MD, Chief Admn Ofcr
Department of Health
3 Capitol Hill
Cannon Building
Room 205
Providence, RI 02908-5097
(401) 277-3855/56/57
Fax: (401) 277-2158

South Carolina State Board of Medical Examiners
Stephen S Serling, JD, Executive Director
P O Box 12243 — *(1220 Pickens Street, 29201)*
Columbia, SC 29211
(803) 734-8901
Fax: (803) 734-8900

South Dakota State Board of Medical & Osteo Examiners
Robert D Johnson, Executive Secretary
1323 South Minnesota Avenue
Sioux Falls, SD 57105
(605) 336-1965

Tennessee State Board of Medical Examiners
Melissa Haggard, Administrator
283 Plus Park Boulevard
Nashville, TN 37247-1010
(615) 367-6231
Fax: (615) 367-6397

Tennessee State Board of Osteopathic Examiners
Anita Van Tiles, Reg Board Admin
283 Plus Park Boulevard
Nashville, TN 37247-1010
(615) 367-6395

Texas State Board of Medical Examiners
Homer Goehrs, MD, Executive Director
P O Box 149134 — *(1812 Centre Creek Drive, 78754)*
Austin, TX 78714-9134
(512) 834-7728
Fax: (512) 834-4597

Utah Physicians Licensing Board
David E Robinson, Director
Division of Occupational & Prof Licensing
P O Box 45805 — *(Heber M Wells Building, 4th Floor,
160 East 300 South, 84145)*
Salt Lake City, UT 84145-0805
(801) 530-6628
Fax: (801) 530-6511

Vermont Board of Medical Practice
Barbara Neuman, JD, Executive Director
109 State Street
(for Federal Express: 26 Terrace Street, 05602)
Montpelier, VT 05609-1106
(802) 828-2673
Fax: (802) 828-2496

Virginia Board of Medicine
Hilary H Conner, MD, Executive Director

6606 West Broad Street, 4th Floor
Richmond, VA 23230-1717
(804) 662-9908
Fax: (804) 662-9943

Virgin Islands Board of Medical Examiners
Jane Aubain, Office Manager
Virgin Islands Department of Health
48 Sugar Estate
St Thomas, VI 00802
(809) 776-8311, ext 201

Washington Department of Health
Gail Zimmerman, Executive Director
BME/MDB Medical Boards
1300 SE Quince Street, MS: EY-25
Olympia, WA 98504
(206) 753-2205
Fax: (206) 586-0998

Washington Board of Osteopathic Medicine & Surgery
Robert Nicoloff, Executive Director
Department of Health
P O Box 47870
1300 SE Quince Street, MS: EY-23
Olympia, WA 98504-7870
(206) 586-8438

West Virginia Board of Medicine
Ronald D Walton, Executive Director
101 Dee Drive
Charleston, WV 25311
(304) 558-2921
Fax: (304) 558-2084

West Virginia Board of Osteopathy
Joseph E Schmelber, DO, Secretary
334 Penco Road
Weirton, WV 26062
(304) 723-4632

Wisconsin Medical Examining Board
Patrick D Browtz, Bureau Director
P O Box 8935 — *(1400 East Washington Avenue, 53703)*
Madison, WI 53708
(608) 266-2811
Fax: (608) 266-0644

Wyoming Board of Medicine
Carole Shotwell, Executive Secretary
2301 Central Avenue, 2nd Floor
Barrett Building, Room 208
Cheyenne, WY 82002
(307) 777-6463 — a.m. #; works at board part-time
(307) 778-7037 — p.m. #; part-time atty position
Fax: (307) 777-6478

Sources

In addition to interviews with victims, law enforcement officials, and other sources, some of whom wish to remain anonymous, official documents and other reference materials were also used in writing this book.

By chapter, the breakdown of written sources is as follows:

Dr. Ming Kow Hah

1. State of New York, Department of Health, State Board For Professional Medical Conduct, In The Matter of Ming Kow Hah, M.D., Commissioner's Recommendation, 4/8/91; Report of the Hearing Committee, 2/26/91; Statement of Charges, 11/16/90; Order of the Commissioner of Education of the State of New York, Ming Kow Hah, Calendar No. 11953.

2. *The New York Times,* January 1, 1992.

3. Ibid, January 14, 1992.

4. *Our Bodies, Ourselves,* by The Boston Women's Health Book Collective, 1979 edition.

Dr. George Burkhardt

1. State of Florida, Department of Professional Regulation, Board of Medicine, Discipline Files of George Burkhardt, M.D., Case Number 0085182, including Administrative Complaint signed 4/27/88 and Final Order signed 6/15/88.

2. *Fort Lauderdale Sun Sentinel,* May 2, 1992.

3. Ibid, March 8, 1992.

4. Ibid, February 2, 1992.

5. Ibid, January 12, 1992.

6. Ibid, April 5, 1991.

7. *For Women First,* August 17, 1992.

Dr. Shakir M. Fattah

1. State Medical Board of Ohio, Report and Recommendation In The Matter of Shakir M. Fattah, M.D., 4/13/92.

2. Court of Common Pleas, Franklin County, Ohio, Case No. 92CVF05-4202, Decision, 2/25/93.

Dr. Abu Hayat

The dialogue in this chapter is reconstructed from records obtained from the New York State Medical Board and from newspaper accounts of the victims' and their relatives' testimony at Dr. Hayat's trial.

1. State of New York, Department of Health, State Board for Professional Medical Conduct, In The Matter of Abu Hayat, M.D., Determination and Order, #BPMC 92-13, 2/17/92; Notice of Hearing, 11/22/91; Statement of Charges, 11/21/91; Hearing Dates, 12/3/91, 12/4/91, and 12/17/91; Deliberation Dates, 1/9/92 and 2/4/92.

2. *Newsday,* February 5, 1993.

3. The *New York Daily News,* January 29, 1993.

4. *The New York Times,* January 29, 1993.

5. Ibid, February 23, 1993.

6. Ibid, February 26, 1992.

Dr. Irvin W. Gilmore

1. Commonwealth of Pennsylvania, Department of State, Bureau of Professional and Occupational Status, Before The State Board of Medicine, In The Matter of the Order to Show Cause Issued Against Irvin W. Gilmore, File No. 83-49-00370, Adjudication and Order, 7/23/91.

Dr. William Dudley

1. Mississippi State Board of Medical Licensure, In The Matter of The Physician's License of William H.C. Dudley, M.D., Determination and Order, 3/21/91.

2. The *Meridian Star,* May 22, 1992.

3. Ibid, March 22, 1991.

Dr. Gary Cohen

1. State of New York, Department of Health, State Board for Professional Medical Conduct, Application to Surrender License, 8/15/90; Statement of Charges.

2. *Newsday,* November 15, 1991.

3. Ibid, October 14, 1991.

4. Ibid, October 8, 1991.

5. Ibid, October 3, 1991.

6. Ibid, February 18, 1990.

7. Ibid, February 1, 1990.

8. Ibid, January 31, 1990.

9. Ibid, January 25, 1990.

Dr. John Story

1. *Lovell Chronicle,* June 20, 1985.

2. Ibid, April 25, 1985.

3. Ibid, April 11, 1985.

4. Ibid, November 29, 1984.

5. Ibid, November 15, 1984.

6. Ibid, July 5, 1984.

7. Ibid, June 21, 1984.

8. Ibid, June 7, 1984.

9. *Doc* by Jack Olsen, published 1989, Atheneum.

Dr. Pravin D. Thakkar

The dialogue in this chapter has been reconstructed on the basis of information supplied by the Indiana State Health Professions Bureau and various newspaper accounts.

1. State of Indiana, Health Professions Bureau, Medical Licensing Board of Indiana, State of Indiana v. Pravin D. Thakkar, M.D., Findings of Fact and Order, Findings of Fact, Order, 2/13/92.
2. *Indianapolis News,* July 31, 1991.
3. Ibid, November 8, 1989.
4. Ibid, June 21, 1989.
5. Ibid, June 1, 1989.
6. Ibid, March 18, 1989.
7. Ibid, February 25, 1989.
8. Ibid, November 16, 1988.

Dr. James Burt

James Burt has had the most extensive amount of coverage of any doctor in this book. His patients have been extensively interviewed by the news media. In particular, the libraries of *The Dayton Daily News* and *Columbus Dispatch* are filled with articles about Burt that would be too numerous to list here. Here are just some of the published articles that were helpful to the author.

1. *The Dayton Daily News,* January 17, 1992.
2. Ibid, November 9, 1991.
3. Ibid, August 16, 1991.
4. Ibid, August 4, 1991.
5. Ibid, June 27, 1991.
6. Ibid, June 23, 1991.
7. Ibid, June 22, 1991.
8. Ibid, June 15, 1991.
9. Ibid, June 14, 1991.

10. Ibid, May 29, 1991.

11. Ibid, May 22, 1991.

12. Ibid, May 17, 1991.

13. Ibid, May 16, 1991.

14. Ibid, January 25, 1989.

15. Ibid, December 21, 1988.

16. Ibid, November 8, 1988.

17. *The New York Times,* September 8, 1991.

18. Ibid, December 9, 1989.

19. Ibid, December 10, 1988.

20. *Fort Worth Star Telegram,* December 20, 1988.

21. *Columbus Dispatch,* December 21, 1988.

22. Ibid, December 1, 1988.

23. Ibid, November 23, 1988.

24. Ibid, November 20, 1988.

25. Ibid, November 14, 1988.

26. Ibid, November 13, 1988.

27. Ibid, November 1, 1988.

28. *Redbook,* July 1989.

29. *Cleveland Plain Dealer,* December 18, 1988.

30. Ibid, October 29, 1988.

31. *Kettering Oakwood News,* November 3, 1988.

32. State Medical Board of Ohio, Entry of Order, 1/26/89.

33. Agreement between James C. Burt, M.D., and the State Medical Board of Ohio, wherein Dr. Burt surrenders his certificate to practice medicine and surgery, dated 1/25/89.

Dr. Kimble McNair

1. Florida Department of Professional Regulation, Board of Medicine, DPR Case Number 0-9894, Final Order, 5/8/91; Administrative Complaint, 12/19/90.

2. *Las Vegas Sun,* February 28, 1992.

3. Ibid, August 17, 1989.

4. Ibid, February 23, 1989.

5. Ibid, February 15, 1989.
6. Ibid, February 10, 1989.
7. Ibid, February 7, 1989.
8. Ibid, February 2, 1989.
9. Ibid, February 1, 1989.
10. Ibid, January 28, 1989.

Dr. Donald L. Weissman

1. Division of Medical Quality, Board of Medical Quality Assurance, Department of Consumer Affairs, State of California, Accusation No. D-3739; Stipulation Re Surrender of License, D-3739.
2. *The Los Angeles Times,* February 27, 1988.
3. Ibid, May 26, 1987.

Dr. Dennis Kleinman

1. State of New Jersey, Department of Law and Public Safety, Division of Consumer Affairs, Board of Medical Examiners, Order to Show Cause; Notice of Hearing and Requirement to File Answer, September 30, 1991; Verified Complaint, September 30, 1991; Consent Order, October 9, 1991; Order of Temporary Suspension, December 12, 1991; Amended Complaint, January 19, 1993; Certification of Deputy Attorney General Paul R. Kenny, January 19, 1993; Notice of Motion to Amend Complaint and Return Matter From the Office of Administrative Law, January 19, 1993; the Order, January 19, 1993.
2. Statement of *Sharon Epson* to law enforcement authorities, September 7, 1991.
3. Statement of Dennis G. Kleinman to law enforcement authorities, September 7, 1991.
4. *The New York Times,* May 6, 1993.
5. The *Daily News,* May 6, 1993.
6. The *New York Post,* May 6, 1993.

Dr. Alan J. Horowitz

1. State of Maryland vs. Alan J. Horowitz, Criminal Trial 7187, Transcript of Proceedings, 8/31/83.

2. State of Maryland, Department of Health and Mental Hygiene, Board of Physician Quality Assurance, Findings of Fact, Conclusions of Law and Order, 11/18/86.

3. Adjudication and Order, Commonwealth of Pennsylvania, Before the State Board of Medicine, File #85-49-00010, 7/26/89.

4. Board of Medical Examiners, of the State of Iowa, Findings of Fact, Conclusions of Law, and Decision, 9/13/84; Complaint and Statement of Charges, 4/12/84.

5. Composite State Board of Medical Examiners, State of Georgia, Consent Order, Findings of Fact, AG. File No. 91893-85, Conclusions of Law, Order, 10/8/86.

6. *The Morning Herald,* July 28, 1992.

7. Ibid, June 30, 1992.

8. Ibid, July 5, 1991.

9. Ibid, November 16, 1985.

10. Ibid, September 1, 1983.

11. Ibid, August 31, 1983.

12. Ibid, April 20, 1983.

Dr. Cecil B. Jacobson

1. United States v. Cecil Jacobson, Judgment in a Criminal Case, 5/8/92.

2. Commonwealth of Virginia, Department of Health Professions, Board of Medicine, Consent Order, Findings of Fact, Order, 6/12/89; Statement of Particulars, 5/1/89.

3. *The Washington Post,* May 9, 1992.

4. *The New York Times,* March 15, 1992.

5. Ibid, March 5, 1992.

6. *USA Today,* March 5, 1992.

Dr. Emanuel Revici

1. Report of the Regents Review Committee, In The Mat-

ter of the Disciplinary Proceeding against Emanuel Revici, No. 8342, 6/27/88, 7/29/88; Terms of Probation; Commissioner's Recommendation, 9/22/87; State of New York, Department of Health, State Board for Professional Medical Conduct, Minutes of Hearing, 8/19/87; Order of the Commissioner of Education of the State of New York, Emanual Revici, Calendar No. 8342, 4/19/86; State of New York, Department of Health, State Board for Professional Medical Conduct, In The Matter of Emanuel Revici, M.D., Respondent, Statement of Charges, 12/22/83; Amended Statement of Charges, 2/17/84; Amended Statement of Charges to Conform to the Evidence, 3/18/85; Answer, 1/3/83; Report of the Hearing Committee, 9/19/85.

2. *The Journal of the American Medical Association,* October 18, 1965.

3. Letter from Anne S. Bohenek, Public Health Representative, Office of Professional Medical Conduct, State of New York, dated 12/24/92.

4. *The New York Times,* December 29, 1983.

Dr. Valentine Birds and Dr. Stephen Herman

1. Before the Medical Board of California, Division of Medical Quality, Department of Consumer Affairs, State of California, In The Matter of the Accusation Against Stephen Herman, M.D., and Valentine Birds, M.D., Case Nos. D-4512, and D-4513, OAH Nos., L-53519, and L-53520, Stipulation for Voluntary Surrender of License, 7/9/91; Accusation, 5/17/91.

2. *The Los Angeles Times,* July 3, 1991.

Dr. George J. Camatsos

1. Mississippi State Board of Medical Licensure, Findings of Fact, Conclusions of Law and Order, In The Matter of the Physician's License of George J. Camatsos, M.D., 8/22/91.

2. *Physician's Desk Reference,* 47th Edition, 1993.

WALK ALONG THE BRINK OF FURY:

THE EDGE SERIES

Westerns By GEORGE G. GILMAN

#20: SULLIVAN'S LAW   (361-7, $3.50/$4.50)

#21: RHAPSODY IN RED   (426-5, $3.50/$4.50)

#22: SLAUGHTER ROAD   (427-3, $3.50/$4.50)

#23: ECHOES OF WAR   (428-1, $3.50/$4.50)

#24: SLAUGHTERDAY   (429-X, $3.50/$4.50)

#25: VIOLENCE TRAIL   (430-3, $3.50/$4.50)

#26: SAVAGE DAWN   (431-1, $3.50/$4.50)

#27: DEATH DRIVE   (515-6, $3.50/$4.50)

#28: EDGE OF EVIL   (526-1, $3.50/$4.50)

#29: THE LIVING, THE DYING AND THE DEAD   (531-8, $3.50/$4.50)

#30: TOWERING NIGHTMARE   (534-2, $3.50/$4.50)

#31: THE GUILTY ONES   (535-0, $3.50/$4.50)

#32: THE FRIGHTENED GUN   (536-9, $3.50/$4.50)

#33: RED FURY   (562-8, $3.50/$4.50)

#34: A RIDE IN THE SUN   (571-7, $3.50/$4.50)